Extended Praise for
Lucy and Linh and Alice Pung

★ "Lyrical, enchanting prose from a narrator with perception so acute she cannot help but share it. Immerses readers into the very heart of every scene. This is highly recommended for classrooms and libraries [and] a superb choice for book discussion groups and world young adult literature survey courses." —*VOYA,* Starred

"Alice Pung is a gem. Her voice is the real thing." —Amy Tan, bestselling author of *The Joy Luck Club*

"Lucy's narration pulls readers alongside her uncertain navigation of two worlds, and we can't help but cheer in solidarity as Lucy recognizes assimilation masquerading as inclusion, refuses to back down, and instead embraces who she is." —*The Horn Book Magazine*

"In a novel filled with strong visual images, Pung draws a sharp contrast between authenticity and deception, integrity and manipulation. Against the vividly painted backdrops of two very different communities, she traces Lucy's struggle to form a new identity without compromising the values she holds closest to her heart." —*Publishers Weekly*

LUCY and LINH

LUCY

and

LINH

ALICE PUNG

EMBER

Text copyright © 2014 by Alice Pung
Cover art and interior illustrations copyright © 2016 by Lucy Kim

All rights reserved. Published in the United States by Ember, an imprint of Random House Children's Books, a division of Penguin Random House LLC, New York. Originally published in Australia by Black Inc., an imprint of Schwartz Publishing Pty Ltd, Collingwood, Australia, in 2014, and in the United States by Alfred A. Knopf, an imprint of Random House Children's Books, New York, in 2016.

Ember and the E colophon are registered trademarks of Penguin Random House LLC.

Visit us on the Web! GetUnderlined.com

Educators and librarians, for a variety of teaching tools,
visit us at RHTeachersLibrarians.com

The Library of Congress has cataloged the hardcover edition of this work as follows:
Names: Pung, Alice
Title: Lucy and Linh / Alice Pung
Other titles: Laurinda
Description: First edition. | New York : Alfred A. Knopf, [2016] |
Originally published in Australia by Black Inc. in 2014 under title: Laurinda. |
Summary: In Australia, Lucy tries to balance her life at home surrounded by her Chinese immigrant family, with her life at a pretentious private school.
Identifiers: LCCN 2015024300 | ISBN 978-0-399-55048-5 (trade) |
ISBN 978-0-399-55049-2 (lib. bdg.) | ISBN 978-0-399-55050-8 (ebook)
Subjects: | CYAC: High schools—Fiction. | Schools—Fiction. | Cliques (Sociology)—Fiction. | Immigrants—Fiction. | Asians—Australia—Fiction. | Australia—Fiction.
Classification: LCC PZ7.1.P86 Lu 2016 | DDC [Fic]—dc23

ISBN 978-0-399-55051-5 (pbk.)

Printed in the United States of America
10 9 8 7 6 5 4 3 2 1
First Ember Edition 2018

For KBH and the Lamb

Life is nothing *but* high school.

—*Kurt Vonnegut*

PROLOGUE

Dear Linh,

Remember how we used to catch the 406 bus after school, past the Victory Carpet Factory and the main hub of Sunray, through to Stanley? What an adventure, we used to think then. What a waste of time, looking back now. It was a waste of time because the bus would always worm its way back to Stanley, following exactly the same route, stopping at the same places and collecting the same people, who did the same things every same day.

Remember that girl from St. Claire's who put her bag on the seat next to her so that no one else could sit down? And how we thought, typical of girls like that. When she got the vibe that we were talking about her behind her back, she turned around and told us to get stuffed. But that wasn't the most shocking thing about her. The most shocking thing was that where we had expected to see white teeth all even like a picket fence, they were herded behind that ugly gate in her mouth. Looking into that paddock of crumbly yellow rocks straining to break free from barbed wire, I thought, no wonder you're going back to Stanley.

This is how I see it now. An old strip of seven shops, each

with an identical metallic snake of a roller shutter coiled at the top. At night, with those iron blinds lowered, the street looked like a long, continuous, dirty warehouse, all graffiti and concrete.

There was the local fish-and-chips shop, the Happy Oyster, which had never seen an oyster, joyous or otherwise, from the first day of its existence. A shop selling smokes, with incredibly expensive and lewd painted plaster figurines in its window—women with serpents and black leather straps instead of clothes. And a hairdresser that still called itself a barber, with a red, white and blue pole at the front and posters in the window of great haircuts from 1983.

The largest shop was the convenience store that tried to pass itself off as a mini-mart, with faded packets of instant noodles and cans of soup not seen in a proper supermarket for years. The whole strip could probably rustle up only two or three trays of vegetables. The place that got the most business was Stanley Spirits on the corner. People went there mostly to get beer—half a dozen cans of VB at a stretch, *VB* standing for *Victoria Bitter,* which could also express the sentiments of the male residents of Stanley aged between seventeen and seventy. My mum never bought anything from this strip. Instead, she caught the bus to neighboring Sunray and its market, where she could get tomatoes for a dollar a pound if she went near closing time.

Ours was the only blue house in Stanley, and I don't mean a pale blue washed out with a lot of white. I mean blue the color of that bubble-gum-flavored ice cream all kids love until they get older and find out how many chemicals are in every scoop. Now I feel the same way about our home. But when I was younger, I loved how it stood out; it was the kind of house a kid would draw, a rectangle in blue and a triangle in red.

To our left were the Donaldsons, a lovely older couple who owned a Dalmatian that barked at all hours of the day. They'd come over once a year, two days after Christmas, to give us cake and handfuls of chocolates that tasted like brown crayons. A few months later, at Chinese New Year, Mum would ask me to walk over with coconut sweets or spring rolls, and sometimes I'd bring moon cakes from the Lunar Festival. "Aren't you a sweetie," they'd say.

The Donaldsons' house was white, and its cement-rendered front was not pimpled with mold. They had a carefully maintained garden of bougainvilleas, cacti and fuchsias, and an upright mailbox—no small feat in a place like Stanley, where teenagers would drive by with cricket bats, in cars that they'd buy for two hundred dollars and spend two thousand tricking out. Most of the mailboxes in Stanley leaned to one side, as if wincing from their blows.

The most enchanting thing about the Donaldsons' house was this: around their front yard were seven little gnomes and a toadstool, each partly hiding behind a flowerpot or shrub. The kids who loved to smash everything that was standing never touched the Donaldsons' peekaboo gnomes.

That's what I see, Linh, but I also remember that our closeness to the Donaldsons didn't stop the kids from knocking over our mailbox. Once they even chucked a rock through our front window. I suggested to my father that it was because our blue house was such an irresistible target, but no way was he going to repaint it. When we first moved in, my father took great care to water the plum tree at the front and the apricot tree at the back. After a while he got too busy and said it was a waste of water. "Let the rain take care of it," he said, but the rain was as half-arsed in its dripping as everything else around here, and eventually the apricot tree dried up. The plum tree survived but bore sour pellets.

Mum spent most of her days indoors, only going out to shop and collect the mail from our mailbox, or to attend church. She'd always wanted me to go to a Catholic school, which was how I ended up at Christ Our Savior. My father, who didn't really believe in God—not since most of his family went missing, presumed dead, in Vietnam—wanted me to win a scholarship to somewhere else.

He also wanted me to stop wasting time doing things for the neighbors and to start hunkering down. "Why do you always interfere with her homework?" he asked my mother. "Where were you when your god was handing out the brains? Holding the door for everyone?"

He wanted me to get out of Stanley. He wanted me out of there for my own good. Where we lived was not a place where good stories began, but a place where bad stories retreated, like small mongrel dogs bitten by much larger, thoroughbred ones.

Reading back through this first letter to you, I can see I knew even then that where I was going, you were not coming along, and that I would have to leave you and all of this behind. But I did not understand then, as I do now, how difficult it would be to create a thoroughbred from mongrel stock.

When my dad dropped us off at the front gate, the first things I saw were the rose garden spreading out on either side of the main driveway, and the enormous sign in iron cursive letters spelling out LAURINDA. No "Ladies' College" after it, of course; the name was meant to speak for itself. Then there was the main building: four sections of sandstone brick, and the giant cream tower in the center. *This place is giving us the finger!* you squawked when you first saw it, Linh.

I thought that in a black-and-white photograph, it could be mistaken for the main house of a plantation in the Deep South of America. I could imagine young ladies in white gloves with lace slingshots, lying in wait to kill a mockingbird or two. It was beautiful, but as it was guarded by a gate and set against the enormous lawn, the beauty snuck up on you, like a femme fatale with a rock.

We could make fun of it because we knew we'd never enter the school itself, only the gym, a massive, windowless box that looked like a giant's shipping container. There was a sign stuck to the door: YEAR TEN SCHOLARSHIP EXAMS THIS WAY. Rows of plastic chairs and tables had been set up, with numbers taped down the sides. It was morgue-cold in there, as though we were going to be strapped into those seats and have our minds dissected in some awful autopsy.

There were over three hundred students in the room but only two of us would make it through this elimination round: a boy for Auburn Academy and a girl for Laurinda. This was the first time Laurinda and Auburn had offered "Equal Access" scholarships, which were supposed to go to kids with parents the school considered broke.

That morning, all the parents were begging the deities, white-knuckled with want, for their kid to be the one who made it through. There were two types, I noticed: the ear pullers, who drove off immediately after giving their kid a serious stare and a punishing pointed finger, and the bum wipers, who stayed as long as they could, until they were kicked out because the exam was about to begin.

It was good to see some familiar faces from Christ Our Savior. Tully was there, and Yvonne and Ivy. They were trying out because they hadn't made it into Hoadley Girls' State Selective School and their parents were giving them a rough time at home. And you, of course, Linh.

I felt sorry for Tully. The way her mother was dragging her to the gym by the elbow, it was as if she was heading for the firing squad. "Your cousin Stephanie got into Hoadley seven years ago," we overheard Mrs. Cho muttering, "and there is no way that you could be dumber than Stephanie."

Now Stephanie was an accountant who sat on her bum churning through numbers all day instead of standing in a factory pulling out chicken gizzards. My parents had taken me to visit her when I was seven. I stared and stared at the badges on her red woolen jacket and her checkered skirt with a big metal pin through it. "She had to take a test to get into the school," my father told me as he drove us home that evening. "She has a good future ahead of her."

As a kid, I wasn't forced to think about The Future much, but I knew I wanted to be dressed like Stephanie in a royal outfit that magically seemed to make adults take you seriously and ask you quiet and sincere questions and listen to your answers. None of that "*Wah,* what a pretty girl you are!" which seemed to be the only way adult strangers behaved toward me back then.

As I walked to my place in the gym, I saw Tully hunched over the desk ahead of me, her back a hard cashew curve and her fingers at her temples. I thought of all those afternoons when she couldn't hang out or even do homework with us because she was being whisked away to some tutoring program or other.

When the exam began, the gym fell so quiet that I could hear myself blink. It must have been like this all the time for Tully, I mused, her whole life one exam after another in white-walled tutoring centers run by dour former math teachers or engineers whose qualifications were not recognized here. She would be used to this silence.

We walked with Tully, Ivy and Yvonne when it was over to catch the bus home. Ivy and Yvonne had been such close friends since Year Seven that they had identical haircuts. They commiserated with each other when their parents made them find after-school work at the local Kumon tutoring center and Kmart, and they planned to run away together when they turned twenty, before their parents could send them back to Vietnam/Malta to get cheap eyelid surgery/nose jobs and/or husbands.

As we walked, we *wah*'ed over houses with roofs like red

bonnets on top of white faces with unblinking bay-window eyes, fanned by decades-old London plane trees. Ivy and Yvonne skipped down the sidewalk, playing the old game of avoiding the cracks in case we broke our mothers' backs. Tully had her fingertips in her jeans pockets; occasionally she would pull out a soggy tissue and wipe her nose.

I could hear Ivy bellowing down the quiet street that Yvonne had stepped on a crack.

"I did not, bitch!" Yvonne screeched back. I noticed the airy curtains of a house ripple.

"Be quiet, youse!" you said. "People are watching us."

"Let them watch!" yelled Ivy in glee.

"We probably interrupted their eleven o'clock croissant."

We caught up with Yvonne and Ivy.

"What did you write about for the final essay?" It was the first time Tully had opened her mouth since the exam. For fifteen minutes, it had been set in a straight line, with a small hook on each end, as if latched to her chin and dragging her head down.

In the last part of the exam, we'd had to write an essay based on a badly photocopied picture of a person sitting behind a desk in the dark, a candle burning. The picture was done in the style of the drawings in the Good News Bible—with swirly lines and no features, so you couldn't see the facial expression.

"I wrote about feeling trapped in an exam that will decide whether my father will disown me," Yvonne joked. "This is my second go! Sixty bucks down the drain again, just because my dad won't accept that I'm not a genius like you, Tully. What did you write about?"

"I wrote about Peter Benenson, who founded Amnesty International," said Tully. "I figured they wanted us to show that we knew about world issues, and they might give bonus credit if we knew about the Universal Declaration of Human Rights."

"Waahh," breathed Ivy, and she whacked Yvonne on the shoulder. "We're stuffed, my friend. I wrote about how when my brother Ming went to prison, he missed Asian food so much that in the exercise yard he watched the pigeons and wanted to kill and roast one, like quail."

I saw the upside-down hooks on Tully's face turn themselves the other way.

"What the hell, Ivy?" Yvonne said, laughing. Then she turned to Tully. "Man, Tully, that is what they call a sophisticated essay. You've got the scholarship in the bag."

"Hear me out!" declared Ivy. "I thought that if I wrote about true life in—what did Mr. Galloway call it?—an 'evocative and poignant' way, those examiners would be amazed by my ability to portray real life *and* feel sorry for me. Two birds with one stone, my friends. Two birds, one massive stone."

Suddenly Tully turned toward you. "What did you write about, Linh?"

You just laughed. "Something stupid."

I noticed that Tully's eyes were two small, desperate fires, but I didn't say anything. I stayed quiet. Tully, who had more As than a wholesale box of batteries, had been sitting in front of me for the whole three hours, distracting me with her rocking backward and forward. Fifty minutes into the exam, she had put her hand up for another blank writing booklet.

Throughout the test, she was practically coughing up her lungs in the near-silent room.

I knew she would get the scholarship. She was like an Olympic gymnast who had been training for this moment her entire life. Nothing else was allowed to matter. She was not allowed to do sports or drama, or take an interest in anything frivolous. She could read about the end of apartheid in South Africa, but she couldn't read the arts pages of the newspaper if her parents were home. That's how crazy they were. She could talk about the Geneva Conventions but she wouldn't know how to boil an egg. She certainly wouldn't know that sleep was something people did to feel rested and more awake.

I felt sorry for Tully. Her parents didn't let her catch the bus by herself, even though she was six months older than the rest of us. But some hidden part of me also did not like her very much. I didn't know what to say to her on the days when we finished school late and I walked her to the train station. Afterward, I would tramp over to my bus stop; by the time I got home, the housework and sewing work would have piled up and my mother would be angry.

Before I'd left that morning for the exam, I had gone into the garage. Mum was sitting there at her table, beneath a fluorescent bulb that glowed like an illuminated mushroom. The dust motes rained down on her head like furry spores. "Two hundred before Wednesday," she told me, slowly turning over a collar-shaped piece of iron-on interfacing in her hands like a manuscript. This was a woman who had never picked up a book in her life; the only literature she looked at was the BI-LO and Safeway ads that arrived in our mailbox every

Tuesday. Yet her fingertips could read that piece of polyester fiber like a blind person read braille.

For some reason, the picture in the exam paper had reminded me of my mother, so I'd written about her. If the other girls had asked, I would have told them. But somehow I did not want to share this with Tully.

"What took you so long?"

My mother was in the kitchen, putting some water on the stove to boil and opening up a packet of ramen, when I arrived home. She lived off those dehydrated noodles, a pack every afternoon.

"I had to wait for the bus and then catch a train."

She wanted to know if the sixty dollars we'd paid for me to take the scholarship exam would be refunded if I didn't get in.

"No, Mum. Where's the Lamb?" I asked.

"Lamb's in his box. Eat first."

I watched her open the sachet of desiccated onions and MSG and pour it into the cooking noodles, then plonk a fried egg on top. My Chinese mother had a profile that I imagined photographers in *National Geographic* would consider noble: born in Hanoi, she had somehow ended up with darker skin and the bone structure of a Montagnard woman, those highland dwellers with strong jaws and long eyes.

We always called my baby brother the Lamb because of our surname, Lam. His real name was Aidan, because Mum wanted a word that our grandmother in Hanoi could pronounce, even though he had never met her. Mum kept saying she wanted to go back, but in thirteen years she had been there only once, and that was to bury Grandpa. "Life gets in the way," she sighed whenever I asked, and then she would stare into the distance like a blind person remembering sight. Because I was so young when we left, I don't remember much about my grandmother except that she smelled like aniseed rings and incense.

The Lamb slept in my parents' bedroom but during the day spent most of his time in the garage with Mum. There were babies with faces like apples and bodies like small blimps, and then there was the Lamb, who looked more like a dried tamarind. Brown and skinny, he even sat in an enormous fruit box, waiting to be picked up. The Lamb was never the sort of baby who'd make it into a Target catalog—he'd more likely be the poster child for Compassion Australia—but he was a healthy and cheerful little pup. His box had cushions and toys, and it was very cozy. We didn't have air-conditioning in our house, but we had a unit in the garage because that was where Mum spent most of the day, and sometimes a big part of the evening too. Sometimes my father helped out, because along with a sewing machine, there was a secondhand overlocker for denim and polar fleece.

"Hello there, Lamby."

Looking at the piles of orange tracksuit pants, I wondered who would ever buy such ugly attire. Then I looked down at the Lamb: with the leftover fabric remnants, Mum had sewn him an orange polar-fleece tracksuit, complete with hood. He looked like a miniature pimp in the making.

"Lamby, we're going to have some noodles now."

The Lamb looked up with his round, unblinking eyes. He

bunched his hand into a small fist with one finger sticking out, and as I leaned down to pick him up, he stuck that finger in my eye.

"Owww!"

The Lamb was beginning to explore the world through his hands. For months it had been his mouth. He put everything he found in it to test it out, including the plastic backs of Fruit Roll-Ups and a powdery dead moth, whose reemergence caused my mother grave alarm.

As I washed my eye out at the sink, the Lamb crawled into the kitchen and rubbed his own eye. Lately he had learned to stand. He was standing now, with one hand splayed on the wall for balance, the index finger of his other hand pointing straight up toward the ceiling and the other fingers balled into a little fist, as if he was having a eureka moment.

"Come here, Lambface." I hoisted him onto my lap.

"He's been in the garage all day," Mum told me. "After you finish your noodles, take him outside for a walk. But don't be too long, because I need you to help me iron a box of shirtsleeves."

The largest box from each new shipment Uncle Sokkha brought over became the Lamb's new playpen, which was just as well because by then he would have decorated the last one with scribbles. Mum only thought to buy him a packet of washable markers when one day he made his open-ended circles with a red permanent pen across a pair of beige shorts she had just sewn.

Uncle Sokkha wasn't our real uncle. He had a mustache and a Cambodian Afro—a Cambofro. I'd never seen one on an Asian man before. He liked patterned shirts and gold chains, and he looked like he should be selling Sunkist soft drinks on television, except for three things:

1. He didn't speak English.

2. He had a scar running from the left corner of his mouth to the edge of his nose, which puckered his lip up a bit at the end so that it looked as if he was constantly snarling at some sick joke.

3. He didn't have the sort of chilled personality required of a soft-drink promoter.

Besides his creepy lip curl, which I didn't think he could help, I'd never seen him smile. Whenever he delivered a new batch of clothes to my mother, he always stressed that it was urgent, like a mob boss directing a hit man. Then he'd drive away in his white van, only to reappear two weeks later with a new batch.

I carried the Lamb outside on my hip and took him to have a look at the Donaldsons' front yard. He pointed to one of the gnomes hiding behind the gerberas and squealed with delight. He also scrambled around in my arms, trying to get down, but I held on tight. I didn't want him trespassing in the neighbors' garden. As friendly as the Donaldsons were, in our neighborhood we all knew our place.

When the letter arrived in the mail a few Fridays later, my first thought was just to throw it in the bin and not tell my father. After all, the envelope felt so thin. But then I thought, what the hell, I'll have a look to see what polite rejection they've come up with, and then call and congratulate Tully. I ripped one end open so carelessly that I ended up tearing off part of the letter.

> *Dear Lucy,*
>
> *As we approach a new century, we must equip our students to become leaders in myriad far-reaching social, economic and cultural fields. Laurinda is proud to introduce and embrace experiences of diversity in our strong tradition.*
>
> *It is with great pleasure that I write to inform you that you have been awarded the inaugural Laurinda Equal Access scholarship.*

It was signed by an E. Grey, Head of High School, with instructions to call the school to arrange for an interview. I think I must have made a noise that sounded like *eeeek, eeeek, eeeek!* because Mum came rushing into the house, thinking the smoke alarm had gone off. "What's wrong with you?" she asked.

I told her.

In an American family sitcom, Linh, this would be the moment when the mother and daughter jump and hug each other and shed some tears. The mother would tell the daughter how proud she was, and then they would joyfully get in the car and go shopping.

"That's good," said Mum. "We don't need to get the refund."

"It was never a refundable deposit, Mum."

In the same sitcom, the mother and daughter would probably sit down over a cup of brewed coffee (and perhaps some cupcakes) to talk about the future. Half a year ago, my mum had bought a can of Nescafé on sale. For her, happiness was hoarding seventeen cans of sweetened condensed milk in the cupboard. We drank our coffee in silence.

"You'd better call your dad," she said finally.

So I did. By the time he came home that evening, he had told his workmates and his friends, and they had passed on the news to their wives and children.

"Lucy Lam!" they were probably exclaiming. "Who would have thought?"

A day later, everyone knew.

As people started calling to congratulate me, at first I felt pride and anxiety in equal measure. They were pleased for me, but not even old Mrs. Giap hid her surprise. That weekend she was coming for a toenail trimming—and even if I was the scholarship winner, my mother would not let me off this task.

"Keep still, Grandma Giap," I told her as I wedged her brown foot between my knees. It reminded me of a mummy's foot, all brown and dry and crumpled in strange places. When I clipped her toenails, I had to close my eyes and mouth because the pieces would fly hard and fast.

"Ah, my girl, you have done more schooling than I ever have in my seventy-eight years," she sighed, and then told me that she had assumed Tully would get the scholarship. "She works harder than you. She's probably smarter than you too." Those Asian old folks had clearly never heard of the white lie. "But she didn't deserve it."

White lies be damned—sometimes I loved the truth.

I thought of Tully, and how her father had got her baptized just so she could get into a Catholic school. He'd called on Mrs. Giap to be her godmother, as if Mrs. Giap's faith were a single-use instrument like a syringe. The difference between Tully and me wasn't our smarts or our parents. The difference, I recognized, was that I was well liked and Tully wasn't.

That didn't alleviate the guilt I was feeling. I'd never thought I would get into Laurinda, and had even supposed that after Tully left Christ Our Savior, things would be less tense without her panic attacks and tears. The only reason Tully had missed out on getting into the state selective school was because she'd been down for a week before the exam with the flu. I had never imagined Tully being left behind.

The following Monday, the start of summer break, I called the number at the end of the letter.

"Laurinda Ladies' College, Eunice Grey speaking."

This was the first time I had spoken to someone from the school, and I was nervous. I introduced myself and she replied, "Ah, yes, Lucy, I was expecting your call." Then there was a pause, as if she'd forgotten something she was supposed to say. For a moment I thought she'd got me mixed up with Tully. Then she remembered: "Congratulations."

"Thanks."

She told me that I needed to come in for an interview next week with my parents, and we'd also sort out a few administrative things.

"Okay."

"Tuesday at eleven?"

"Okay."

"I look forward to meeting you then."

"Okay." Then I added again, "Thank you."

It was only after I hung up that I realized I had not thought to check with my father to see if he was working a shift then. Mrs. Grey had spoken so authoritatively that I presumed our meeting time was set. If my father couldn't make it, I decided, I would go alone.

I was used to sorting out phone billing errors, insurance claims and doctors' appointments for my parents. Sometimes, to avoid the hassle of explaining that I was acting on their behalf, I simply pretended to be my mother over the phone. She even let me forge her signature on forms. I'd never understood the brats on television who threw tantrums when their dads missed their soccer matches, as if the world of adults revolved around their games. If the Lamb grew up to be one of those boys who resented our father working on Saturdays and missing his school football finals, he'd get a slap on the bum from either Mum or me for his selfishness. That was the way things were with our family.

But Dad was taking this unexpected miracle of a scholarship so seriously that he got some time off work.

My father parked his Camry beside the only other car at the school, a silver BMW. The college was deserted, but the wooden front door of the main building opened when I pushed it. A stained-glass window depicting the college crest took up an entire wall. On the mahogany reception desk was a vase of heavy flowers, the likes of which I'd never seen in Stanley—they looked as if they'd been plucked from some heady Brazilian rain forest. Behind the desk was a framed oil painting of a woman staring myopically into the distance; she was wearing an academic gown and a hat that looked like a deflated jester's cap.

"Where do we go?" my father asked. I had no idea. Perhaps we were meant to sit on the dark brown leather chairs and wait. Then we heard a door open somewhere down the corridor. There were footsteps, and a tall, broad woman stepped into the reception area. "You must be Lucy Lam." She smiled at me as if she wasn't used to smiling, her white eggshell face cracking, her features scrambling around. Then she turned to my dad. "And you must be Mr. Lam. Welcome to our school."

Mrs. Grey had short hair dyed the color of rust and wore a wasabi-colored blouse. She towered over us, so I got a clear view of the sharp pyramid of her nasal cavity and also her mouth, with the maroon lipstick seeping through her tiny lip wrinkles. As she led us down a corridor of polished wooden doors, all closed, I felt like I was going to confession: against the wall outside each door was a wooden pew long enough to seat three girls.

The first thing I noticed on entering Mrs. Grey's office was how empty it was. There was a small shelf of books against one corner of the room, a fireplace in the other, and an enormous, shiny desk in the middle that seemed to be made of a single slab of wood picked up off a forest floor, sandpapered and polished. Mrs. Grey sat down behind the desk, which was completely bare except for a silver penholder. My father and I each took one of the two brocade-upholstered chairs on the other side.

Mrs. Grey told my father that my results on the exam were very good, and that my essay was outstanding. "You must be tremendously proud of her."

"You are too kind," my father said, "but my daughter Lucy here, she really isn't so smart. We never knew she had smarts in her. We didn't even think to get her extra tutoring. That's why we were so surprised that she won the scholarship. Ha!"

"At Laurinda, we are looking for well-rounded students," explained Mrs. Grey. "And we frown upon coached students."

My father looked confused, and I knew he was wondering why I had been chosen if they preferred untutored fat girls.

"At Laurinda, we pride ourselves on our diversity, hence this new Equal Access program," Mrs. Grey continued. "We are looking for natural talent and leadership potential. A student who goes to cram school and rote-learns things to pass exams does not meet the criteria."

I was beginning to feel pretty good about myself.

"We are very pleased that you will be joining our college, Lucy," she told me. "In your letter with your application, you mentioned that you were very involved in voluntary activities, and that your hobbies include fashion design?"

I did not tell her that this was because Mum sometimes sent me to church on the Sundays when she couldn't make it, and that she made me do kitchen duty and visit the older ladies in the neighborhood who didn't have grandchildren who could help them translate their mail. Or that by *fashion design* I meant helping Mum translate the designs of Coast & Co. fashions into tangibles that could be made for below minimum wage.

"You also mentioned," Mrs. Grey continued, "that you were a representative on your student council last year."

I looked down at my hands.

"Here we don't have a student representative body, as we feel there is no need for one. The girls are engaged in all types of enriching activities—debating, music, theater, musical theater, sports. We do hope that you will be able to partake in many of these activities while you are here."

I nodded, hoping to indicate that I would be an upstanding Laurinda citizen.

She told us about the history of the school, how it was one of the oldest ladies' colleges in the state, and how it was a Christian institution, so we would have to go to church once every term.

Once every term! Back at Christ Our Savior, church was once a week. Here the girls focused on Latin and art history. I had come too late to learn the latter, Mrs. Grey told me, but it was something I might have liked.

She handed me a navy blue book and matching folder. "This is the student handbook, and in it you will find all you need to know about Laurinda," she announced, as if the school itself were a great lady I was supposed to study up on. "And in this folder is our uniform list. Note that we have only one supplier, Edmondsons."

She put both hands on her desk and stood. "Now I will show you around." I noticed that her nails were painted the same color as her lips.

"The rendering is very beautiful," my father commented as we stood in front of the main building. "My Italian nephew Claude is a renderer on the Gold Coast."

Dad was taking the "displaying diversity" part too far, I thought.

"It's actually sandstone," explained Mrs. Grey. "Sydney Basin Hawkesbury sandstone. Very few buildings in Melbourne around the turn of the century were built with this material, which was imported from New South Wales."

It was only much later that I realized sandstone was not the same as a rendered façade—back then I was just as lost as my father, and we stood there willingly being edified by a being who knew so much more than we did.

"We have three campuses at Laurinda," Mrs. Grey told us as she led us away from the main building. "The junior school is down the road. This is the middle school campus, for Years Seven to Ten. Next year, when Lucy is in senior school, she will go to the campus on Arcadia Avenue."

We stood on the small lawn at the center of the school, and Mrs. Grey pointed up. The bells in the tower, she explained, were shipped from London in 1886. They stood in the Barry

Wing, the oldest part of the school, named after Sir Redmond Barry, the judge who had sentenced Ned Kelly to hang.

She shuttled us down some more corridors, all the while continuing her commentary: In this wing, Dame Nellie Melba once had dinner with the attorney general. In that wing, two weeks ago, the vice-chancellor of the University of Melbourne had held a meeting about the future of higher education with the leaders of the nation's other top five universities. "It was an honor to host that delegation," said Mrs. Grey, with as much reverence as the nuns at Christ Our Savior would have shown had a flock of archangels descended to announce the Second Coming.

She then showed us the new performing arts center, a massive spherical affair made of glass and metal that could seat five hundred people, and the seven individual rehearsal rooms, each containing a different set of musical instruments. My father made the appropriate wide-mouthed sounds of awe.

After the tour, Mrs. Grey took us back to the main wing. "We're looking forward to having you join the Laurinda community next year, Lucy," she said to me, and then shook my father's hand.

And so, Linh, my final term at Christ Our Savior went by very, very quickly. If I had known how quickly it would pass, I would not have spent so much time in class daydreaming about when my new uniform would arrive. I would not have walked around comparing our school's rented, pale green, three-bedroom cement music house across the road with Laurinda's performing arts center. I would not have looked at our teachers and thought, geez, Mr. Galloway is really nice but he spelled *liaise* wrong on the board. And I would not have been miffed when Ivy and Yvonne kept riling me. "We will miss you sooo much," Ivy said. "Don't forget us when you go to your rich school, bitch!"

But you kept bringing me back to myself, Linh, forcing me to notice those moments. You'd laugh like a mad person at Ivy's awful jokes.

"What's the definition of a smart-arse?" she'd ask.

"I dunno," you'd reply.

"Someone who can sit on a tub of ice cream and tell you what flavor it is!"

"Ha! I have a better one. What's brown and sticky?"

"Gross . . . we don't want to know."

"A stick! Ha!"

When old Mr. Warren wore shorts to school, you said, "Hey, sir, nice legs! You should be on a catwalk!"

"Linh, you watch it, or one day you'll have a harassment claim against your name," he retorted, but then he did a mock sashay with one hand on his hip and wiggled his bum. Those teachers, they cracked us up.

Tully sat quietly and miserably in our group, occasionally smiling like a moribund old lady who wanted relatives to think she was going to be okay. When we got our end-of-year science tests back, you could see that Tully had got near full marks again. "Wow, Tully, you're the smartest person I know," you told her.

"Piss off, Linh. I don't want to hear your bullshit!" She got up and left.

On my last day, the teachers took us Year Nines to the

botanical gardens for a picnic. Even Sister Clarke came along. It was one of those days when the sky was all one bright shade of blue and stretched high, as though you were living inside a balloon, warm and giddy. The sunshine slowed our heartbeats down bit by bit as we sat on the grass in our small satellite groups, but close to one another. Even the popular girls—Alessandra, Toula and their gang—were huddled nearby. Of course we had a hierarchy, but on days like this, when we shared all our food, and when Mr. Warren and four other girls were strumming soft classics like "Stand by Me" on guitars they'd lugged from the music house, I was reminded what a nice place this was. The only break in the mood was when Alessandra turned to Yvonne and said, "Hey, nice blouse, Yvonne. Is it from the eighties?"

Yvonne just shrugged, but you replied, "I heard that the 1980s are coming back into fashion, Alessandra."

"Oh, I didn't mean the 1980s," Alessandra said. "I meant the *1880s*."

Before you could think of a comeback, there were five loud claps and we looked up to see Sister Clarke calling for Tully and me to stand up. Bewildered, we did. "I would like us all to congratulate these girls, your elected student representatives, for the superb job they have done this year." People cheered. "Not only have they been tireless and enthusiastic in organizing the Red Cross door-knock appeal, the Tournament of Minds team and the Meet the Year Sevens barbecue, but they have successfully petitioned for the introduction of trousers as part of your uniform, so next year you'll be warm during winter!"

Loud cheers erupted. Tully smiled at me wanly.

For years, we had been trying to get out of wearing ridiculous woolen skirts that kept our legs cold no matter how many pairs of tights we had on. Tully and I had argued that it was sexist and old-fashioned. The compromise we had reached with the school was that we would be allowed to wear woolen pants, but the school would also introduce blazers. Otherwise, in our all-gray woolen sweater-and-trousers combos, we'd look like a prison work gang.

Until then, the entire school had only twelve black blazers of different sizes, which students borrowed whenever we had to do out-of-school presentations or debating. But every girl next year would have her own smart new jacket. With no trimmings on the sleeves or collar, and a detachable college logo on the pocket, the blazer could also double as a suit jacket for job interviews. For mothers who could sew, it could be made from Butterick pattern no. 6578. All you had to do was buy and attach the embroidered Christ Our Savior crest. My mother had made a mock-up of the jacket, and Tully and I had advocated for it in student-staff meetings.

Sister Clarke brought out a surprise cake. It was only a Safeway mud cake, and she had six more in plastic bags on the barbecue bench for the whole of Year Nine, but this one had white lettering on it that someone had done with an icing pen. "FAREWELL," it said, with my name below in cursive.

"It has been a wonderful three years having you at our college," Sister Clarke said. "You have contributed so much to the school, not only by being involved in so many activities, but also through your strong friendships with your classmates. You will be dearly missed. We wish you all the very best at your new school. Remember, you will always be welcome here at Christ Our Savior—"

"Whoa!" you interrupted, because you didn't want me to

get too emotional in front of the class—that's how good a friend you were, Linh. "This cake is awesome! Mr. Warren, you'd better not stand too close, because the knife's coming out and the first cut is the deepest!"

When the buses dropped us back at the school to collect our bags, we saw a group of St. Andrew's boys loitering near our fence.

"Ooh, Yvonne, your lover boy is here!" teased the girls.

"Shut up," said Yvonne.

We all knew that one of the boys, Hai, had the hots for Yvonne. When we grabbed our bags and headed toward the gate, he and his mates were there to greet us, every one of them dressed in black T-shirt and jacket and jeans. "Yo, Yvonne, check this out, me and ma homies are going to sing you a song, baby gurrllll."

"Oh my God, so embarrassing," said Yvonne, covering her face with one hand.

All his mates made gangsta gestures, pointing toward him like he was a Southeast Asian pop star, and he started to belt out a popular American song—but *in Maltese*. As the only Viet kid in a class full of kids from Malta, he spoke Maltese better than he spoke English because all his mates were Maltese. When he finished serenading Yvonne, we all clapped, and then Hai dropped to one knee and asked if Yvonne would be his girlfriend.

She squealed and laughed and said, "Oh, you are too embarrassing," and of course we egged her on until she eventually said yes, which was what she had wanted to do in the first place. Hai jumped up and squeezed Yvonne in a massive bear hug and then kissed her cheek, and all the while she was shrieking, "Eww, gross!"

I sighed inwardly. Boys, I thought. I would sure miss those boys when I went to the new school.

Suddenly Ivy hollered, "Hey, guys, it's her last day!" She pointed, and all eyes turned to me and I went red. The paradoxes of being a teenager: I didn't like this attention, and yet secretly I *loved* it.

"Oh yeah? Where you going?" the tallest boy asked.

These cute Maltese boys—I just knew Ivy was going to explain to them that I had won a scholarship to Laurinda, like it was a huge deal—and of course it was, except not to these guys. It was the sort of thing that would make them think I was a snob who reckoned she was too good for this suburb. That thought suddenly made me feel very sad.

Luckily, you jumped in. "*I'm* going away," you lied, but I didn't mind. I never minded when you did those crazy things, Linh. "It's *my* last day!"

"Oh yeah? Where're you going to?"

"Juvie, yo."

The tall boy knew you were BS'ing, but he played along. "What for, gangsta?"

"Give her a kiss on the cheek and she'll tell you."

Holy Mary! Even you could not believe Ivy had blurted that out, Linh. But it was our last day of term, and you were in a reckless mood. You grinned and turned your cheek to one side.

The tall boy smiled and came closer. Everyone whooped. Then you turned the other cheek.

"Wow," you breathed afterward, flapping your hands as if you'd just stuck them in hot coals. "Discount day. Two for the price of one!"

As we walked home that last afternoon, you with that

dopey grin stamped on your face, I thought about the summer before I had started Year Seven at Christ Our Savior. I was a pretty shy kid, but I had read every edition of *Smash Hits* and *TV Hits* at the library over those holidays to train myself to be a teenager. I thought that if I knew what was in them, I would have things to talk about with the cool girls. It never occurred to me that what I knew wouldn't alter the personality I had—not until I came to that first homeroom and Mrs. Abrams sat me next to Melissa for roll call. All year I had nothing much to say to her, because she lived the life the magazines assumed teenagers lived: sneaking out at night to go to parties and buying the same brand of T-shirt that others did. She didn't have to *read* about it.

But you, Linh, you managed to make a place for yourself at Christ Our Savior by watching, not by showing off with try-hard knowledge of popular culture. Your jokes and pranks were good-natured and self-effacing and never pissed people off like some of the backhanded things girls like Alessandra said did.

Do you remember how, before we left for the picnic that morning, we heard Melissa crying in the girls' bathroom, refusing to come out? You leaned against the door and quietly told her, "Don't worry, Melissa, at least you're really *highbrow* now, not like the rest of those hussies."

She finally emerged from her stall, realizing you weren't going to offer her false reassurance like everyone else, but also that it wasn't that big a deal that her drawn-on eyebrows were half an inch higher than the two pale and hairless half-moons created by her terrible waxing mistake.

Melissa stood in front of the mirror, cleaning her face and

sniffling. After a few moments, you both cackled like crazy. Then she looked at me. "Oh, man, I'm going to miss you!"

It was really nice that she said that, since you were the one she really liked. Even if it wasn't true, at that moment it felt good.

When I arrived home, our lounge room was packed with new boxes, which meant that Uncle Sokkha had paid a visit. My mother was crouched on the floor, peeling the masking tape from the tops of the boxes. "*Wah,* who would wear this?" she asked, holding up the sample she was meant to replicate, a very short, dark red skirt with buttons up the front. I did not tell her that some of the girls at Christ Our Savior would commit unholy acts for a thing like that.

"Hey, Ma, will you have any of that material left?" I asked.

"Yes."

"Can I have some?"

"What do you want it for?"

"I want to make a skirt."

"No."

"What do you mean, no?"

"Don't waste your time."

"It won't be a short one," I promised.

"You've got better things to do now," she told me.

Dad sat on our mustard-yellow sofa, which had been donated to us thirteen years earlier by the Brotherhood of St.

Laurence. He was looking through the navy folder that Mrs. Grey had given us. *"Wah!"* he suddenly exclaimed. "Look here, Quyen! Look at this!"

My mother eased herself off the floor and sat next to my father. "One hundred and thirty-five dollars!" she exclaimed.

They were looking at the uniform list from Edmondsons. "And that's only the jacket," said my father. "Look at this skirt!"

He held up the booklet and showed us the winter uniform, a pleated tartan kilt worn by a smug girl who obviously did not care about having cold legs in winter.

"Let me see that." My mother took the booklet from him and put it up close to her face. All the sewing had made her nearsighted. Then she said the five words I dreaded most: "I could make you that."

"But where would you get the material?" I hoped to put her off, but I knew she would try to find it in the Vietnamese fabric stores. I also knew she would never find an exact match, because the fabric was probably imported from England for a hundred dollars a yard. She would pick a polyester tartan in a close-enough pattern, and for the double-buckle belt link at the top of the kilt, she would go to the fabric store and find a plastic-painted-to-look-like-metal one. She had no idea how worlds apart her homemade skirt would be, even if her couture skills were just as good as those of the tailors of Edmondsons, if not better.

"No one will know the difference," she said.

"Old woman," my father sighed (though in fact he was five years older), "she is not going to have one of your peasant homemade outfits for this school. What will the teachers think of this cheapskate family? They're already providing her with a full scholarship!"

Even though he had insulted my mother's sewing skills and implied she was stingy, Linh, I did not say anything to contradict my father. I was on his side, because he was on mine.

TERM ONE

Dear Linh,

On my first day, when I entered our homeroom, I had no idea where to sit, so I headed for the first empty seat I saw, next to a girl with very long hair braided into a plait and a pound-cake face flecked with freckles.

"You're the new girl, aren't you?" she asked.

"Yes—how did you know?"

"All your clothes are new."

I looked down, embarrassed. Not a thread of my new uniform had been in the wash. My shirt had crease lines from being folded in the packet. Around the room, the other girls' clothes had a lived-in, everyday look. Later I would see how they chucked their jackets on the backseats of buses, tied their sweaters around their waists, not caring if the sleeves stretched, and hiked up the hems of their summer skirts. No one wore the blue hair ribbons—I was the only one dumb enough to have taken that part of the uniform code seriously.

The girl next to me was named Katie. "Don't worry," she told me, "you look great."

I didn't detect any sarcasm. She was being genuinely kind, and at that moment I learned two things about Katie. By telling me that she noticed my clothes were new, she showed that she was honest, but she could also tell the occasional white lie if the circumstances called for it.

After homeroom, we marched to the performing arts center for assembly. Years Seven and Eight sat level with the stage, while Years Nine and Ten sat in the raised seating areas. Looking down, I could see a moving blanket of blue and maroon. I had never seen anything so ordered before in real life, so . . . well, uniform. Even though we had a uniform at Christ Our Savior, we got away with wearing whatever socks we wanted as long as they were white, and whatever shirt we wanted as long as it was blue. Remember how some girls came in with all kinds of casual shirts, while others pulled their socks so high that they looked like tights, Linh?

Here, every girl in the auditorium had her hair tied back if it was below shoulder length. Here, every girl wore a blazer. Here, every girl sat still, no matter how long she had to wait. If she couldn't sit still, she was probably told to sit on her hands, as I saw many of the Year Sevens doing. I had been to assemblies before, but this was the model of an assembly. Suddenly I understood what it was to *assemble,* just as a few moments before I had truly understood *uniform.*

I heard the sound of bagpipes, and everyone began to stand. Then I saw a girl playing *actual* bagpipes march through the stained-glass double doors of the auditorium.

Following her were two girls carrying long white flags emblazoned with the Laurinda motto—one in Latin (*Concordia Prorsum*) and the other in English (Forward in Harmony). The girls had more badges and pins on their lapels than a World War II veteran. Following them were four girls carrying red, blue, yellow and green flags. These, I presumed, were the prefects.

Finally the staff of the college marched by, all decked out in black academic gowns. Some had sashes of green or orange, while others had tassels and other scholarly insignia. I recognized Mrs. Grey by her red hood.

When they all had taken their seats onstage, Mrs. Grey stood up and looked around the auditorium. A few students were still quietly talking to each other. Mrs. Grey raised her right hand in the air, as if in parody of a bored student waiting to answer a question.

Then something strange happened. Students in the middle row—Year Eights—also raised their right arms in the air. Then the Year Nines followed. Meanwhile, the teachers at each end of the aisles raised their right arms. The befuddled Year Sevens, with whom I could identify, slowly began to copy the motion. Soon everyone on the ground floor of the auditorium had raised an arm and was quiet. That's when I noticed that all the girls on the top level also had their right arms raised. The entire school did! I quickly shot mine up. The room was now dead silent—you could hear every suppressed cough.

Over the next few weeks I grew used to this technique, which the staff and teachers used to quiet the girls. I saw how effective it was: it required barely any effort on their part, and you could see almost immediately who had caught on and who hadn't, and how we silently policed each other.

When all was quiet, the hands went down. The principal, Mrs. Ellison, walked to the podium. A petite and pretty woman in a pale pink silk shirt and a navy double-breasted suit with small gold buttons, she resembled a geriatric Princess Diana. She even had a string of pearls around her neck. I almost laughed—she was nothing like good old Sister Clarke with her frizzy hair and brown A-line skirts!

"It is good to see you all back, young ladies. I hope you had a refreshing break over the summer in readiness for a new school year." She then told us what the young ladies of Laurinda could expect from the year ahead. First, the stained-glass windows of the main wing were being restored to their former glory with glass flown in from England. This term we would have seven more guest speakers than last year, including chocolatier queen Angela Piper. The girls cheered; apparently, Penelope had come from a rival girls' school so it was a coup to have her. Also, the girls were probably thinking, free samples, woo-hoo. Then, after the applause and cheering, Mrs. Ellison reminded us once more to take the academic year seriously.

A musical interlude followed. A girl named Trisha sat at the side of the stage in front of a grand piano. I hadn't even noticed the piano until then, so big was the auditorium. She started to play.

She was possessed. Her hands seemed to drag her body left and right, up and down the keys of the piano, at one point almost toppling her out of her seat. It was as if her fingers were playing some mad game of chase with her torso, except that every time they landed on a key, they made magical sounds that made me think of ice cubes in clear cups, floors of buildings collapsing with tiles tinkling unbroken, the first chink of daylight through castle windows in faraway countries, flying fish, volcanoes erupting with fireworks, the Lamb in his white beanie, my mother's Singer in full swing.

When she finished, Trisha stood up and took a small bow. It was the most incredible thing I had ever seen a fifteen-year-old do. She was a genius, Linh. At Christ Our Savior she would have been on the cover of the school magazine— they'd have made her play the organ in church every week and given her a nickname like "Magic Digits."

But even more incredible than Trisha's talent was the applause: I was the only one clapping like a grinning monkey-and-cymbal toy. Embarrassed, realizing that everyone else was offering only a polite palm patting, I toned it down.

When assembly ended, none of the girls mentioned Trisha's playing as we moved off to our first classes. It was only after I'd been to a couple of assemblies that I realized every musical offering would be just as intense as the first, and every reaction would be just as tepid.

Ms. Vanderwerp taught my first class of the week, history. Wearing a long aquamarine dress that ended in wavy lines halfway down her calves, she looked like a Pac-Man ghost. She had enormous convex glasses, so thick that her eyes seemed to swim around in each lens.

Ms. Vanderwerp explained that we would be studying twentieth-century history, from the causes of World War I to the Vietnam War. She had a trembly voice, but she wasn't even that old. When she wrote on the whiteboard, her hand was shaky too. On her desk sat a cylinder of wipes. Sometimes she would emit a nervous laugh, but most of the time her mouth drooped as if she'd had a stroke.

I was seated next to a girl named Amber Leslie. Ms. Vanderwerp had arranged us in alphabetical last-name order around the room. "Easier for me to remember you in the first few weeks," she told us.

When she called out my name, she got my first name, middle name and surname mixed up. She apologized when her watery-bowl eyes found me in the room.

"Just call me Lucy," I said.

She smiled. "Thank you, Lucy," she said, as if I had just invented some kind of life-changing supermop to free her from many hours of housekeeping.

Out of the corner of my eye, I saw Amber Leslie smile. I turned toward her, and the first thing I noticed was that she had very unusual lips. Her top lip was puffier than her bottom lip and jutted forward a little—not because buckteeth were giving it a nudge, for Amber had small, perfect white teeth, but almost as if her chin was shyly pushing her bottom lip behind her top one. She had the endearing jaw of a baby, gazelle-brown eyes and bangs that were trimmed so that two-thirds of her forehead lay bare.

I'm not doing a very good job of description, Linh, because those features and haircut sound as if they belong to a drooling asylum inmate, but on Amber Leslie they were mesmerizing. Because each one of her features was individually so striking, it took me a moment to realize that her face as a whole was stammeringly beautiful, a rare combination of beauty, innocence and experience that would surely provoke asthmatic lust in boys and mute envy in girls. She also smelled like the Body Shop's Fuzzy Peach perfume oil.

Distracted by Amber, I didn't notice that Ms. Vanderwerp was handing out term outlines, until one of the girls piped up: "Ms. V, hey, Ms. V, this term outline is for the Year Eights."

"Oh," she exclaimed, taking a closer look, "I'm afraid it is. Oh, dear. My apologies, girls." At least she didn't call us "young ladies." "I must have left the others by the photocopier. Won't be long!"

After she left the room, some of the students looked at each other. It was a look that made me realize Ms. Vanderwerp was prone to such mistakes. At Christ Our Savior, whenever teachers left the class, girls would start calling out to each other across the room: "Hey, Melissa, lift up your bangs and give us a look! Aww, come on, they're not that bad. They'll grow back!" Or: "Quick, Tully, give us the answer!" But quietness at Laurinda didn't necessarily mean good behavior, I saw, or even indifference. Many things were going on in that quiet—a raised eyebrow, a rolling eyeball, a deliberate sniff. The room was soon reeking with the odorless stench of collective contempt.

When Ms. Vanderwerp returned, she passed around the correct handouts. She had been gone for less than three minutes, but I could feel something had shifted. "Thank you," I said automatically when she came around to my desk, but Amber Leslie didn't.

There was another girl I noticed on that first day, Linh, and that was because she was so rude. "Typical," she muttered when Ms. Vanderwerp called the roll and made us all change seats. "Typical," she groaned when Ms. Vanderwerp told us that we would be studying twentieth-century history. When I heard her sigh her third "Typical" as Ms. Vanderwerp left the room, I realized that here was a sagacious reincarnate who could predict the turn of events with pinpoint accuracy, which was probably why life bored her so much.

Her name was Chelsea White. Unlike Amber's Angelina Jolie appeal, she was more the Jennifer Aniston kind of pretty, the kind that only other girls made a fuss about. She had curly doll hair and pink cheeks, as if someone had slapped her twice. She looked like one of those imitation Franklin Mint porcelain dolls, with the features painted a couple of millimeters above the grooves—the ones that would turn on you when you went to sleep at night.

When Ms. Vanderwerp handed her the correct document and requested the Year Eight outline back, Chelsea showed Ms. Vanderwerp that she had torn it into four pieces.

How had she managed that, I wondered, when I hadn't heard the sound of paper ripping?

"Chelsea White!" scolded Ms. Vanderwerp. "Now, tell me, why on earth did you do that?"

"You gave us the wrong class outline, Ms. V," Chelsea replied innocently. "I didn't think you needed this anymore."

"Well, I did need it!" protested Ms. Vanderwerp. Next to me, Amber Leslie was calmly peeling her cuticles. Ms. Vanderwerp had been the careless one, and Chelsea was making her pay.

That was when I learned a very important early lesson: here at Laurinda, mistakes meant annihilation.

At recess, I was called to Mrs. Grey's office. I had not spoken to her since our "interview" almost a month before. Her office was as bare as when I had first seen it, and when I sat down, I had the curious feeling that I should have asked her for permission.

"So, Miss Lam. How are you finding your first day?"

"Fine," I replied.

"You know, you are our inaugural Equal Access student," she said. "That means you are the first one we have ever had."

"Yes, Mrs. Grey," I answered.

"You are aware that Laurinda is making a big investment in you? In committing to fund your education for the next three years, we are gambling on an unknown quantity."

"Yes, Mrs. Grey." And then, "Thank you, Mrs. Grey."

"What does your father do?" she asked me point-blank.

I was appalled by the directness of her question—and by how much adults thought they could get away with when they were dealing with minors and there was no one else in the room.

"Dad works."

"Where?"

"At Victory."

"What's that?"

"A carpet factory."

"What about your mother? Home duties?"

I nodded. I didn't want to tell her about the sewing.

"Do you speak English at home?"

"No," I answered.

She gave me that smile again. "Now, Miss Lam, tell me what books you studied last year."

"*The Perks of Being a Wallflower.*"

She looked at me blankly.

"By Stephen Chbosky."

Her brow furrowed. She'd clearly not heard of it and was not interested. "What else?"

"*Romeo and Juliet.*"

"What else?"

"*Stand by Me.* But that wasn't a book." I wasn't sure why I added this. "It was a film."

"Ah, yes, based on a Stephen King novel," remarked Mrs. Grey, in the same way a person might say, *ah, yes, that ingrown toenail, part of my foot.* "You are aware that at Laurinda we don't study movies?"

"Yes."

"And we don't study any books considered young adult literature. For instance, your Stephen Chbosky."

So she *had* heard of him.

"*Romeo and Juliet* is a play we study in our first year of high school. We consider it a good introduction to Shakespeare at the elementary level." She paused. "Now, I don't blame you for your school's choice of reading, but here at Laurinda we are a serious academic college, as evidenced by our English curriculum. We study the classics—Dickens, Austen, the poetry of Donne, Keats—as well as contemporary classics—Brecht, Graham Greene, Edith Wharton, Fitzgerald."

I nodded mutely. Aside from Dickens and Austen, I had no idea who these writers were.

"We think it is wise for you to participate in a bridging course."

I wanted to protest, did you not read the reference that Mr. Shipp gave me? *Lucy Lam is one of our strongest English students. Her dramatic monologue from the perspective of Charlie from* The Perks of Being a Wallflower *was one of the most creative pieces of extended fiction in the class.*

"Now, you realize that we are not picking on you," she explained, in the way a doctor tells you that an anesthetic is not going to hurt before the amputation. "In fact, Lucy, it was your English essay that gained you this scholarship in the first place. It was outstanding. Many of the students who sat the exam, who appeared to have crammed for mathematics, neglected their writing. Many pieces were, I'm afraid to say, very poor. There was even an essay where the candidate thought he was some kind of hoodlum from the Bronx whose brother was in prison. Although we commend great imaginative feats, that one was the unfortunate result of a mind subjected to too much American television." I didn't say anything while she cast her eyes heavenward in silent lamentation. "Naturally, that student did not make it into Auburn Academy."

"Weren't there some other good essays, though?" I asked, and immediately realized my mistake—that I was implying most of the essays were crap and mine was outstanding. Back at our old school, Linh, this would have been taken as a simple question, a display of polite humility. Here it was a judgment, one I was not entitled to make.

"Fishing for compliments, are we, Miss Lam?" Mrs. Grey asked, one eyebrow raised. Once more I realized that at Laurinda, you had to think very, very carefully every time you considered opening your mouth. "Of course there were. In fact, there was one other remarkable piece, the runner-up essay, about the founder of Amnesty International."

"How come you didn't pick her?" I asked. It was yet another mistake, turning me transparent like the curtainless window of our house, where outsiders could peer in on a place where there was nothing worth stealing. How could I have known it was a *her*? "Or him," I added.

"We found *her* piece—yes, it was a she, and she was close competition for you, you may be interested to know—we found her piece too stilted. Her grammar was perfect, her writing was fluent and sophisticated, but there was just something off-kilter about it. Almost as if she'd memorized a speech."

Here you could not be mediocre, but you had to be well balanced. Not too real, yet not too fake. Tully tried to be someone she was not, Ivy was exactly who she was, and both were unacceptable at this school. That was probably what made me the ideal scholarship recipient. I was smart enough, but I had no particular sense of ownership over my thoughts. It was you who gave me a sense of belonging, Linh, with your magnetic ways and madcap schemes. Without you, I felt like a cipher.

"This is what will happen," Mrs. Grey continued. "You

will take some remedial lessons to get you up to scratch, and then you will be transferred back to ordinary English."

If you'd been with me, you would have thrown a fit. How dare the school think I was not ready for Green and Fitzsimmons and whoever else when they'd given me a scholarship based on my essay writing? You would have prodded me to defend myself. But you weren't there, and I didn't want to make ripples.

"You should feel very lucky," instructed Mrs. Grey. "I have arranged for you to have a one-on-one tutor twice a week. Mrs. Leslie is a Laurindan herself, and also the president of the Laurinda Book Club. She knows the English syllabus inside out."

The last time I had one-on-one lessons with anyone was in Grade One with the school speech pathologist, because I pronounced all my *r*'s as *w*'s. That was to fix a flaw that, although "weally endeawing" as a little kid, would have screwed me up big-time as a teenager. I wondered whether there was something about me that only Mrs. Grey could see, something that, without intervention, would doom me to failure.

Gina was another girl who stood out from that first day's blur of faces, because she had dyed hair the hue of a cherry lollipop, cut in a bob that ended beneath her chin. You could easily locate her in any classroom—she was like a round sale sticker on a plain carton of eggs. We weren't allowed to have any earrings except small studs, but Gina had tiny diamonds that she hoped no teacher would notice. Also, while the rest of us had blank nails, hers were white-tipped and glossy with clear paint.

Gina had the hots for Mr. Sinclair, badly. He was a new teacher, I learned, and when we first entered the room we could see only the back of his suit because he was at the whiteboard. It seemed that all male staff were required to wear suits to work; the women had to be dressed in the female equivalent, which was usually an elegantly sculpted work dress, a cashmere twinset, or slacks and a blouse.

When Mr. Sinclair finished, he stepped back, and we saw what he had written: *POLITICS: From the Greek—"poly" meaning "many," and "ticks" meaning "bloodsucking creatures."* All the girls except Gina made a kind of *huh* noise, as if they were too clever for such a bad pun.

When Mr. Sinclair turned around, the girls expected to see some sort of "hangin' wid ma homies in da hood" teacher. You know the type, Linh: forty years old, dadlike but still thinking he's funny as hell. Instead, they saw how young Mr. Sinclair was, and how attractive. Take a bunch of girls and separate them from the boys from kindergarten on, and that is the kind of thing they will notice.

Gina was noticing it more than anyone. I swear, Linh, you could see the impure thoughts forming on her features. Secretly, I liked this about her, that she didn't seem to have a filter between her thoughts and her face.

We expected Mr. Sinclair to point to the board and read out what he had written, after which all the girls would laugh, just because he was so cute and they wanted to make a good impression. But he didn't. Instead, he introduced himself and started the lesson. Politics, Mr. Sinclair told us, was about governments. "But if you want to break it down further, it is essentially the study of people and power."

Glancing around the room, I could already see how this was playing out in our class. The desks were arranged in a U shape around Mr. Sinclair's front table. "Socratic learning," he called it, but Chelsea pointed out that Socrates had never included any women in his teachings. She wasn't a bimbo after all, I saw, but was just prone to say snide things every seven minutes or so, as if she had bitch Tourette's. She, Amber and a girl named Brodie Newberry were seated at the bottom end of the U, as far away from the teacher as possible, but also with the best view of the whole show.

Brodie was a tall, dark-haired girl who didn't say much, but it was an unsettling silence. She had dark eyes that were neither green nor gray; they seemed to absorb rather than reflect your image if you looked into them. I had the feeling that there were things beneath the surface waiting to float up when they stopped swimming. I realized then that I had seen Brodie before: she was one of the prefects who had marched into the auditorium bearing the school banner.

At the other end of the U, directly opposite me, was Gina. It turned out, Linh, that she would not budge from that position all term. She told us she was so close she could smell Mr. Sinclair's aftershave, and it smelled like CK One.

A pattern was set that first day: Chelsea or Brodie would offer their views, or shoot questions at Mr. Sinclair, and sometimes Amber would back up her friends. Because the three girls were hogging Mr. Sinclair's attention so regally, often for twenty minutes at a stretch, the rest of us felt like we were watching a trial on a television set we could not switch off. At times it seemed the girls were judges and Mr. Sinclair was a defense lawyer, and we were the bored jury listening to the case of some white-collar crime we did not understand.

"Why do people think the Whitlam dismissal was such a bad thing if the government was in such a shambles that no bills were being passed?" demanded Chelsea, as if her life depended on it.

Mr. Sinclair was the ever-patient explainer, but his Socratic method wasn't working. I wasn't understanding very much at all. How did these girls know so much about the world, enough to be able to form opinions about it? I still didn't know who Whitlam was, and these conversations in class didn't offer me any firm foothold.

Sometimes I detected an answer that was not quite right,

and I waited patiently for an opening, a small gap of silence in which I could say something or ask a question. But the moment I opened my mouth to say, "Amber, I think your definition of a constitutional monarchy . . . ," the gap would close again. Already they were talking about a referendum for a republic, and my half sentence would be left dangling. Often I felt ridiculous, like a choir member still singing the chorus when everyone else had moved on to the next verse.

Pretty quickly I learned the nicknames of all the teachers. Mrs. Grey was known as the Growler, probably because if you were stuck in her office with the door closed for longer than fifteen minutes, you usually came out in tears. Ms. Vanderwerp was Ms. V and Mr. Sinclair was simply H.O., standing for "Hot One," even after Gina found out that he was married and had an infant son.

I saw his wife picking him up one day after school in a car that had a baby seat in the back; as he approached, she wound down her window and stuck out her tongue at him. It is hard to explain why, but I found that charming, Linh. Probably it had something to do with how *ordinary* she was. Even from a distance I could tell that she was not as attractive as he was, though I would never agree with Gina, who muttered, "Why is he with that fugly cow?"

Gina was a bit of a loner, but she didn't seem too bothered by it. She was the sort of girl who wanted a boyfriend so badly that she gravitated toward whichever group happened to be discussing their crushes or their boy troubles. I'm not sure how the other girls felt about this, but I think sometimes they were just happy that Gina put herself forward so they didn't have to look so desperate or dumb. They would be like, "Oh, we usually talk about intellectual stuff like the role of class in Ruth Park's novels, but since Gina is here . . ."

On that first day at lunchtime, I found my first friend. Or, more accurately, she found me. Katie sought me out and gave me a more interesting tour of the school than Mrs. Grey had, that was for sure. I discovered that all the opulence my father and I had seen on the official tour was in contrast to the student corridors, which were littered with rubbish.

Our lockers were our only private spaces, and some girls lined them with photos of their pets or pop icons, and inspirational cards. The inside of my locker was completely blank, which was the way I wanted it, and I always shoved my bag in there. I decided not to leave it on top of the lockers, because Katie had warned me that some girls would trawl through bags; anything inside was fair game.

There weren't many places to go at lunchtime. So that the grass would stay perfectly green, we weren't allowed on the lawn at the front of the school. According to Katie, the performing arts center had taken up most of the space where an oval used to be, and we weren't allowed in there during lunch or recess. Yet even back when there was an oval, the girls weren't allowed on it, because it was connected to a little park reserve and the teachers were scared that pedophiles or flashers might be loitering nearby.

There were two tennis courts, but those were usually locked during lunch and recess, as were the seven music rooms. You weren't allowed to go in there to jam with the guitars, because that kind of thing was reserved for the talented.

Katie, who had been at Laurinda since kindergarten, pointed out all the occupied places: this corner was where the musicians hung out, in that stairwell dwelled the debaters, on this patch of concrete were the high-achieving Mediterranean girls (at Christ Our Savior we called them the Smart Wogs, remember? Yvonne was the smartest of them all), and here and there sat the little satellite groups of Year Sevens, Eights or Nines, who might as well have been invisible.

There was one unoccupied bench, near the rose garden—in fact, with a direct view of the blooms—but Katie steered me away from it. "The Cabinet sits there," she said. "They'd start a War of the Roses if anyone took their spot." She laughed.

"What's the Cabinet?" I asked.

Katie told me how, in the 1890s, Laurinda had been a finishing school for young ladies. After the girls were educated, they were said to be "in the Cabinet"—which meant on display to eligible bachelors who might become their husbands. Those who did not get picked from the Cabinet were left on the shelf, shoved to the very back, where they were condemned never to appear in the wedding announcements of newspapers. Many of them had returned here to teach.

Although most girls these days aimed to go to university, not to sit at home embroidering linen for their hope chests, the things that mattered then—attractiveness, wealth, personality—still mattered in determining your Cabinet position. Over time the term had evolved to name the unspoken hierarchy at Laurinda: a trio of girls so powerful they were collectively known as "the Cabinet." It seemed that the Cabinet had always existed, although its members constantly changed, morphing into new faces every few years. They were the ones responsible for keeping the elusive "Laurinda spirit" alive.

This year it was Amber, Chelsea and Brodie, three top-shelfers who were protected like finest porcelain by the administration and taken out regularly to show off their kiln marks, the stamp of the school's quality.

But I didn't understand why it was Amber, Chelsea and Brodie who were at the top, Linh. Sure, they were pretty enough, but (with the exception of Amber) there were a dozen more beautiful girls on campus. Amber and Brodie were also teacher's pets of a kind, and in any other school that did not lead to high status. But here, strangely enough, it seemed to increase their power.

Amber's beauty was so distracting that she didn't need to develop much of a personality. Brodie, on the other hand, reminded me of Tully in her steely ambition and competitiveness. You didn't want to be a threat to Tully because you'd wound her fragile sense of self—jealousy and insecurity and fear would flash across her face so transparently that you'd feel bad. But I had the feeling that you didn't want to be a threat to Brodie because she would cut you down.

Unlike Tully, Brodie did not seem assailed by self-doubt over her intelligence, or by the fear that her future would be determined by her performance on exams. The difference was that Tully wanted so desperately to be in, whereas Brodie was already in. She had been in since she was in kindergarten, and she was determined to keep others out. Brodie did not smile very often, but when she did, it was not an invitation to friendship but a signal to ward off closeness. It seemed that if she looked at you, you had to pay your dues. Other girls were always smiling at her, but I wondered if they were baring their teeth from fear—like animals did when threatened.

Katie and I found some steps outside the maintenance shed, near the side entrance of the school, and that became our spot. We watched as Mrs. Grey conducted tours for the occasional visiting families of prospective international students, declaring with expansive hand gestures, "Here is where the girls play tennis" and "The young ladies like to hold music recitals in our new music rooms. Do you play an instrument, Swee Ling?"

When this happened, Katie would smile at me and I would smile back, and I felt like we were in this together. It didn't take me very long to figure out that Katie was a loner, and why she was. She just couldn't stop talking. But I liked Katie and I let her talk.

The Cabinet paraded through the college at lunchtime. They could talk to everyone and anyone, even though they did not do so too often, but no one talked to them for fear of being ignored.

"Oh my God, that was *sooo* hard," Brodie exclaimed after a math test one afternoon.

"I know, hey?" said Chelsea. "That last page was crazy scary."

Brodie turned to the girl behind her. "Did you find it difficult, Nicola?"

"Not really," replied Nicola, flattered to be asked. "I've been studying really hard for it for a week."

"You mean you didn't find it very difficult?" asked Brodie. "Wow, Nicola. Wow. *Everyone* found the last page impossible. I thought there were some trick questions in there. In fact, I'm sure there were."

Nicola's face crumpled. "What do you mean?"

"You know."

"No, I don't."

"Oh, then don't worry about it. You must have aced the test! You *are* a math genius, Nicola."

And with that they walked away, leaving poor Nicola to fret for days until the results came back.

It was bad timing that Laurinda held the annual Senior School Art Retrospective Exhibition on Valentine's Day, especially as it was at Auburn Academy. The exhibition was supposed to showcase the works of last year's students, but nobody cared about them when the fresh scent of hormones from this year's male cohort was in the air.

We were walking to the boys' school, a little way up the street, when Mrs. Grey noticed that Gina's face had the flat brown color and texture of an unsliced supermarket bread loaf. "Gina Grant, what is that on your face?" she yelled.

We all turned back to look. Even a neighborhood old guy watering his camellias jolted, his hose making an arc across the footpath.

"My features, miss."

"Answer my question seriously! I'm sick of your antics. Are you wearing makeup?"

Gina was sent back to Laurinda to wipe it off. "Look at the shitload of makeup on your face, Growler," she muttered as she turned back.

Just as she passed the Cabinet, Amber sang in a whispery voice, very quietly and almost imperceptibly, "Slut, slutty slut slut."

★ ★ ★

At the exhibition, we went around looking at paintings and sculptures on themes such as despair and anorexia and war, while the boys snaked their way around us in sniggering huddles. Basically, we pretended that they were there to inconvenience us, blocking our view.

Gina was the only one making it obvious that she was excited to be around the opposite sex. Others were more discreet, although I noticed the Cabinet was not immune to the charms of the Auburn boys. They had begun acting coy. You'd never think that these were the same girls who planned world domination in our politics class.

I happened to be standing near them, beside a pink papier-mâché sculpture of a brain with electrical wires jutting out of it, when an Asian boy with glasses walked by. Amber nudged me. "Look, there's one for you." She and Chelsea giggled.

It was incredible how they assumed that I would not be interested in any other type of boy, but that's how they were. From their white-daisy bouquet of slim pickings, they cast out all the yellow chrysanthemums, and anything brown was considered wilted.

Back at Christ Our Savior, a cute boy was a cute boy, even if he was a bit of a loser. But here it seemed that cuteness had to be filtered through quite a few lenses. It reminded me of going to the optometrist and having to read the letters on the wall, how each lens would be placed before my eyes until the fuzziness disappeared and the letters became sharp and distinct. That's how Laurindans saw their boys—in fine, fine detail, down to the cut of their button-up shirts.

But it seemed to me that all these girls were myopic, because the guys they considered popular were not necessarily the hottest. Some were downright dweeby. And the hotter guys from Auburn Academy—a tall, dark, handsome one called Harshan, and the Marlon Brando look-alike Emilio— were treated like outsiders. Maybe these guys were too visceral for them. Laurinda girls were into Jane Austen heroes, not hunks.

Harshan had skin the color of a violin and an earring in one ear; I noticed it as he leaned over to poke a finger at one of the wires of the brain sculpture. When Chelsea spoke to him, she didn't ask what he thought of the sculpture. Instead, she seemed to want to foster some cultural cohesion by asking, "So what part of India are you from?"

"I was born here, actually," he said in a friendly way. "My parents are Sri Lankan, from Fiji."

Even someone like Harshan was not immune to the charms of the Cabinet, I saw, particularly with Amber standing there. Here was the thing about the accidental artwork of her face—a few millimeters off and her eyes would be set too close together; a few millimeters apart and her mouth would make her chin look sunken. It was this tenuousness that made her so hot, that made boys feel they were living on the edge just by looking at her.

"Same diff," said Amber, and she and Chelsea giggled. They were flirting with him; they assumed Harshan understood they were not racist, because they had deigned to speak to him. But they had no real idea what the difference between Sri Lanka and India was—and, making it worse, they didn't care. One was Dilmah tea and the other Gandhi. We didn't study South Asian history at this school.

"Ignorant bitches," he muttered under his breath.

"Excuse me?" Amber's eyes widened.

"What did you call us?" Chelsea turned toward him. "That is sooo offensive. Oh my God. Geez, some people can't take a joke," she pouted. I could see she was wounded because her eyes glittered like anthracite. Suddenly, it seemed, this was all Harshan's fault—he was the brute, insulting these two young Laurinda diplomats who meant well, who were curious about his culture. They were *nice* girls, and he was a condescending, sexist pig.

Harshan looked down at them, and I could tell that all the beauty he'd seen there had dissolved. Then he did something completely unexpected, which made them squeal. He lowered his head and bowed from the waist—a long, drawn-out bow that came to just above the hem of their skirts, his back straight as an ironing board. He slowly came up and held his hands in the prayer position. Bobbing his head from side to side, he said, "Oh, golly gee, ma'am, I'm welly, welly solly— please accept my most humble apologies." His face was hard but, unlike Chelsea's, it was not brittle. He turned and walked away.

Amber and Chelsea burst into laughter. "Stupid curry muncher," said Chelsea, and then told a story about how guys like that were always trying to pick her up at Urban nightclub and how they couldn't dance for shit.

I moved away from the brain sculpture.

Amber returned from Auburn Academy with a pen. It had a plastic heart at the top that lit up, and it played a tinny song when you wrote with it. I'm not sure which boy had given it to her, but Amber was ecstatic, flashing it around class, showing teachers and using it to write, until Mrs. Trengrove said that the music was too distracting; could she please use a normal pen like everyone else? Even that did not ruin her heart-thumping joy, and she bounded to class, skipping and leaping, showing off her gazelle legs.

There was love elsewhere too.

In politics, someone had put a single heart-shaped chocolate wrapped in gold foil on Mr. Sinclair's desk. We all knew it was Gina. He walked to his desk, put down his planner and lesson folder, and pretended not to see it.

"Sir!" Chelsea called out. "Sir, someone left something for you!"

He also pretended to be deaf.

"Sir," Chelsea repeated, "I think someone left you a present."

He looked down at his desk, at the very spot where the chocolate was, so we knew that he knew it was there. As much as he tried, he wasn't very good at feigning surprise. His face was turning as red as his hair.

"Oh," he exclaimed.

Poor guy. Perhaps teachers' college hadn't taught him what to do in this scenario. We could tell he was wishing for the chocolate to disappear. To acknowledge that it was there, and that it was intended for him, would be like, well . . . like taking candy from a minor.

We all started to laugh, which gave him an opportunity to try to be a teacher again. "All right, cut it out. That's enough carrying on."

"What are you going to do with it, Mr. Sinclair?"

"Ooh, you have a secret admirer!"

"I wonder who it is!"

"Someone loves you, sir!"

"Yes, very funny," he said drily. "Now, where did we leave off last class? The American electoral system, I believe."

You had to hand it to him—no one gave a toss about how the Americans elected their president, but he plowed on regardless. The girls were too distracted by that little gold object on his desk, a symbol of their power over this awkward but endearingly attractive man.

I could look at them all, Linh, and tell myself how ridiculously these girls were carrying on, but during recess, sitting with Katie, who genuinely didn't care about the art show visit or about getting presents, I felt a pang. As she talked, I started to fall into my usual reverie about the sort of year I might have had if I hadn't changed schools. Maybe, if I had stayed at Christ Our Savior, I might have had a boyfriend from St. Andrew's. . . .

There's a secret to getting a boyfriend at fifteen, and it is this: you have to have a group of friends. You'll never get picked up alone unless by creeps, or unless you are extremely beautiful (and even then you'll mostly get creeps), because alone you have no personality. It's only when you're with your friends that you start to shine.

Boys are the same. You see a boy around his mates, and you can pick whether he is the clown of the group, the quiet philosopher or the alpha male. Alone, you can't tell because he'd act differently, and of course he can't tell anything about your personality either. When alone with a member of the opposite sex, we feign indifference, even though we yearn to be exaggerated versions of ourselves, filled with extra bravado or extra niceness.

My problem this year was that I no longer had a group. I had lost you and Yvonne and Ivy. Even Tully had been worth tolerating. As much as I liked Katie, we weren't really a group. We never did anything together outside of class or lunch break. We never called each other up in the evening. And our dynamic was that Katie talked and I listened.

In my first week, Katie had asked me, "What do you do during school holidays?" but before giving me a chance to reply, she said, "I usually spend them on my cousin's place near the countryside, in Mallah. They have seven acres and four cows and some sheep. It's only a hobby farm, though, because my uncle owns a small business in town. It's beautiful and real peaceful there. My cousin Dick and I ride horses. You should come up with me next school holidays!"

Oh my God, Linh, this girl was straight out of a 1950s picture book! She had called her cousin "Dick" with no sense of irony whatsoever.

I wondered what it would be like to be admired or desired by a boy, and thought about how lucky Amber was. I guess Gina was thinking the same thing, because she came up to us at recess. "Did you hear what Amber called me when the Growler sent me back to school to wash my face off?"

"No," Katie lied. "What did she call you, Gina?"

Just as Gina was about to tell us what we already knew, she spotted something that made her jaw clamp like a clam. The Cabinet was approaching!

If the rest of the school had not taken them so seriously, I would have laughed then, because they walked like a movie mean-girl gang, with heads held high and each with one hand (the right) in her blazer pocket. What was this, some kind of Western where they'd pull out their pistols and have a shoot-out?

Gina bared her teeth in what she hoped was a smile.

Brodie acknowledged Katie and me by giving us a small nod that barely tilted her chin. Then she turned to Gina. "Hey there, Regina. We hear you've been going around the school telling all and sundry that Amber has damaged your good name."

She actually used the words *all and sundry*, Linh.

"Oh yeah?" demanded Gina, but her voice was fearful. "Who told you that?"

"It doesn't matter who told who what." That was Chelsea—she was less articulate. "If you have a problem with any of us, you should have the guts to say it to our faces."

"Yeah," said Amber. "I thought we were friends."

Gina looked stunned: she'd never so much as contemplated the possibility that the Cabinet would consider her a friend.

"I'm hurt that you've been backstabbing me, Gina," said Amber. "I thought that, as friends, we could joke around about stuff like that. I didn't mean it! If anyone is the slut, it is obviously *me*."

Gina was even more flabbergasted.

"Come on, who was the harlot who came back with the tacky pen?" Amber pulled it out and waved it around for emphasis.

"Yeah," Chelsea added. "Imagine all the tricks Amber had to turn to get her cheap, materialistic thrills."

"She has no shame," added Brodie.

Gina cracked a tentative smile. Then, seeing it was okay by the Cabinet, she started to laugh.

Amber flung an arm around Gina's shoulder. "Here, my fellow ho." Then she did something that took Gina completely by surprise. "Have this." She handed Gina her flashing pink pen.

"Oh," stammered Gina. "Oh . . . are you sure?"

"Of course! Chicks before dicks!"

After they left, Gina was in shock. "Oh my God, Amber just gave me this!" she said, as if Katie and I hadn't just witnessed the whole thing. But I knew that Amber's enthusiasm over her gift was all a show. She had only pretended to be proud of the thing to heighten its value before she off-loaded it. Gina had pen envy, and the Cabinet knew just how to fuel it.

"I feel so bad," confessed Gina. "I was a backstabbing bitch to her over some stupid joke."

"Yeah, that was real nice of them," said Katie wistfully, and I looked at my friend, stunned.

After school that day I got off the train at Sunray and headed for the indoor market. "Bring meat home, one pound of beef," my mother had instructed me the night before. "Don't pick the pieces that are brown, and don't loiter."

At Vinh and Robina's Meats, Tully's mother greeted me as I walked in the store. "*Wah,* look at you, so smart in your uniform!"

At school I may have looked like a try-hard, superpolished version of everyone else in my immaculate uniform, but in this neighborhood I stood out like a beacon, a sign to small business owners and factory workers that the next generation would belong to a different class. This was an outfit not made for messing up, or for hacking away at cow carcasses, or for hiding in back rooms threading needles. This outfit was made for a seated life, a life of air-conditioning, long lunches and weekends away in semi-rural cottages.

"How are you finding the work at the school?" asked Tully's mother.

"Okay, Mrs. Cho," I answered. "There's a lot more of it than at Christ Our Savior."

"Of course there is!" she exclaimed. "Those good schools always give you more work. It's how they get students used to working hard at university. Afterward, when they all become professionals, they have good work habits and get promoted sooner."

Tully's mother didn't just talk to you; she lectured. She also had a pretty warped idea of how the world worked.

"So what subjects did you pick this year?"

I listed them, one by one. Mrs. Cho's eyes widened when I finished. "No advanced math?"

"No."

"Why not?"

"I'm no good at it, Mrs. Cho."

"But how are you going to get into university without taking an advanced subject?"

I didn't dare tell her that I also intended to drop most of my science subjects when I got to Year Eleven next year, Linh. She would have had a heart attack and collapsed on her tray of duck livers. Instead, I smiled, because within our community a smile often seemed to be the right answer to anything if you were a girl. "I don't want to be a doctor or anything like that."

"What do you think you will do, then? Law?"

"No," I confessed. "I'd like to get into teaching."

"*Wah!* What a waste, with you being so smart. *Aiyoh,* such a waste. So much smarter than Tully!"

I didn't take the bait. "Not sure about that."

"Ah, that Tully!" Mrs. Cho sighed. "Uncle says she's lazy and, well, you know, that kind of ding-dong way she has—so helpless and impractical. We despair. What will she ever make of herself? She's not as stable or as hardworking as you are."

Even though I didn't really like Tully, it seemed unfair that her own mother would talk about her like this.

"Ay, ay," she said, waving me closer. "I know why Tully did not get into the school. Her English is not as good as yours. I remember now, you won the Year Eight poetry competition! Yes! You!"

I smiled again, although by now my jaw was beginning to feel sore.

"Maybe you can come over and give Tully some lessons in English, huh?" she asked. I said yes to be polite, knowing that the last thing Tully needed was tutoring from me.

Mrs. Cho handed me the bloodied block of steak in a plastic bag with a knot tied at the top. "Well, pass on our regards to your mum and dad. They must be very proud of you."

"Yes, I will. Thanks, Mrs. Cho."

There was a letter from the school in our mailbox when I arrived home.

> *Dear Mr. Lam,*
>
> *It appears that your daughter is not participating in Laurinda's extracurricular physical education program. We stress the importance of physical education for the overall health of every student, and for the beneficial effects of teamwork.*
>
> *Lucy has been signed up for netball but has not attended any games this term. Please ensure that she . . .*

I dropped the letter in the kitchen bin and went to the garage, where I found the Lamb in his cardboard box. He listlessly banged his rattle and one-eyed terry-cloth duck together.

"Yo, Lamb," I said, picking him up. "What have you been up to today?"

His nose was running, so I tore a sheet from a roll of toilet paper Mum had left nearby and wiped his face. A streak of blue stained his cheek. That was strange, I thought; I hadn't seen markers in his box today. Then I looked at the wad in my hands and realized that the tissue was also daubed blue. I looked back at the Lamb, and wiped his nose again. His snot was the same blue that a Toilet Duck cube would turn the water after you flushed.

"Ma!" I yelled. "Ma, come and have a look at this!"

"Coming, coming. No need to yell the house down." My mother came back into the garage with Lamb's bottle and set it down next to her overlocker. "What is it?"

"His snot is blue!"

"Let me see."

I showed her the tissue, and as she took it from me I noticed that her fingertips were the same blue. After examining the tissue, she looked at the pile of denim jeans by her sewing machine. "Oh, crap," she sighed. "He's breathing it all in."

She was right: the Lamb had been inhaling the floating blue-dyed dust motes whenever my mother shook out a pair of jeans or trimmed their edges in preparation for the over-locker. I imagined the branches on the tiny trees of his lungs overhanging with blue threads. Enough time and breathing, I imagined, and each organ would be encased in a little knitted blue pouch.

"Aiyoh," my mother sighed. "We need to find a better place for him to sit during the day." Then she added, needlessly, "Don't tell your father."

She took the Lamb back in her arms. "Poor little Lamby." She handed him to me. "Take him to the kitchen and sit him down in his high chair while you do your homework. Give him his bottle too."

Later, when my mother came out for a coffee break and saw the crumpled letter in the bin, she pulled it out. "Why did you throw this away? What does it say?"

"It's nothing, Mum. The school just wants us to play sports on Saturdays."

"Then go if you want."

"Nah."

"Aha! You can even take the Lamb with you. Then he won't have to stay with me in the garage."

My mum didn't understand some things, Linh, like the way you couldn't have a baby on a hockey field or netball court. To her, sport was play, and if I wanted to play with some of the girls in my class, then the Lamb could come too, and the ones who were off the court could look after him. She had no idea that we would have to go to Alberdine Park on Saturday mornings and stay there for four or five hours. There was even a compulsory sports uniform, which consisted of twelve different items, all bearing the college crest: two polo tops and two swim caps (one for school events and one for house events), a bathing suit, a water-resistant jacket, micro-fiber track pants, leggings, athletic shorts, a netball skirt, a cap and socks, plus a sports bag.

My mother had no idea how seriously Laurinda took its play.

Mrs. Leslie, my remedial English teacher, was the most attractive older lady I had ever seen. She was skinny in a way that women my mother's age in Stanley weren't, and the warm lines around her eyes made her even more lovely. All her blouses were silky and pastel, and all her cardigans were the color of small woodland animals. She came in two times a week, *just for me*. The two of us sat in the corner of the library when everyone else was in normal English class.

I felt very lucky indeed.

She was also Amber's mother.

We were studying a book called *The Great Gatsby,* which was about a rich man in a pink suit who had huge parties in his house on a long island shaped like an egg. I thought that he was possibly gay, with his fashion sense, and that his love for that rich, cotton-candy Daisy was fake, because all she did was play tennis and complain about the heat. Who Gatsby really wanted to be with was Tom, which is why he killed Tom's mistress. There was a line in it that said Gatsby would never look at another man's wife, which supported my theory.

I was really looking forward to sharing my insight with Mrs. Leslie. I never spoke up in normal English class, but I thought that we'd have deep and meaningful talks since she was the head of the book club. But no, in the first lesson she gave me an essay structure to learn (introduction, body and conclusion). She had also come armed with vocabulary lists based on the book.

She told me she liked how I expressed things so concisely and asked if I had read *Lord of the Flies*.

"No, but I might know him."

"Pardon?"

"I know the leading distributor of jeans zippers in Australia," I joked, but she didn't find it funny. I guessed it wasn't the time to tell her your joke, Linh, about how Hamlet was the son of Piglet.

So I sat there miserably as Mrs. Leslie tested me on words I didn't know, like *extemporize* and *supercilious*.

Then she read passages out to me and asked me to explain what they meant. I had no idea why she was testing my comprehension as if I were ten years old, so at first I replied with stuff like, "This passage shows that the story is set in New York, which is a rich and cultured part of America."

"Have you been to New York, Lucy?" she asked me.

"No."

"Then you can't make generalizations like that. Not all of New York is wealthy or cultured. Think about the valley of ashes."

Eventually I started to cotton on to what Mrs. Leslie wanted. My answers became more detailed, and not all about plot. I learned to judge the characters as I'd judge real people. *Nick secretly admires Gatsby, but due to his class and circumstances, and also to him being related to Daisy, he can't openly admit it. To do so would be to admit that he hangs around shady people and condones their dodge,* I would write in my essays. Or: *The green light is supposed to be a metaphor for Gatsby's hope, because it is far away and flashes and blinks, to emphasize that hope is often elusive. But no one ever speaks about Gatsby's envy, which the green could also symbolize.*

I had no idea why, but this last comment really did it for Mrs. Leslie. Her brown eyes lit up. "You are really engaging with the text and learning the skill of analysis," she praised. "What do you mean by Gatsby's envy?"

I thought of all the people I knew in Stanley who looked at the houses along Ambient Estates with the same metal-rimmed, wide-eyed Eckleburg yearning as those living in the valley of ashes. I thought of how hard we tried—you, me, Yvonne, Ivy—to look sophisticated with our imitation perfumes and gold buttons and makeup, when true Laurindans never wore such stuff, and how the plainness of their clothes did not conceal the fact that their tops were made of angora and their shoes of calfskin. I'd been at the school for only a few weeks when I realized that we were the ones standing on the shore in our pink suits, suddenly tacky, suddenly left so far behind, and that—unlike Gatsby—most of us could not afford a boat to take us across to the other side. The only way to get there was to do it individually, sink or swim, and of course very few swimmers made it.

"Gatsby wants the status they have, but he can't get it no matter how rich he becomes, because his wealth is shady . . . I mean, ill gotten."

"Spot on, Lucy!" cheered Mrs. Leslie.

Then she asked me how I was settling into the school.

"Good," I said. "Katie has been a good friend to me."

"Katie," Mrs. Leslie said slowly. "Is that Katherine Gladrock?"

"Yes," I replied.

Then she chuckled. "Sweet girl. But awfully dull."

For my first history essay for Ms. Vanderwerp, I received thirteen out of twenty. Thirteen out of twenty! A bare pass. She had also written a note: *A good effort, but your argumentative skills need improving. Please come and see me.* And she got my name wrong again. I don't know how difficult it is to forget "Lucy," but somehow she did.

Ms. Vanderwerp's office was a small, cramped corner thing, bigger than a broom closet but only just. It smelled of Pine-Sol, and on an overhead shelf she had three cartons of wipes and two boxes of tissues.

"Don't worry," she reassured me. "I can see that this is the first history essay you've written. It was a good attempt. But you didn't sustain a consistent argument about what could have caused World War I."

"My argument is that many things happened to cause the war, and no one thing made it happen."

Ms. Vanderwerp looked at me for a while, then told me that my conclusion was satisfactory but that I had to structure my argument to reflect it. She allowed me to resubmit because it was my first essay. When she returned it with a sixteen out of twenty—a mark that would have made Tully weep inconsolably—I felt like I'd got the hang of things.

So for my next two assignments, I followed the same formula. Many things in history happened to cause X, Y or Z. There was no decisive moment.

"Lucy, your writing skills are vastly improved," Ms. Vanderwerp told me, "but the questions are asking you to choose a side and argue for it."

"But why do I have to choose a side? There are so many sides to a historical event, as you've taught us."

"Yes, Lucy. But the nature of the task is to write argumentatively. So you have to choose a side, acknowledge the other side and then defeat its arguments. Am I making sense to you?"

She was making sense, but I wasn't sure whether I should be forming opinions about grave historical events in six hundred words or less. What did an argument I made about who started World War I have to do with anything? I didn't even get to decide what we'd eat for dinner, or when I could go out, or who I could sit next to in class. Who cared what a fifteen-year-old thought?

When the bell rang, we stood up to leave. I watched Ms. Vanderwerp walk away to her next class. There was something slightly blurred about her whole being, as if she were a watercolor painting that someone couldn't be bothered finishing; not only that, but they didn't even care enough not to smudge it with their smock sleeve.

No one had explained to me why Ms. Vanderwerp carried wipes around with her at all times, but after my fourth history class I figured it out. The Cabinet showed me.

One afternoon Amber came to class looking pallid and

unwell. She took out a pocket pack of tissues and placed it on her desk. "Are you okay?" I asked. She hadn't seemed sick that morning.

She nodded. When Ms. Vanderwerp was handing out a photocopy about America's involvement in World War II, Amber let out a massive, whooping sneeze just as the teacher was near her desk. Ms. Vanderwerp jumped backward, almost falling over Katie. All the beige seeped out of her face as she righted herself. Instead of saying, "Bless you, Amber," Ms. Vanderwerp kept her distance and opened all the windows of the room. "Amber, dear, would you like to go to the sick bay? You look quite unwell."

"No, I should be all right, Ms. V."

Then I noticed Amber's smile, and how the color of her face didn't particularly match her neck. I saw what I hadn't noticed before—that whenever anyone coughed, Ms. Vanderwerp would open a window. Whenever anyone sneezed, she would turn around toward the whiteboard as if she needed to write something or rub something out.

I heard Brodie snigger behind Ms. Vanderwerp's back while she busied herself writing on the board, and I realized that what Amber had done was all an act—an act of talcumpowder torture, carefully timed to churn up Ms. Vanderwerp's worst fears.

That same afternoon, when I returned home, Mum had fixed the Lamb's blue snot problem. She had caught a bus to Sunray's fabric store and bought five yards of very, very fine bridal netting, which she hemmed at the top and passed a drawstring through. At the bottom she sewed an enormous circle of stiff copper wire. She gathered the drawstring at the top and hung the contraption from a ceiling beam, trapping the Lamb's box inside like a bee inside a butterfly net.

"Mr. Lamb, look at you!" I squealed. "You have your own little hideaway!" I squatted on the floor and lifted up the circular base to peer at him.

"Gah!" he said, dribbling. He was eating one of those iced cakes in plastic wrappers, the cakes that never went bad.

"He only stays in here with me during the day while you are at school," Mum told me. "Take him into the kitchen and give him some mashed soup from the pot on the stove top. Then let him walk in his baby walker while you are doing your homework."

Although Lamb had recently learned to walk, we often put him in his playpen to prevent him from bumping into boxes or sharp corners or crawling toward dangerous objects, like the fabric cutter or the ironing board.

I lifted the Lamb from his box, and he was still holding on to his one-eyed duck. But the moment I set him down on my lap, he decided to pee on my blazer.

"Oh, no! Crap, Mum!"

"What happened?" My mother was panicking. "Did he fall?" She came rushing toward us. Then she noticed the rivulet running down my pocket, collecting in dark droplets on the concrete floor.

"Why didn't you put a nappy on him?" I shouted.

"He has a rash on his bum." She picked him up and showed me.

"Eww, I don't need to see that!"

81

"It'll come out with a wash," she said, patting my damp sleeve with her hand, but that only made me angrier.

"You can't put something like this through a machine! You have to dry-clean it!"

I had forgotten that I was talking to a textiles expert, and my mother had had enough of me. "For the last six months, all you have been going on about is your clothes," she yelled. "Summer dress this, winter kilt that. How do you think a three-hundred-dollar uniform will help you study better, huh?" She washed the sleeve of my blazer with Imperial Leather soap, then dried it with a hair dryer. It did not shrink.

The truth was that I'd always felt grimier than most of the girls at Laurinda, even before the Lamb peed on me. I felt grimy because Stanley was a grimy place, Linh. When the wind blew the wrong way, you knew how foul the fumes of the Victory Carpet Factory could be.

Not long before, Mrs. Leslie had made me write about a childhood memory which evoked a sense of place that no longer existed except in memory. I wrote about being a really young kid and standing next to my grandma in Hanoi, helping her sell boiled eggs. Of course, I didn't remember very much except the way the market smelled, and how there were sometimes runaway chickens on the ground.

"I cried when I read this," Mrs. Leslie said.

"Sorry," I replied. "Was it that bad?"

"Oh, no! No, no, Lucy!" she insisted, not getting that I was joking. "No, darling. It was just too beautiful. It was just so special."

I wasn't exactly sure what was so special about using a cute toddler as a cheap marketing tool, Linh, but hey, it seemed to push Mrs. Leslie's buttons in a good way. I was glad, because although I had mixed feelings about her daughter, I really liked Mrs. Leslie.

The boys had their sports. Every weekend they would play tennis and cricket against the other schools in their league. Their sport was serious, a way for them to exercise their competitive streaks, for those streaks to burst into glowing colors for the school and smear their rivals. If an Auburn boy played particularly well, he was celebrated by his team. An individual skill or talent brought them all a step closer to victory.

We had sports too, but our sports always seemed an inferior imitation of the boys'. They had cricket, we had softball. They had basketball, we had netball. Girls wanted to play the former; no boys wanted to play the latter. While some of the girls went to see the boys play, none of the boys ever came to Laurinda games. And then some of the girls had ballet, which was more a daily practice in perfectionism than a sport.

If we tried to do four or five jumping jacks to warm up before class, we would be met with "Girls, don't be silly. You're not freshmen." The gym was the only place for that kind of behavior, and we had gym only once a week for two hours. The girls had to get their kicks another way.

Over the weekend Gina had gone into the city, and when she was at the Dux department store, she ran into the lead singer of Mercury Stool, her favorite band. She grabbed a blue notebook and pen from the stationery department she had been standing in and ran after him.

"Let us have a look, hey, Gina?" Brodie said, and the girls milling around Gina parted like the Red Sea. Brodie took the book from her and examined it. "Wow, this is amazing," she marveled to Amber, and passed it along.

Amber held the book up to the light. "Incredible."

"You are so lucky!" fawned Chelsea.

"Thank God they didn't charge me extra because it had his signature on it!" Gina said, suddenly shy, realizing these girls held her sacred object in the same reverence.

"My father will get it valued for you by his friend Gregory Mitchell," Amber offered, handing it back.

"No, thanks, Amber. I'm never going to sell this!" Gina hugged the blue notebook to her chest.

"Come on, Gina. I mean, I know you think it's priceless and all, but Gregory can tell you how much it will be worth in ten years' time," said Chelsea. "Gregory valued a *Neighbours* swap card my mum's had since 1987, and you wouldn't believe how much it's worth today."

"I don't care how much it's worth to others," said Gina. "It can't mean more to anyone else than it does to me."

I saw Chelsea rolling her eyes at Brodie.

"Well, he can at least tell you how to mount and frame it properly for your room," said Brodie gently. "Come on. We'd like to do this for you."

Week after week, Gina asked about her notebook. Week after week, Amber told her it was with Gregory, getting valued . . . until one morning. A crowd milled around Amber, who sat slumped at her desk. "I'm so sorry," she said, her huge eyes filling with tears when Gina arrived. "I feel so guilty. Gregory lost it. He said he would look into it, and must have left it around somewhere. . . . He thinks his wife put it out in the recycling."

"On the bright side, I suppose it must not have been worth as much as we thought," Chelsea said, patting Amber on the back. Because Amber was crying so much, Gina could not. But I watched her as she tried to keep her chin under control. This school sure taught you stoicism.

Another time, the Cabinet turned on Katie. "What are you doing your oral assignment on?" Brodie asked Katie, who considered herself a Russian history expert.

"Tsar Nicholas's family, and the mystery of Anastasia. Lucy and I are thinking of reenacting the murder of the royal family, but from a modern-day forensic scientist's perspective." For two days, this project had been all Katie would talk about at lunchtime.

"I don't think it's a group assignment, Katie."

"Ms. Vanderwerp said that we could work together."

"Well, Ms. Vanderwerp told me that it was an oral presentation, to assess our speaking skills. That's what she said to *me*. But if you want to make a song and dance about Tsar Nicholas and his family, by all means go ahead."

"I'll go and ask Ms. Vanderwerp."

"Sure, and of course she'll say yes to *you,* Katie—if you really want to torture us with fifteen minutes of your version of *Bill & Ted's Excellent Adventure.*"

Katie made no move to see Ms. Vanderwerp.

"But we could totally do it," I told her at recess. She was sitting glumly, the quietest she had ever been. "Come on, Katie, it'll be fun."

"Nah."

"But you said you've already started writing the script."

"Nah," Katie said sadly. "Don't want to look like a fool."

When the week of the presentations arrived, Katie stood up and read from two pages of notes. "Nikolay Aleksandrovich Romanov was the last emperor of Russia and grand duke of Finland, known as Bloody Nicholas to his enemies because of his approval of anti–Jewish massacres and pogroms, and his execution of political rivals."

Katie's sentences were far too long and left her breathless; she'd forgotten that words typed on a page were different from spoken words. In the middle of her talk, the Cabinet stood up and left the room. Katie noticed and looked up, losing her place. She looked back down at her notes and finished her talk, but when she walked back to her desk I could see that she was shaking.

Suddenly the Cabinet reappeared, in full costume—Brodie in a fake beard and a greatcoat with epaulettes, Amber in a long gown and tiara. Chelsea was a younger girl with a frock that fell beneath her knees and a yellow ribbon in her hair. They had created a slide show of images that, when projected onto the wall behind them, served as historical backdrops: the tsar's palace, the carriage ride in the night, the murders, the forensic scientists and their theories. The last slide was a picture of a bookshelf, with Brodie replacing a book titled *Shelving the Enigma*.

At the end, the whole class clapped.

"They copied us!" Katie hissed to me.

"It's not copying when no one else has done this sort of thing before," Chelsea said, smiling.

Katie looked pleadingly at Ms. Vanderwerp.

Fortunately, it was Katie, and not Brodie, who had spent entire lunchtimes last year sitting in Ms. Vanderwerp's little office with her Russian dolls, her photos and postcards of Moscow's underground railway. It was Katie who had regaled Ms. Vanderwerp with stories of seeing Lenin embalmed in his glass coffin and her theories of the tsar's missing daughter. It was Katie who had made sure that she did not sneeze or cough in Ms. Vanderwerp's presence.

After class, as Katie and I were walking out, the Cabinet followed us. "I know you feel like we stole your idea," said Brodie. Damn it, the Cabinet was always a step ahead—they even denied us the pleasure of backstabbing them! "But do you two seriously think you could have pulled off something like this?"

"You guys were great," Katie conceded. "Really."

"Thanks, Katie," said Brodie generously. "But you know what? You were our inspiration. When we saw how revved up you were, we thought, hey, why not? Why not go all out? After all, if Katie Gladrock is not afraid to put herself out there, even risk embarrassment, well, neither are we!"

"You are a champ, Katie," gushed Chelsea. "A champ."

Linh, these girls were like the disembodied clowns' heads you find at carnivals, the ones with the open mouths. The game looked so easy, but only when you played it did you realize that the heads were always turning from side to side, reminding you, *"No! You can't win!"*

When the Cabinet left us alone, we found our usual spot near the maintenance shed.

"They're kind of mean, aren't they?" I asked Katie.

"Oh, no, the Cabinet's all right," she reassured me. "Once you get over their pranks, you'll see they're okay. I mean, they were really nice to get Gina all those Mercury Stool posters."

"But they lost her notebook!"

"Yeah, but they felt really bad about it. Amber was crying, didn't you see?"

Was Katie blind? *"But they stole your idea!"*

"It was a bad one anyway," Katie said. "They improved it. Come on, Lucy, as if we were going to get up there and do what they did."

"We were!" I said. "We were so going to do it!"

"Well, you would have been the only one up there, because I wasn't going to."

For the first time, I heard a hint of defensiveness in Katie's voice. I'd assumed that she and I felt the same way about the Cabinet. I'd assumed we saw them through the same lens.

"Our parents used to be friends," Katie confessed. "In fact, it was Brodie's mum who introduced my mum to my step-father. They were really close back then."

It now dawned on me that I was like a brand-new camera; all my snapshots were only a few months old. But Katie was an old Kodak with a very long roll of film inside, filled with images and events from a decade spent at Laurinda.

Poor Katie, I thought. She acted as if this tenuous link to the Cabinet actually meant something.

★ ★ ★

The next week, when results came in, Ms. Vanderwerp read them out to the class:

Katie: A+

Brodie, Amber and Chelsea: B+

"What?" Chelsea whined.

"I assessed you not just on this one assignment, but on your work across the whole term," said Ms. Vanderwerp.

"That's not fair!" protested Amber. "You never told us you were going to do that!"

"Our assignment alone would have bumped up our term's marks to an A at least, wouldn't you say, Ms. Vanderwerp?" Brodie was using her most reasonable voice, which was like a knife dipped in Nutella: so sweet and soft on top that you could easily overlook the menace that lay beneath.

"Your group assignment was excellent," Ms. Vanderwerp said. "But all term, you three girls have been distracted—and, what's worse, distracting others too. You don't seem to take history seriously. So I am afraid I had to deduct marks for effort. You need to learn to apply yourselves consistently, not just when it suits you. I'm sorry, girls."

"You're not, but you will be," Chelsea muttered quietly, and then blew her nose loudly into a tissue. It was like a trumpet heralding war.

I had the feeling that something was about to happen, but I couldn't talk to Katie about it at school. She was so garrulous that she could speak for thirty minutes straight, and her pet topic this week was Mussolini and fascism in Italy. I had to think of a way to make her *listen*.

I decided I would telephone her at home. That way we would be free from the eavesdropping of other girls, and I might just get a chance to say something that would not be interrupted.

Linh, I really didn't need you to be there, but you came anyway, and I was grateful. You still found my Laurinda life fascinating back then. We sat on my bed, and you had the Lamb in your lap. *Do this,* you instructed me in a crazed Southern preacher drawl. *Lead the poor blind soul out of the dark! Switch the lights on in the Cabinet for her!*

We waited for the Lamb to stop squealing and clapping over your performance before I picked up the phone and dialed.

"Who is this, dear?" her grandmother said when I asked to speak to Katie.

"A friend from school," I replied.

When Katie answered, she said, "Oh, hi, Lucy!" all excited to hear from me. I guessed that no one ever called her.

"Hi, Katie," I said. "Listen, I'm a bit worried about stuff going on at school. So I thought we could talk about it."

And—hallelujah!—she asked me to explain. I managed to get through a minute's worth of words before she cut me off.

"Lucy, you're worried about nothing," she said. "I get that you're coming to a new school and everything must seem so weird, but it really is nothing to stress over, I swear. All the girls at Laurinda are nice."

"But I am worried," I said. "I've been here long enough now to see the way things are and it creeps me out."

"No," Katie replied firmly, "Lucy Lam, you see things as *you* are. And you see them wrong. I get that you're Asian and respectful and came from a Catholic school and all that, but you don't understand pranks."

At that point, you pulled the phone from my hands and switched it off. You hung up on her! You said, *What kind of racist shit is that?*

She's not racist, I explained. She likes Asians.

Don't say I don't look out for you! you told me as you redialed her number. "Katie," you said before I could stop you, "why do you keep defending those bitches?"

"What?" I could hear Katie on the other end. "Who is this?"

"Lucy."

"No, it's not. You sound nothing like her."

"Oh yeah? Not Asian and respectful enough, I guess. But screw that. Katie, these girls are real pieces of work. Kicking others when they're down. Stealing credit. Parading through the school like princesses." I almost laughed, Linh—your attempts to sound like a Laurinda girl were hilarious. "Treating the rest of the students like crap."

But I could tell you'd got under Katie's skin, as this time it was her turn to hang up.

The next day, Katie pretended that our bizarre, passive-aggressive, interrupted phone conversation had never happened. She just kept talking as she had before, with me occasionally asking a question. But there was a strange new vibe between us, and I got the feeling that I'd crossed a line. I was the new girl, and I wasn't supposed to have opinions about Laurinda yet.

I had been hoping my honesty would bring us closer, but instead it made me keep my distance. There was something off about this school, and the more Katie rabbited on, the harder it was for me to pay attention. It all seemed so trivial—how Gina was leaving a single flower she pilfered from a neighbor's gardens in front of Mr. Sinclair's office every morning; how Amber was organizing a Mother's Day high tea for Laurindans and their mums; and how Katie was bringing her grandmother to it.

At Christ Our Savior, this harmless gossip was what connected us and got us through the school day. But here, in light of the other things going on—how at lunchtime a girl had pulled a lettuce leaf out of her salad, rinsed it under the tap, walked behind Ms. V and pretended to cough violently while flicking her with it; or how the flowers Gina left were accompanied by notes that, although not exactly dirty, tiptoed around the edge of decency (*If you had a band, I'd play the central organ*)—it felt like Katie was living in a bubble.

One lunchtime I shut myself away in the library.

"Hey," said Katie when she found me. "What are you doing?"

"I've got a lot of work to finish for Mrs. Leslie," I lied.

"Do you know what Gina put under Mr. Sinclair's door today?" she asked me, about to sit down and chew my ear for half an hour. "You'll never believe it, but—"

"Sorry, Katie, I really need some time to finish this off."

"Sure," she said, and left me alone.

The next two lunchtimes I did the same thing, and each time Katie came to find me, I was very pleasant to her. "I'm sorry, Katie," I said the first time, "I've got to finish off some work for politics." The next time it was: "I'm a bit stuck on this unit in biology about genetics."

The final time she came, I sighed and said, "More work from Mrs. Leslie. Apparently I'm really behind." I looked back down at the exercise book in front of me, filled with lists of words from *Gatsby* and a paragraph about the Jazz Age.

"Oh," said Katie. I knew she had spotted that paragraph, and I cursed myself, because I had the feeling that she might be about to give me a twenty-minute lecture on the era. But she didn't sit down. "Well, good luck," she muttered, and left.

I could now hear my own thoughts, something that had become harder and harder to do the more I hung around Katie. I didn't need new friends anyway, Linh, when I still had you to confirm I wasn't going mad or seeing things. You were now coming over after school every day, minding the Lamb as I did my homework. It was such a relief. You made me feel more myself again.

★ ★ ★

94

In history the next day, instead of our usual work, Ms. Vanderwerp had brought in a copy of Aung San Suu Kyi's *Freedom from Fear*.

She handed us some photocopied passages from it, including: *It is not power that corrupts but fear. Fear of losing power corrupts those who wield it and fear of the scourge of power corrupts those who are subject to it.*

"I disagree with this," commented Katie. "How can those who are oppressed be considered corrupt? I mean, it's not their fault they're living under dictatorships. They're not the ones doing the bad things."

I put my hand up.

"Lucy?" Ms. Vanderwerp was always happy when I spoke up, because it was so rare.

"It's not saying it's their fault," I explained. "It's just saying that fear corrupts them. Like, people living under dictatorships turn in their own families to the authorities."

"Well, then," Ms. Vanderwerp said, "let's explore the effect of fear and power on . . ."

"Excuse me, miss," Chelsea interrupted, "but we've already done this with Mr. Sinclair."

"You mean you've talked about the political situation in Myanmar?"

"No, we've talked about how power is used and abused, and all that stuff."

"Well, for those of you who were not lucky enough to be in Mr. Sinclair's politics class, this discussion will be of interest, I'm sure," continued Ms. Vanderwerp.

"Umm, no, it's not," said Gina bluntly.

"Discussions about history and war are always interesting," Ms. Vanderwerp went on. But what she didn't see was that you can't teach anyone about power when you don't have much of it yourself. "Live in peace, or die in pieces," she said. No one laughed, so she laughed by herself.

Ms. Vanderwerp laughed at her own joke.

I saw Chelsea roll her eyes at Amber.

Amber pretended to pull out her own fingernails with the fingers of her left hand as tweezers.

Chelsea stuck out her thumb and forefinger to make a gun. She then pointed the gun at her own temple and pulled the trigger. *Shoot me now.*

Then came the incident that altered the course of our year. Afterward, some girls blamed Ms. Vanderwerp, but the saddest thing was that she was doing it all inadvertently, with her wet eyes always looking on the verge of tears, and that catch in her voice when she spoke, like a zipper that would not go all the way up, revealing an embarrassing gap. There was something about her that reminded me of an aunt who was always knitting scarves you'd never wear.

When I arrived for history the next morning, I could not sit in my usual spot because Brodie and Chelsea were crowding around Amber. As I entered the room, I heard Chelsea squealing, "Quick! She's coming!"

For a second I thought they were working on some plot they planned to unleash against me. But when the three girls looked up and saw it was me, they seemed relieved. "Quick, shut the door!" they hissed. I did as instructed, and realized that my paranoia was misplaced vanity. Of course they were plotting against someone else. Why would they target me?

I didn't dare tap either Brodie or Chelsea on the shoulder and ask for my seat back. But I edged closer, hoping they would notice me and leave so that I could sit down. I saw

Amber had a thick red marker in one hand with the top off. I could smell the ink in the air, the same strangely delicious artificial scent of nail polish.

Chelsea was crouched on the floor. In front of her was a silver thermos cup emblazoned with the school logo; you could buy it for twenty-five dollars at Edmondsons. Steam was coming from its open top. And in her lap, on top of a pile of tissues laid flat against the material of her kilt, was something red.

I saw what it was, but it seemed so bizarre, so repulsively wrong, that I couldn't be sure. I couldn't look again because Chelsea picked the taboo object off her lap and plonked it into the thermos of hot water like a tea bag.

Pulling it out by its string, she got up and ran toward the door with Brodie. Just at that moment the door opened, and Katie stumbled in. "Hey, what's happening?"

"Katie, get in your seat *now*!" yelled Brodie.

"But what are you doing?"

"Bloody hell, Katie, just sit down!"

The Cabinet had always been cruel in a silky, nice way, never before so crudely as this. Stunned, Katie found her seat and sat down.

"Quick, the tape!" Brodie hissed, and Chelsea tore a strip of masking tape from a roll and handed it to her. Chelsea then passed Brodie the offensive object. Brodie, who was the tallest girl in their group and could reach the top of the doorframe, taped it firmly in place.

And so the deed was done.

Stuck there, dead in the middle of the doorframe, the thing swung from its string like some kind of eyeless cotton roadkill.

Chelsea and Brodie ran back to their desks and sat down. The door of the room was still closed. "No one say a word!"

We all sat at our desks straighter than usual. No one moved. It was only for a few seconds, but we all looked in toxic shock at the object, colored with a red permanent marker and dipped in hot water, steaming there, swinging there, like a sick abortive art project, in the middle of the doorframe, but low enough so that when the door eventually did open— and it would open any second now—Ms. Vanderwerp would walk in, oblivious, carrying her green spiral-bound teacher's planner and cylinder of wipes. She would walk in, and she would not know what had whacked her in the middle of the forehead until she turned back to take a second look.

And that is exactly what happened.

The door swung open, because Ms. Vanderwerp was always a minute or so late.

She stumbled in, and was hit in the forehead.

Immediately, her hand shot up to wipe away the unexpected moisture.

Looking at her hand, she saw that it was now covered in a streak of watery red.

She looked back to see what had struck her, and when she turned to face the class, she looked at the room like a person who had unexpectedly found herself blinded. Her eyes had never swum so much behind her glasses, like blue fish whose water was rapidly draining out of their bowls.

All this seemed to happen much slower than I imagined it would, which made the incident even more awfully slapstick.

Now, any reasonable person would quickly spot that that watery red was not the color of blood, and that the fluid didn't even smell like blood. But Ms. Vanderwerp had no time to reason this through in her head.

Why would such a thing still be warm? And yet it was the icky warmth of the water, the diluted hue of red and the steaming wad of expanded cotton swaying from side to side, that escalated her disgust and confusion. Her mouth turned into an infinity sign of horror.

No one laughed, or said, "Miss, miss, it's a joke!"

"Argh!" she screamed, and it was a rough scream. I had always imagined that if Ms. Vanderwerp were to raise her voice, it would be high. But this was the scream of a cement truck on its first rotation. It was a scream of breaking rock. It was the first time that tremulous, gentle voice had made a noise that was clear and full of conviction.

For a moment, the blue fish behind her glasses looked as if they could be saved: I could see the tears filling up their bowls, overflowing down the sides of her face. Then she was out of the room.

"Quick, someone shut the door!" shouted Brodie, and Amber dashed from her seat and grabbed the handle. She had the presence of mind not to slam it and so draw attention to Room 105.

"She was crying. Did you see? Tears were coming out of her eyes!" That was Katie, whose mouth was an O.

"Shit. Shit. Shit!" Amber panicked. Her panic was like an actress's, her hands wrung at the wrists as if doing an imitation of alarm.

We all looked up at the doorframe, and it was still there, a macabre microphone amplifying what they had done to poor Ms. Vanderwerp.

Still standing by the door, Amber jumped up and pulled the tampon from the doorframe. She held it out in front of her as if it had somehow transformed into an actual used sanitary item, and it suddenly seemed as nauseating as the real thing. She headed toward the only bin in the room.

"No, no!" hissed Brodie. "What if they search the bin?"

"Well, I'm not putting that back in my bag!"

"Put it in your thermos, Chelsea," ordered Brodie.

"Eww," Chelsea complained.

Amber ran to Chelsea's desk, opened her thermos and dropped the tampon in. She screwed the lid back on as if she were screwing down the cover of a black manhole that could unleash zombies. Some water spilled onto Chelsea's desk and she wiped it off with her sleeve, scowling.

Then Amber paced back to her own seat next to me. I could hear her breath, like a series of sighs, both exhausted and excited. A creepy thought snuck up on me, Linh, that this reaction sounded almost postcoital. Gross.

There was movement from the other side of the room. Katie stood up.

"Katie, what the hell do you think you're doing?" demanded Brodie in a whisper.

"I can't take this," Katie said.

"Stop being a drama queen. Sit down."

"You're all so dead," warned Katie.

"Yeah?" challenged Chelsea. "Well, you're part of this too, so don't pretend not to know about it, you self-righteous bitch. You sat in the classroom and did nothing. You wanted to see what would happen."

Brodie examined the room with her murky lion's eyes. "All of you are part of this," she said.

"I need to go to the bathroom." I stood up.

"Oh, for crying out loud!" Chelsea didn't know whether I was being funny or smart or what. "Piss in your pants."

I sat back down.

"No one say a word," hissed Chelsea.

We sat for a minute or so in silence, broken only by Chelsea giggling once or twice in panic. I didn't dare look at Amber, in case she saw the expression on my face. Stupid bitches, I thought.

The wait seemed like a small eternity, even though it was less than a minute; I wondered why we sat there glued to our seats instead of dispersing because there was no longer a teacher in the room. But deep down, we knew that there was nowhere for us to go, and that if we did that we'd get into even more trouble.

In some self-denying parts of their brains, the Cabinet probably thought that things could continue as normal, that if they did what we were trained to do at this school—be Young Ladies, innocuous, innocent and well behaved—the repercussions would not be so bad, that the incident would be put down to Ms. Vanderwerp's fragility, and how she could not control a class.

But I knew that every teacher would see through this lie.

After a time, we heard heavy, determined footsteps outside. The Growler stormed into the room, looking around, making sure we felt her gaze. "Who is responsible for this?" she hollered.

No one said a word.

She slammed the door shut. "Despicable, vile act of bullying!" We would all get detention and stay in at lunchtime unless someone spoke, she announced. "Come on, own up—all of you are witnesses."

Then it dawned on us. As if we thought we could lie about it! As if we could pretend it had never happened! All that time wasted hiding evidence, when the Cabinet could have spent the remaining moments of the class devising one good collective story.

Mrs. Grey looked around. Her eyes were like a sniper's, and when they stopped on a student, her words became ammunition. "Siobhan?"

Siobhan looked down at her desk.

"Meredith? Isabelle? Stella?"

They all remained silent. Then she turned her gaze on me. Thin red trees of veins had etched themselves into her cheeks. "Lucy?"

I kept my jaw clamped and lowered my head.

"Oh, for heaven's sake! None of you are going out to lunch until somebody owns up. You'll have a whole hour to think about what you have done. I expected better than this from Year Tens."

An hour. I could see Amber's back relaxing, curving down into the chair. During that hour, she would be able to rally the troops and concoct a convincing story. She looked at Chelsea—but that was a mistake, because Chelsea could not stop a smirk from insinuating itself on her sharp little face.

"Chelsea!" hammered the Growler. "What do you have to smile about?"

Chelsea looked down at her desk again.

It was peculiar: the Growler had not asked Chelsea whether she knew who was responsible for this vile act. In fact, she'd not asked any of the Cabinet; she hadn't even glanced their way. Surely the next person to be asked to report on school transgressions would be Brodie, the prefect? But no.

"When I leave, the teacher on yard duty will stay with you through lunchtime," the Growler said.

Amber's shoulders slumped. All plans of insurrection were thwarted.

The teacher on duty was Mr. Sinclair. He came into the classroom and didn't say a word as he closed the door behind him.

From his seat behind his desk, he looked at us for a long while. It was not a good look. Even Gina, who would have given anything to have Mr. Sinclair look at her for longer than three seconds, suddenly did not want his eyes on her.

Finally he spoke. "You girls are in serious trouble, I hear."

At first, they tried to get Mr. Sinclair on their side. "But, sir, it was only a joke." Amber was thick—she hadn't noticed that Mr. Sinclair had begun not with a question but with a statement. Still, they tried to buddy up to him.

"We didn't mean to," whined Gina.

I'd never seen such a look on Mr. Sinclair's face, and I never wanted to again. I doubted that even his wife or mother had seen it. It was a look of incredulity, but not a "do you take me for some kind of fool" look. No, it was a look that reflected the lie back to the liar.

"How dare you?" bellowed Mr. Sinclair—Mr. Sinclair the Hot One, Mr. Sinclair who had awkwardly ignored his Valentine's Day gifts, Mr. Sinclair with his Socratic classroom. "How dare you do this to a colleague of mine? One of the nicest people in this college."

104

Ms. Vanderwerp was genuinely kind, it was true, and no genuine kindness could exist without vulnerability here.

"You girls should be ashamed of yourselves."

And all of a sudden, we were.

Even Chelsea's sneer was wiped from her face. We were all ashamed, deeply ashamed. This was not like the Growler growling at us, telling us we should be ashamed of ourselves, all day, every day, for every trivial transgression, like wearing our ribbons crisscrossed around our ponytails or speaking up accidentally at the same time a teacher was speaking. This was real shame, because we respected Mr. Sinclair.

"All of you—you, Sammy. You, Caitlin. You, Gina . . ."

"But, sir, I didn't do anything!" protested Gina.

He looked at her. He didn't have to say anything. He was telling her off with his eyes, and it probably dawned on Gina at that moment that having this achingly handsome older man telling her off did not elicit the same sweetly masochistic feelings that Elizabeth Bennet had when Mr. Darcy yelled at her.

It was frightening to be really *put in your place*.

"You girls think that your charm will get you things in life," Mr. Sinclair said to us. "But let me tell you how wrong you are."

And he did. Chelsea became defensive. Her chin was up, and her light brown ponytail sashayed like a thoroughbred pony.

While the Growler had been focused on catching the culprits, waiting to see which one of us would rat on our mates, Mr. Sinclair didn't seem to care who had done it. In his eyes, we all had.

"In your adult lives, if you did anything like what you've done here today, you would be fired from your jobs. You're insulated because of your privilege, but you won't be insulated forever."

Gina had her head down. Little gasping sounds were coming from her corner of the room, and Meredith put an arm around her.

"Now, tell me, why did you feel the need to pull something like this?"

I saw in an instant how self-deluded we'd been, thinking that a class of fifteen-year-olds could make a grown man feel bumbling and awkward. We had nothing over Mr. Sinclair. He was his own person, with his own wife and son, and he didn't care what we thought. Even his bumbling charm might have been an act. This didn't make me lose respect for him; I saw it as a necessary strategy against us.

None of us could look at him.

We were kept back again for fifteen minutes after school, so that the Growler could again try to weed out the culprit. When she finally let us go, Chelsea burst out laughing. *"Vile, dees-pick-able act of bullying,"* she shrieked in a theatrical voice. "Stupid old cow."

"Now, tell me"—Gina, who was following behind, did her own imitation—*"why did you feel the need to pull something like this? The only thing he pulls is himself!"* Her face was still blotchy red, though, and I expected the waterworks would resume as soon as she got in her mother's car.

I had missed my bus back to the station and my train back to Stanley. I came home an hour late, but I couldn't tell my parents the reason. Can you imagine, Linh? I don't think Dad even knew what the offending object was, and Mum thought that using one meant you were no longer chaste.

What I thought about that evening was something strange Mrs. Grey had said. She'd called the stunt a vile, despicable act of bullying. But couldn't students only bully other students? No student was supposed to be able to bully a teacher. But the Cabinet had done just that.

When things go well at a girls' school, they go soaringly well. Gallons of self-esteem, girls allowing their comic genius or sporting prowess to shine through, no boys around to make them feel coy. Do you remember, back at Christ Our Savior, when Zarhar did such a good Elvis impersonation that she was picked to play the male lead in our school production of *Grease*? We whooped and stomped and clapped at her performance; I think one or two girls even discovered their true sexual orientation watching her perform.

At Christ Our Savior, girls were people, not female-impersonator shells of their true selves; they ate with gusto and kept their brothers in line at home; they manned their houses with brooms and mops and whacked any muddy legs in their way.

There was something creepy about the femininity at Laurinda, something so cloistered and yet brimming with stifled sex that it reminded me of the Victorian whalebone corsets we once saw at the Werribee Park Mansion, which kept everything cramped tight, until the stitches unraveled and out poured mounds of naked pink and white. It was the femininity of tiny éclairs and teacups, crocheted collars and little pearl earrings, the young-girl-to-old-woman transition that skipped sexuality altogether, so that when you saw it—in Gina, for instance—it was as garish as a scarlet *A* on the chest.

This was how "niceness" was policed—not through directives about virtue, but through conformity in dress and manners. The result was that anyone who was slightly different, who had a heartbeat that didn't race at the latest Laura Ashley creation but instead at George-with-the-one-eyebrow on the Auburn Academy soccer team, anyone who liked her colors bold and not pastel, who loved her jokes explicit and not coy—any of those types were automatically cast as sluts, and so became pariahs.

Gina wasn't in class the next day. When Mr. Sinclair called the roll and there was a silence after her name, you could feel the significance of that sink in. I suppose the detention must have been the worst thing to have happened in Gina's life so far, Linh. Not being able to impress the object of her affections, and then—worse—getting told off by him.

As far as Gina was concerned, Mr. Sinclair had called the entire class rich bitches, because that was what "insulated by privilege" meant to her. Her wealth and power left no room for nuance. If you had been told off the way we had, you'd feel pretty shamefaced. With the exception of Katie, these girls did not. Or, if they did, they rolled their shame over to expose the softest part of its underbelly, then gave it a swift, sharp kick with their designer boots. Finished it off once and for all.

So after Gina's mother had sat in her Volvo fuming that her daughter was being made half an hour late for ballet practice, and after Gina had bounded out of detention with tears running down her face, they both exploded in hot outrage, and their anger cast a deep shadow over what had really happened.

Gina's mother reported Mr. Sinclair's meanness to the ladies at her Wednesday midmorning yoga lesson, and then— get out the smelling salts now, Linh—word began to spread that there was a teacher harassing all the young ladies at Laurinda, shaming them for being who they were.

This was Gina's chance to redeem herself, to show that she was an extremely proper young lady who could not stomach rude men. It was also her chance to get back at the object of her obsessions, who, she had found out, was not flattered by her attentions. He had become a disciplinarian, a megalomaniac who couldn't take a joke. A wounded ego and a wounded heart are the same thing when your love is unrequited.

Mr. Sinclair's every word was analyzed at the Langham Hotel's Sunday high tea, a treat for Gina from her father to help her overcome the trauma of being unjustly vilified. "He puts the hot girls in the center of the room so he can watch them more closely," cried Gina, out of a murky mixture of jealousy and wrath. "That Socratic classroom is bullshit." She wiped away fresh tears. "And during the whole lunchtime detention, he spent *at least* fifteen minutes staring at us, without even saying anything."

Her father patted her on the hand. "There, there, Reggie baby, it's all right. I am very proud of you for being so strong through all of this."

Finally, the expansive hand gestures Mr. Sinclair used to illustrate a point in class were translated by Gina's mother— through two glasses of champagne and a Peking duck pancake—to mean that he had *busy hands*.

When Katie reported this to me, I should not have been surprised to learn that the tale had been stretched out to the very edges of its perversity, like one of those cells we made turgid with blue-black dye and then examined beneath a microscope in biology.

Word reached the school administration, and politics with Mr. Sinclair was never the same again. Before the incident, his lessons had been dotted with interesting anecdotes. He once told us, for instance, that our former prime minister had left school at fourteen, and another time that he'd managed a band called the Ramrods. Some girls cracked up at hearing their hot teacher use the word *ramrod* without irony.

But then Gina had left that note about playing in his band, a note that probably left Mr. Sinclair wondering with cold dread what else he might inadvertently have let slip.

Now it was like someone had ripped out all the life from behind his face and replaced it with wires and cogs. Although he was not a teacher who feared us—I think he had too much contempt for us now to be afraid—we could tell that he didn't trust us at all.

All teenage girls are drama queens inside their minds, even the mousiest of us. We load and reload movies of ourselves in heroic postures and outlandish triumphs, movies that, if they were ever to be played in front of an audience of people we know and love, would cause us to shrivel in shame.

I had been practicing my line, polishing it, making sure I got every word exactly as it should be. I aimed to deliver it flawlessly; it would be a gem of truth, stunning in its brevity.

I'd arranged to meet Mrs. Grey, even if it meant I might miss the bus and be home late again. I'd stayed quiet during the attack on Ms. Vanderwerp, and I wasn't going to keep quiet a second time.

When I opened her door, she looked at me and slowly closed her eyes. She looked tired, her skin sallow beneath the powder. She opened her eyes again as I sat down. "What is it, Miss Lam?"

"Mrs. Grey, about the other week in history class . . ."

"Go on." She sat very still, waiting for me to tattle on the culprits. I remembered how, in Stanley, Ivy's brother had vowed that when he got out of jail, he would rearrange some faces. "Snitches get stitches," Ivy used to repeat to us.

"Well, you know how Mr. Sinclair was supervising us during our lunchtime detention," I began.

The corners of her mouth dropped. She probably thought that I was as sensitive as Gina.

I wanted to deliver my line with conviction, but because the Growler was looking at me as if every moment spent on me was a moment she would never get back, I stumbled over it too quickly. "Mr. Sinclair didn't do anything to those girls, and he didn't say anything that was not true." Instead of an unassailable declarative statement, it had become an apology.

"Is that all?" Mrs. Grey asked me.

"Yes, Mrs. Grey. I just wanted to say this because Mr. Sinclair—"

She cut me off. "Thank you, Lucy." But she sounded far from grateful. She sounded annoyed. She heaved a sigh that could have inflated a hot-air balloon, and repeated, "Thank you, Lucy. Other students—Siobhan, Katie and Stella—have already come to talk to me about this."

There was nothing more I could say, except a baffled "That's good."

She dismissed me by closing her eyes again slowly. In that state, which was not a resting one, her face looked like one at a morgue, a face made up by an artist who had not known the deceased in real life and so had given her green eye shadow and plum lips. I wondered whether Mrs. Grey had been wearing the wrong makeup all her life, or the wrong face.

I left her office feeling deflated. It seemed as if all my words were a waste of time, and all of Katie's and Siobhan's and Stella's too. The way Mrs. Grey treated me in her office, in that two minutes, it was as if she wanted me to keep my nose out of her important business, the adult business of making decisions; the only relevance I might have for her decisions was if I snitched and turned someone in.

The whole meeting had left me feeling vulnerable too, as if I'd exposed something about myself that I had not meant to. From then on, I wasn't sure whether it was my paranoia or whether Mrs. Grey had started to appraise me differently, but she definitely took more notice of me.

Maybe she had believed at first that I was a detached high achiever out to milk this scholarship for all it was worth academically so I could get into a good university and become a dentist, but now she knew that there was more to me than that. Mrs. Grey had seen I was more involved in the happenings of the school than she gave me credit for, and I suspected she might not have liked this kind of involvement.

Beneath my despair, I also felt a sense of solidarity. If Katie,

Siobhan and Stella had each gone to see Mrs. Grey, then there were some girls at this school who thought the same way I did. I vowed I would talk about it with Katie the next opportunity I got.

I waited for the right moment, but she was always in a different class, or talking to others at her locker, or in crowded spaces like the cafeteria. After a week I understood that a shift had occurred. It was true that Katie would talk to anyone—she was the sort of girl you could imagine in a decade's time being a nurse, and then in two decades a round, friendly housewife with two small children, and then in five decades a jolly old granny. Once I had seen her grandmother come to pick her up from school; they both had the same way of smiling like contented house cats.

But that week I noticed Siobhan and Stella were hanging around Katie's locker more and more. Then, in politics class, the three of them sat together near the front. That was when I knew they'd formed a trinity—and triangles, the most stable shapes in geometry, were impenetrable. So there was no way I could talk with Katie about my time in Mrs. Grey's office now. To speak to Katie alone would have been a debrief; to talk in front of all three girls would have been a declaration. The three of them had already done their debrief, and I was stranded.

I noticed them exchanging glances in politics, smug in their knowledge that they had done the right thing, allies helping Mr. Sinclair in his hour of need. I felt sadness for them, knowing that no one really gave a stuff about their actions, or mine for that matter. Like me, they weren't in the Cabinet but were gathering dust in some bottom drawer. No one cared what they said.

They had no important parents to back them up. Katie lived with her elderly grandparents; Siobhan's mother was a librarian, and her father a public servant; Stella's father was a minister. They had no skills or talents that brought special honor to the school, although they were all pretty decent students. These were girls who enthusiastically sang in the choir even though they would never get solos, who volunteered for Clean Up Australia Day, who happily played the piano by rote to entertain their relatives at Christmas—Nice Girls in a little bubble of goodwill.

I didn't dislike them. I just saw right through them, and through all that niceness. "How could Gina do that to Mr. Sinclair?" I could imagine them exclaiming over their lunches of Vegemite and cheese sandwiches and Oranginas. "It's just so mean." Of course, they would never use the word *bitch* or call Gina a slut. But I knew they thought things like that—we all did.

I was beginning to understand more about this insular world of Laurinda. And the more I saw of it, the more disquieted I felt.

You know how, back at Christ Our Savior, it was okay to drift in and out of friendship groups, so long as you weren't a backstabber or someone with an annoying habit like a tendency to squeal in a high-pitched voice or lie pathologically about your boyfriends? Remember the self-contained satellites like Carol, who would occasionally join us for recess but could be just as happy playing chess in the library with other girls?

At Laurinda it didn't happen like that. Floaters didn't exist here: you had to attach yourself to the bottom of some massive Friend Ship like a clinging barnacle, and if you were at the bottom of the ship, you had to go wherever that ship sailed.

Well, I was sick of it all, Linh. I was going to detach myself, and see if I would sink or swim.

TERM TWO

Dear Linh,

How strange high school is, that our reputations are in the hands of people we barely know, people we see every day and even sit close enough to that we can smell their sweat and see their bra straps falling from their short-sleeved summer uniforms. At Laurinda, what made a girl popular or unpopular wasn't wealth (otherwise, some of the Mediterranean students would have reigned) or attractiveness (Tharusha was possibly the most beautiful girl at the school, but you barely saw her face because she was so shy) or talent (as I'd seen from the muted response when Trisha played the piano). Popularity—and power—was based on things that could not be seen or felt—on ideas planted in other people's minds.

Term Two began with a massive infusion of the Laurinda spirit—such an enormous shot of it that we'd feel too sick and dizzy to get up to no good. This concoction was the idea of the Growler, of course, in league with the Cabinet.

At our chapel service, Reverend Mathes delivered a sermon about compassion—Ephesians 4:32, "Be kind and tender-hearted to one another." Then Brodie walked up to the front of the church and stood at the altar. I could not believe it, Linh. Brodie, of all people! She was going to make a speech.

"Compassion," she began, "is a rare quality that must be demonstrated to those who are less fortunate than us." She paused. "We are aware of the immense privileges that being a student at Laurinda brings, but with great power comes great responsibility." Pause. "We must be responsible for how our words and actions affect others." Pause. "We must lead by example." Pause.

These pauses were part of her speaking technique, I realized, probably to let the profundity of her words sink in, as though she were Dr. Martin Luther King.

"We must reach out to others!"

And as she said this, she did something so stupid that I almost burst out laughing, Linh—she extended her right arm, fingers splayed, her school colors flashing on the sleeve. Then I noticed she was looking directly *at me*. She was extending her helping hand to me! And she wasn't even winking. I looked around and could see the Growler smiling.

"Our school was one of the first ladies' colleges in the state," Brodie continued, "and we uphold a strong tradition of supporting the rights of women in a nurturing environment." On and on she went, until she turned toward the Growler. "If I may be so flippantly audacious—and I hope you will indulge me here, Mrs. Grey, as you do such an excellent job providing pastoral care to girls—while other private schools are hierarchical and based on a top-down approach, we are like this cup of wine at the table"—and she pointed to Reverend Mathes's goblet—"open and giving, and open to giving."

She extended both arms again, like Jesus summoning his flock, and continued: "You could even say that instead of adopting a hard and rigid phallus model of leadership"—and here she pretended to grasp something in her hand, and even moved her fist *up and down* a couple of times!—"we have adopted a receptive chalice model"—and now she cupped her hands. "This is the Laurinda spirit!"

The girls whooped and applauded, and some even stamped their feet. In church! I sat there, my hands clenched tight beneath my kilt. You had to hand it to Brodie: she knew how to play it both ways. Just when you thought that her speech was going to become so toadying that you would have to chuck a cushion onstage for her genuflecting knees, she compared the school to a dick and a fanny, a move so unexpected that a ripple of orgiastic hilarity flowed through the crowd. The applause was deafening.

Brodie had pulled such a swift one that even the teachers were applauding her ability to imbue four hundred girls with the Laurinda spirit. Some—the weaker ones—were chuckling, even though they found the joke distasteful, to show that they had a sense of humor. Others laughed outright, convinced it was just another example of student high jinks.

Mr. Sinclair had a grimace on his face, the look you'd have if you were watching someone embarrass themselves by telling a very unfunny fart joke. Mrs. Grey's expression was one of carefully contrived neutrality, giving nothing away. The person who was least impressed was Reverend Mathes, standing there in his robes.

We did not see Ms. Vanderwerp in Term Two. "Maybe she's offed herself!" Gina suggested, with no small amount of vicious glee.

Although the staff never spoke about it, we knew Ms. Vanderwerp had gone away on stress leave. Mr. Abraham took her place, a towering man with an Easter Island face and gray hair in his ears. He walked into the classroom and gave us a look as if to say, go on, try the tampon trick on me.

But we would never have done it to a male teacher, Linh. There would have been shame in pulling something like that on a man—but not a shame about hurting him, because men aren't hurt that way. They are the ones who bond over poop- and piss-themed road trip movies, after all. It was the stigma of being female. We'd have been too embarrassed to hear a man rail about how disgusting our bodies were.

I also found out why the girls called Mrs. Grey the Growler. Back at Christ Our Savior, although we had a bulging arsenal of multilingual profanities, we didn't know Aussie colloquialisms so well. Once I discovered what this nickname meant, I understood all its associations in a different way: the Hairy Growler, the Red Gaping Jaws of Growler. And all the while

I had thought that they were just describing her demeanor! I also worked out that Ms. Vanderwerp was called Ms. V not just as a shortening of her long surname . . . the *V* stood for something else.

I was learning a new language here, the language of Laurinda's snarky and disgruntled majority. A language that was peppered with sexual innuendo, because *proper* Laurinda girls simply did not do sex. It was too visceral. No one except Gina acknowledged that we might have crushes or want boyfriends just as badly as the girls from Christ Our Savior. No one faced up to the reality that maybe some girls were already having sex, and a lot of it. We were meant to be above all that.

Yet the teachers who called us "young ladies" treated us as anything but. And the more repressed the students felt, the more colorful their hidden hateful language became. It was a thousand times more obscene than anything a Stanley druggie might blurt out in an angry haze, because it was so calculated and deliberate. What a dichotomy—these nice girls and their foul language!

And here you were either being told off or being backed by the school, depending on your standing. If any other girl had made the joke that Brodie had in chapel, she would have been suspended. But Brodie had diplomatic immunity. It was ages until I figured out why, but when I did, a heavy weight dropped inside of me, a weight I could not dislodge.

The Cabinet had weeded out one of the weaker teachers. The collective belief among the other girls was that Ms. Vanderwerp had been unfit to teach. "My father said that they shouldn't let teachers like her into the class anyway, if she couldn't control the students," I overheard a girl named

Tiffany tell her friend Cynthia. That was when I understood why the school didn't have a student representative council. The Cabinet would always be around to make sure things were kept in order.

"Mrs. Leslie, I can't concentrate," I blurted out the next time we had a tutorial. "Something really bad has happened."

I needed to tell another adult, someone responsible, and someone who seemed to care about things other than the Laurinda spirit. I sensed that, of the teachers, only Mrs. Leslie might understand. A woman who cried over my essay about selling eggs with my grandma might not even know that her daughter was part of the Cabinet. After all, my parents had only a vague idea what I did at school.

"What is it, dear?" she asked, concerned. "Bad things at home?"

"No," I said. "At this school."

There was a long pause. "Oh? That's interesting," she finally said, although she didn't seem that interested. "What sort of thing, Lucy?"

How could I tell her that her virtuous daughter had contributed to a teacher's nervous breakdown?

"Well, I, umm . . . I think something bad has happened to Ms. Vanderwerp."

"What do you mean, dear?"

"We screwed her over massively" was how you'd put it, Linh, but I'd learned that unless you put things in a palatable way here, no one was ever going to listen to you. "I think we caused Ms. Vanderwerp to quit."

She laughed, indulgently. "Surely you must be mistaken, Lucy?"

"What?"

"We don't say 'what,' we say 'pardon,'" she corrected. "How do you mean you caused her to 'quit'?" She said it as if we'd helped Ms. Vanderwerp stop smoking.

"Well, what we did in class . . ."

"Oh, Lucy! Sweetie, you have been worried about this? Ms. Vanderwerp has just gone on long-service leave. Family-related matters. I thought there was an announcement at assembly?"

I didn't even know Ms. Vanderwerp had a family. I'd always imagined her living alone with a cat and a box of tea bags. "But the last day of Term One—"

She cut me off. "Students will always play pranks, Lucy. It's part of being young. Mind you, not all students are as mature and well behaved as you, and not all pranks are acceptable, but growing up sometimes means testing your boundaries."

"But, Mrs. Leslie, it wasn't—"

I couldn't continue, because Mrs. Leslie had decided she wanted to tell me a story. "Lucy, when I was a student here we had a teacher—mean as anything—named Mrs. May. She taught home economics. Back then, we all had to learn to cook, believe it or not. And if Mrs. May was displeased with your pie or your stew, she would tip it on the floor—right there on the floor!—and make you clean it up.

"So one day we all hid our oven timers around the classroom. She was an older lady, so we climbed on top of the kitchen benches and hid them in the fan vents where she couldn't reach. We timed them to go off every two minutes. Thirty girls, thirty timers! Can you imagine?"

Mrs. Leslie's eyes grew distant and unfocused even as she laughed. She was back at Laurinda and a student again, with a draconian teacher like Mrs. May, who was their version of Mrs. Grey, I suppose. Amber's mum was fourteen again. There was no getting through to her now.

After two weeks, I was surprised that no one had so much as mentioned Ms. Vanderwerp. She was gone, like an embarrassing passing of wind in a perfumed sitting room. Yet something had fundamentally changed about this school. Beneath the sandstone, tectonic plates were shifting and new formations were about to rise to the surface.

The first of these changes came to light in Mrs. Grey's office. By now I refused to call her the Growler. I did not like or respect her any more than I had at the start of the year—it was more that I respected myself. I had learned from Harshan's example that you did not need to kowtow to the Cabinet. So at least in my mind, she would revert to her surname, that nebulous hue between black and white.

"Come in, Miss Lam."

I entered her office and closed the door. Her nose whistled like a kettle sometimes, the only sign that something unsettling was going on inside. Otherwise, she always seemed as calm as a stainless steel urn. Her nose was whistling now.

She wasted no time on small talk. "Miss Lam, where do you see yourself in the scheme of things?"

"Pardon, Mrs. Grey?"

"Where is your place at Laurinda?"

"Here," I replied, confused, and then rushed to explain. "I mean, not in this room, of course, because this is your office."

She looked at me for a long while before speaking, and as I watched I could hear waves crashing in my eardrums. "Tell me, Miss Lam, where did you learn this very frustrating method of making irrelevant distinctions and not answering what you are asked?"

She'd asked me questions about my life, things I was sure she would never ask any other student—how much my parents made, and whether my mother collected welfare. Now I had no idea what she was talking about or what she wanted from me.

"Miss Lam, it seems to me that you have been remedied, so to speak."

"Pardon, Mrs. Grey?"

"Mrs. Leslie tells me that you've shown marked improvement. As a result, you will move back to your ordinary English classes. No more remedial English. Do you feel ready, Miss Lam?"

"No."

She had not expected this answer.

"Mrs. Leslie feels you are ready. Why do you believe that you aren't?"

"I'm not." I spent almost every other class with the Cabinet and Katie. My time with Mrs. Leslie was a refuge from the madness.

"Why do you insist on lying, Miss Lam? Did your Catholic school not teach you the eighth commandment?"

"But I'm not lying, miss," I replied. "I still don't know whether . . ."

She stared so hard and long at me that I stopped talking and looked away.

"Let me tell you something, Miss Lam." She leaned in

close. "From the very beginning I sensed that you were displeased to be doing remedial English. We organized that for your benefit, so you would be able to catch up. You have been resentful, and now not only have you progressed to wasting Mrs. Leslie's valuable time by talking about things other than the texts, you have also presumed a familiarity with staff that is disrespectful."

"That's not true. I really like Mrs. Leslie."

"I have known Mrs. Leslie for decades. I know she has a tendency to be soft on students. That woman will make a girl feel she is her greatest champion and confidante." She paused. "She will be very upset with me about this, but I am not gentle like her, so let me tell you, Miss Lam, that she is not there to gossip with you about the goings-on of your teachers."

I suddenly wanted to be out of there, away from the searing eyes of Mrs. Grey. I knew now that Mrs. Leslie had mentioned—most likely in passing, most likely innocuously—my concerns about Ms. Vanderwerp.

"Here is what will happen this term," she told me. "You will move to the regular English class. You will no longer have lessons with Mrs. Leslie."

This was not how it was supposed to happen. Mrs. Grey had let me win a Pyrrhic victory: I was in the regular English class not as an acknowledgment of how good I was, but as a punishment.

At lunchtime I would go to the library before anyone could find me. Some days the world seemed too full of people, and I would tuck myself away in the back corner where the larger-folio books were, the books about art and architecture that didn't fit on the ordinary shelves, and I would pull one off the shelf and look through it. I saw from the date stamps that the last time some of them had been borrowed was before I was born.

One day I discovered a stack of Laurinda yearbooks. I'd seen the long row of navy blue spines every time I went there, but they didn't have any writing so I had assumed they were useless old journals. They dated back to 1902 in that format; there were also older ones, which were smaller and had black cloth covers.

I spent quite a few lunchtimes leafing through those yearbooks. I would usually get through about ten—a decade's worth—in the hour, before I got hungry and had to go to my locker to get my sandwich. They were mostly dreary, identical images of grinning girls in sports uniforms, the same cute pictures of kindergarten students painting, the same reports on the Red Cross appeal. Yet after looking through so many of them, I noticed that certain faces seemed to repeat: a freckle-faced girl named Claire from 1971 would reappear in a plumper form as Cecilia in 1979, but they would not share the same last name.

Each decade had its own look—the long, straight hair and the part down the middle in the seventies, the poufy under-skirts in the school plays of the fifties, the feathered haircuts in the eighties. The most fascinating period for me was the early 1900s. Even then, more than a hundred years ago, if you looked carefully, you could detect the differences between the girls. All fourteen girls in the 1903 photograph were wearing white gloves, but while most girls had just plain ones, some had gloves with three or four pearl buttons down the sides. Those girls also had the best seats—in the front, on either side of the teacher in her long, dark dress—while most of the group were left standing.

One afternoon, when Mrs. Leslie was returning some books to the library, she spotted me getting a yearbook from the shelves. I quickly shoved it back and pretended to look at the spine of a book about Caravaggio.

"Lucy!" she called out, sauntering over. "It's so wonderful to see you!"

I smiled.

"You're in Amber's English class now! How are you doing there?"

"Good."

"I've missed your insights," she said. "You must be studying *Emma* now. How I love that book! How far into it are you, Lucy?"

"The very beginning."

She asked if I was enjoying it, and I lied. This was what I was learning at Laurinda, Linh: in order to be nice or polite, you had to lie. Back at Christ Our Savior, you could tell a teacher straight-out that you did not like a book, so long as you didn't use swear words. But here I felt I was constantly tiptoeing around egos like they were eggs, and one clumsy step could mean someone's self-esteem would come leaking out.

"I have the BBC collection of *Emma* and *Pride and Prejudice*," Mrs. Leslie told me. "Amber just adores Mr. Darcy. Perhaps you could come over after school one day and watch it with us?"

I marveled at the naïveté of Mrs. Leslie, Linh, a grown-up who thought she could put her daughter and me together to watch a few videos and we would become best friends while she brought us milk and cookies.

"Sure, Mrs. Leslie," I said. "That sounds like fun."

As you know, my mother never did anything slowly. She gulped down her coffee. She slurped up her food, even laying down sheets of newspaper on the table when she was eating so that the splatters could just be scrunched up and tossed in the bin. She'd eat grapes from a bowl next to her sewing machine with a wet towel folded beside her to wipe her fingers on, so that they wouldn't stain the denim or polar fleece pieces.

When she was pregnant with the Lamb, she had bad morning sickness; once she ate a bowl of pho and vomited it back out again within half an hour. I had to clean it up, and in the sick were long white tendrils of noodles, and beef slices that were still disk-shaped. My mother barely even chewed her food. If her sewing machine were a car, she'd constantly be driving way past the speed limit, her foot jammed down flat on the accelerator pedal.

Mrs. Leslie did everything as if she had all the time in the world. She waited for me patiently after school in her dark blue BMW, just as she said she would. The seats were warm, as if the car had been sitting in the sun on a ninety-degree day, except that it was sixty degrees outside. She saw me touch the leather. "Oh, they're heated," she explained. When I gave her a blank look, she told me that if I pressed a button to my left, I could turn it off.

She was taking me to her house for a cup of tea and a catch-up. When I had told my father about it last week, he had just about been ready to take the day off work and drive me there himself. That was how excited he was, Linh. "Make sure you ask her lots of questions about things you are stuck on," he advised me.

As Mrs. Leslie pulled out of the parking lot, I asked, "Where's Amber?"

"She has band rehearsal. She'll catch the school bus back at five." The school had four buses to ferry students to and from their after-school activities, although they never went as far as Stanley.

I felt relieved that it was just me and Mrs. Leslie. I felt more comfortable with her than with her daughter. While she was driving, she asked me the usual questions about school and whether I felt I had now adapted. "It's never easy, is it?" she sighed. "You're very brave, Lucy. Amber's been at Laurinda since kindergarten. Sometimes I wonder whether we did the right thing by her."

She paused, and I knew she wanted me to say something affirming, but I had no idea what that might be. "Amber's nice," I reassured her.

Linh, what has become of me? I lied to fill in a moment of silent awkwardness, becoming a simpering people pleaser, when I could have stayed quiet.

"But she's so insular. I wish the two of you could be friends, Lucy. You'd open up her world—I dare say even open her eyes to her self-centered ways."

Where was this heading, Linh? I thought only Asian mothers did this kind of thing.

"I worry about her," Mrs. Leslie confided. "She's always been so sensitive, but never that sensible. She's been friends with Brodie for so long that sometimes I feel the friendship has held Amber back from becoming her own person." She paused. "Now, I do think Brodie is a very talented young woman, but she is so brilliant that Amber seems to get lost in her shadow. I think she doesn't try very hard because she feels there's no way she could ever measure up to Brodie."

It felt strange, being privy to this. It was a bit like when Mrs. Cho started running down Tully to me. Yet this time I wasn't sure that Mrs. Leslie was aware she was speaking aloud—she almost seemed to be talking to herself.

"But you, Lucy," she concluded, "you're just such a hardworking, self-contained little hive of industry. You never let things get you down."

I knew Mrs. Leslie was itching to remind me how proud my parents must be and what a great contribution to this country we refugees made. I felt awkward because she did not know the real us; I wondered how she'd feel about Ivy's brother Ming, with his prison time. Her naïveté was a beautiful thing, I decided, because it meant she would always see the best in us. Although Ming's parents would probably never be able to excuse his vices and habits, there would always be someone like Mrs. Leslie, far away from our lives, who would.

Luckily, we had arrived at our destination. Their house was really something, Linh. The first thing I noticed was the wooden floors. "Wooden floors are what villagers have," my father had said when we ripped up our dark and grimy carpets five years ago and discovered the old floorboards. "Let's tile over them." And so he and cousin Claude had spent a week and a half mixing cement and grouting, aligning the little plastic plus symbols to keep the corners of the white tiles even, and cutting ceramics to shape.

Not only was Amber's house uncarpeted, but the floorboards were bare. They were so shiny that you could almost see your reflection, your face lost in swirls of wood-grain waves in the timber ocean.

There was a polished wooden sculpture in one corner of the living room that was like a tree branch kissing the floor with its wider end, an invisible tap pouring a puddle of wood onto the ground. I was afraid to ask what it was in case it was phallic, but Mrs. Leslie caught me looking at it.

"Oh, that's a didgeridoo," she said, almost as if we were back in remedial class.

I told her I'd never seen a didgeridoo like that before.

"It's a pared-down one." Mrs. Leslie laughed in an embarrassed way, though I didn't understand why she felt embarrassed. Somehow I knew that there was another, more complicated name for it, or for that style of art. There was no way Mrs. Leslie would buy a random "pared-down" hollow tree branch.

"Where does it come from?" I asked.

"An art gallery in the city," she replied.

"What's the gallery called?"

"Oh, Lucy, it's just a little art gallery in the city," she said with a small laugh, and I felt ashamed to have sounded so pushy, although really I was only thinking that if I passed it one day I could go in and have a look. But I suspected the art would be heart-stoppingly expensive.

"Would you like a cup of tea, Lucy? We have oolong or jasmine."

"Black tea is fine with me, Mrs. Leslie."

She went into the kitchen and, not knowing what else to do, I followed. Her kitchen looked like something from a magazine, all granite and pure white cupboards and stainless steel. I noticed small things, like the soft paper towels that they wasted wiping spills—the sort of thing, if we had them, we would use to wipe the Lamb's face after a meal instead of pilfered McDonald's napkins or plain old toilet paper.

There was a cabinet where all the nice plates and bowls were on display, some on special stands so that the pictures on the plates faced you like paintings. What awed me most about her house was that Mrs. Leslie had all this expensive stuff lying around. My mum and dad always told me to hide our valuables if any visitors came by.

On the kitchen bench, next to a phone, I suddenly spotted a familiar object—a blue notebook. No, I thought, that can't be the same Mercury Stool–signed article. Because this one had pages torn out and phone messages scrawled all over it.

"What's she doing here?" Amber asked when she arrived home at five-thirty and saw me sitting at the Leslies' dining table, drinking tea from a cup on a saucer. A little plate next to me was filled with Oreos.

"I beg your pardon?" For a moment Mrs. Leslie sounded scarily like a teacher.

"*Sorry.* Lucy, what are you doing here?" she asked me.

I didn't know what to say. This was embarrassing, but I

wasn't sure why. All I knew was that, somehow, my presence was annoying to Amber.

"Lucy and I are having a little catch-up," said Mrs. Leslie. "Would you like to join us?"

"Oh, I see," said Amber. "Well, she's not going to disappear, because she's in my English class now."

"Yes, I know," replied Mrs. Leslie.

"So she's not like Zi Wei or June Moon." Amber turned toward me. "Two Asian girls that came here on exchange a few years ago. They went back home to China and Korea, back to their rich mums and dads, but my mum here—you should have seen her carry on. It was as if the girls were going back to kneeling on broken glass or something."

"That's enough, young lady."

"You're not supposed to have favorites anyhow."

"Enough!"

Amber ignored her mother and busied herself making a snack. I noticed how she used half a dozen utensils to make a sandwich.

"Hey, Amber, you have an interesting-looking jotter," I said.

"Pardon?"

"Next to your phone."

"Oh," she said, barely glancing at it, "that piece of crap. I think Gina gave it to me."

"Amber Leslie, watch your language!" fired Mrs. Leslie.

My father came to collect me half an hour later. Amber opened the door, and Mrs. Leslie came to tell him how much she had enjoyed having me over.

"*Wah,* look at the size of that place," my father exclaimed after he'd pulled out of the driveway. "What does her father do?"

"I don't know, Dad. Some sort of engineer."

"Your friend looks like a movie star."

I could see how pleased my father was that I was friends with Amber, whose mother worked at the school and who lived in such a fairy-tale house. "I'm glad you are making good friends."

My father was happy on the drive back from Amber's house, because he thought that I had made progress. But I felt the opposite. I was regressing as a person. Those two hours with Mrs. Leslie and Amber had drained me, Linh. It was exhausting to be the sort of person they expected me to be.

When I was six years old, Dad bought a cheap one-pound bag of mixed candy from Tien, who worked at the Allens' factory. He made me stand outside the front of my elementary school and hand them out to the neighborhood kids walking home. He hung back behind me. It had been a hot day, the bag was heavy and I was not interested in either the candy or the other kids. I just wanted to get home and watch *Fat Cat and Friends*.

Nor were the other kids interested in me. They would come up, grab a handful of candy and walk off. Some parents made their kids say, "Thank you." Other parents said it on their kids' behalf and smiled warmly at me. One mum pulled her little boy away from my bag when she saw my dad hovering behind me, even though he was smiling broadly at them. In fact, that probably creeped them out even more.

When my father walked me home that afternoon, he said, "Well, Lucy, now that you've had a chance to get to know the kids at the school, some of the older ones will look after you."

Maybe you could pull a trick like that in Hanoi, because people were so broke, and older kids knew to look after younger ones, but here in Stanley my poor father had no idea of the difference between exploitation and friendship.

So when he proposed that I invite some Laurinda girls over for a movie night, I had to quash the idea.

"This is the first time it will be on television!" he said. "It is a huge event, and it would be nice for you to share our culture with your friends."

"No, Dad, I really don't think the girls will want to watch *Hope in Hanoi*."

My father had been waiting for this movie, which was set during the Vietnam War, to come on TV for years. All movies ended up on the television eventually, he reasoned, which was why we never, ever went to the cinema. Someone at the factory had told Dad that the movie was going to screen that Friday night.

"We could have a little party, order some takeout food."

"No."

"I can't believe I have a daughter who is ashamed of her culture. So ashamed she won't even have her friends over to see a movie about it."

My father made me livid with rage. If Dad thought that the war represented the sum of our culture, I couldn't be bothered arguing with him. "We'll see," I said, to shut him up. But he seemed to sense something else I was thinking.

"Do you think that a lovely girl like Amber will care what our house looks like?" he asked me.

"Yes," I retorted. "Amber would care. But Mrs. Leslie wouldn't—she'd just feel sorry for us."

"And what is wrong with that?"

At that moment, I could not stand my father.

"What is wrong with living humbly?" he continued, determined to make his point—a point that he knew was wrong, which was why he had to twist words and call it "humble" instead of what it was. Even his voice made me want to snap a chopstick in half. "They would see how hard we work, and feel admiration for how hard you try at school."

He wanted us to act like stoic refugees when it worked to our advantage. According to my father, it was an easy role to play—all I had to do was keep my head down, keep quiet and work hard, and then everyone would like me. There was no such thing as having trouble fitting in if you presented the right image to your audience.

"You have to be sociable at the new school," he advised. "It's not like Christ Our Savior, where girls just stuck with each other because they were Asian or Spanish or Greek or whatever."

That Friday evening, Dad came home with three big bags of McDonald's. Enough food for a family three times our size.

"*Wah,* what's with all this food, old man?" my mother asked.

My father looked at me as if I'd poured one of the plastic cups of Coke over his head. It was a wordless look of exorbitant disappointment. "I thought you were bringing some friends home."

I didn't want to make the situation worse, so I didn't tell him that the types of girls I now hung around with didn't consider McDonald's the epitome of modern, hygienic, healthy food. They considered it the food of poor, fat rednecks.

My father's adoration of McDonald's was completely without irony. "The Australian government would never allow advertisements to lie on television," he once told me. I knew the Laurinda girls would not share his love of the perfect golden fry, or marvel over the milky nutritional glory of the ninety-nine-cent cone.

"Let's have a look at what's inside, Lamb," I said, shame preventing me from looking at my dad. I opened up one of the Happy Meal boxes and rummaged for the surprise toy.

"Who is going to eat all this, I ask you?" my mother scolded.

"Our daughter said that she would bring some friends."

"You should have asked her how many people were coming."

"I didn't say anyone was coming!" I protested.

There was silence. The Lamb found the toy and started to bite away the plastic packaging with his four front teeth. "Lamby," I said to him, "let me open that for you."

"Indeed," my father lamented, "who is going to eat all this food?"

I sighed. "I will. I love this stuff. I will eat both the Big Macs—one for dinner and one for breakfast."

"Don't be ridiculous," said my father. "Do you want to turn into a fat pig like the white girls here in Stanley with their bums hanging out of their pants?"

At this point in an American sitcom, there would be canned laughter. Then the teenage protagonist would run to her room and slam the door. The American mum would hold her hand up to her mouth and exclaim, "Rich, you can't say things like that!"

But this was our cement house, we never locked our parents out and we could never make a comedy about the people who let us live in their suburb and their country and put up with our ethnic ways.

We just looked at the television, all three of us, and didn't say another word, because the movie was about to begin. I had the Lamb on my lap, and I inserted fries into his mouth at regular intervals.

Nothing much excited my parents these days, but movies like this one did. It began in a small Vietnamese village and told the life story of one woman. It was also about a white war veteran who had always wanted an Asian wife. He took the village woman to the United States and she adapted there, but he couldn't go back to his old life so he shot himself in the head. It was one of those movies you would call intense and epic.

But these times—sitting with my family and watching Vietnam War movies filled with limbs being blown off, rapes and women digging their own graves—were the happiest of my childhood. I was glad that people kept making these films, which were bonding Asian families together all over Australia.

Ivy called me up afterward to talk. She was excited because her family had made a night of it too. And then I talked to you about it, Linh.

I think my dad is pissed off at me, I said.

Why does he want your new friends to come over so badly? you wondered. *It's not like he ever wanted Yvonne or Ivy to come over when you were still at Christ Our Savior.*

Yeah, I mused. In fact, he asked me if I was still hanging around those "gangsta girls," and told me to watch out because it would be my ruin.

My father had once marveled at Ivy's big, fat birthday cake of a house in Sunray, with its Italian pillars at the front and granite tabletops inside. But now that he had seen a different type of wealth, he didn't want me hanging around with her. Ivy's family might have money, but they weren't that different from us. In their double garage, Ivy's mother had set up not one but five sewing machines, and various cousins and aunties came over regularly to earn some money. Ivy's parents' wealth was a wealth without power, my dad believed, a hot, stressed and determined wealth that was insular and left them unable to fully enjoy its rewards.

"Her parents work all the time in the garage, so she goes tramping about at the shopping center with her designer clothes and her airy attitude, and when it's time to hunker down and do some real work, she turns to you," my father reprimanded. So that had been the end of Ivy's visits.

As for Yvonne—forget about it, she was with that gangsta Viet boyfriend now. "A beautiful white girl like that, hanging around with that hooligan!" was how my father put it.

In fact, besides a couple of times when you visited me, visits that my father bore grudgingly, none of my Christ Our Savior friends came over to study anymore. My father didn't want them "using" me.

The second time Mrs. Leslie picked me up, Amber was there too, because she didn't have band practice that evening. Mrs. Leslie turned to face us before she started the car. "Girls, I just have to run a few errands. They won't take long—do you mind?"

I was in her car, she was the driver—what else could I say? I would have jumped at the chance to exchange my errands for hers any day, because I was sure that hers would not be as tedious as mine: read out letters from the phone and gas companies, mop the floors, interpret at the clinic when the Lamb got his vaccinations . . .

I was right: Mrs. Leslie's errands were in another league. The first thing she did was park near a café and treat us to an afternoon snack. "This is one of our favorite cafés, isn't it, Amber?" I imagined the two of them sitting there on a Saturday morning on the quaint wrought iron chairs, talking about what dress to get for Valedictory Dinner. But then Amber deliberately looked the other way, forcing me to modify the image in my mind: now the two of them were sitting there with Amber not speaking while Mrs. Leslie complained, "Why can't you be more like Lucy Lam, that paragon of brilliance?"

"I think you'll like this place too, Lucy," Mrs. Leslie said. "Now, what would you like?" She handed me the menu, a sheet of parchment paper attached to a wooden clipboard.

But I couldn't understand a single thing written there. I could read the individual words, but they made no sense. Even the coffees sounded like fancy desserts. "Wow. 'Cinnamon-infused sourdough loaf with sun-ripened vine fruit,'" I read.

Amber sighed. "That's just raisin toast." She then turned her bored face toward the window, so as not to hear her mother telling her off.

Mrs. Leslie laughed. "Oh, Lucy, they do have some pretentious names here, but some excellent breads. What would you like?"

"The raisin toast?"

"Sultana bread it is for you, then!"

Amber rolled her eyes.

When the waitress came, Mrs. Leslie and I ordered something to eat, but Amber just wanted a pineapple juice.

The waitress returned, setting a pastry called a chocolate brioche in front of Mrs. Leslie. "Oh, dear me," she sighed after she took the first bite, "this is very wicked."

I thought of how my parents would never refer to food as wicked. Food was the gift of the gods—it was the stuff they had hoarded and saved on the boat, and something they would never, ever be stingy with when they had guests over.

Mrs. Leslie patted her stomach and smiled at me, as if we were sharing some private joke or she had got herself knocked up. "It's going straight here!"

After our meal, Mrs. Leslie bought two long rolls for

home, and we walked farther down the strip of shops to a place called Lennie's ("Purveyors of Fine Foods"), where she bought a small block of cheese. The guy behind the counter spoke about the cheeses in such a way that you'd imagine he went home every evening and retreated to his room with a copy of *Food & Wine* instead of *Playboy*.

"This cheese is one of my favorites, fresh from Tasmania and infused with hand-picked wasabi leaves. You'll find it has a full-bodied kick to it."

"I'd like to give him a full-bodied kick," muttered Amber as we walked out of the store, and for the first time that afternoon I thought she wasn't so bad.

We walked farther down the strip, which was packed with girls from all the elementary schools and their mothers, and I tried to block out thoughts of how I would just have bought some meat from Tully's mum, and vegetables from the Sunray market, before heading home on the bus. My father had told Mum that I was receiving special tutoring from Mrs. Leslie. That's what he thought we were doing.

The final place we stopped that day was Spencer's Event Specialists. It stocked everything you needed for a party except the food, but to call it a party store was like calling Barney's Clint's Crazy Bargains. Spencer's was not a store for children. Everything was neatly packed on shelves with hand-lettered labels at the bottom, written using a calligraphy pen you could buy for $29.95.

There were fifty different types of invitations, for every occasion. Rolls and rolls of ribbons in every color and pattern. Balloons sold singly by theme (Happy 60th/Christening/Anniversary/Sweet Sixteen!). On one shelf were beautiful objects for the home, such as candle holders, glass bowls and plastic flower arrangements, and when I looked at the sign below, I could not believe my eyes. These were single-use decorations. I saw printed tape for $7.99 a roll. I took it all in while Mrs. Leslie and Amber went off to look for whatever it was they wanted.

Standing there, I thought about how my mother bought stationery—like a roll of tape or outdated journals for two dollars a third of the way into the year. She would never keep a diary or a scrapbook; she just liked having the stuff around and palming it off on me. She had no idea what I did in school—she must have thought my schoolwork required a lot of sticking or stapling.

"Never underestimate the power of a scented candle!" declared a sign beneath a display of colored candles.

Yes, I thought. Buy two and invade Russia!

I found Mrs. Leslie and Amber in front of the organza bags with drawstring ribbon tops like miniature party skirts. There were ones with "Sweet Sixteen!" printed on them, but Mrs. Leslie said she preferred the plain ones.

"Yeah, the gold lettering is so tacky," added Amber.

"What color should we have?" Mrs. Leslie asked Amber.

Amber pointed to the fuchsia ones.

"Bit bright, aren't they?"

"Well, you asked!"

"But, darling, they won't match your invitations."

"Why does everything have to match? It's not like we're living in the 1950s, bloody hell!"

"I've just about had enough of you!" hissed Mrs. Leslie as she went to pay for the bags. They came in packets of six, at twelve dollars a packet. She needed ten packets. I could barely watch as she paid, but luckily she did it with a credit card, so the transaction seemed kind of unreal. I supposed that was why rich people used credit cards so often: they didn't need to painstakingly count out banknotes, as they'd reached a point in life when money was just numerical and not frustratingly finite and concrete.

"So, Lucy, you'll come, of course, won't you?" We were back in the car and Mrs. Leslie had turned on the engine.

"Sure, Mrs. Leslie," I replied automatically. Then I added, "If Amber would like me there." How rude of me to invite myself to Amber's birthday in her presence, even if her mother had asked! But maybe my reply sounded passive-aggressive?

This was terrible. Hanging around the two of them had me forever doubting whether I was saying or doing the right thing, or wondering whether I was offending either of them.

"Good."

Amber didn't say anything. She didn't need to, because whatever she said would have been a lie.

"Would you like me to bring anything?" I asked.

"Just your dear self!"

"What about food?"

"It's all catered." Then Mrs. Leslie paused, perhaps thinking that hiring catering for a party was obscenely indulgent, like her chocolate brioche. "Well, Lucy, are there any special foods you would like to bring?"

"Umm, my mum could make something."

"That would be lovely, Lucy, but I don't want your mother to go to any trouble at all."

It was funny, the sorts of things Mrs. Leslie said, as if you could prepare some food without going to any trouble at all, as if it would magically materialize—like the pie Snow White "baked" for the dwarves, when really her animal friends had done all the work for her.

I sat in the backseat of my father's Camry with two enormous white plastic trays of rice-paper rolls—one balanced on my lap and one in the empty space across from the Lamb's safety seat—and wished you were coming with me. At the last minute Mum had wanted me to take the Lamb too.

"What are you asking, old woman?" my father demanded.

"Old man, I have work to do." She pointed to the pile of pockets that needed interfacing ironed into them. There were several hundred. "And she's just going to a party."

"No!" My father took the Lamb from her. "He stays here. I'll look after him."

"But I need you to help me with these shirts! They're due on Monday."

Suddenly I felt very guilty and weary. All this fuss for a party I didn't even want to attend. "I don't *have* to go," I began.

"But your mother's made all these rice-paper rolls for you to take!"

My mother had originally suggested frying up some Teochew rice cakes. I had talked her out of it, not because they weren't delicious but because they were fried in oil; a party with bespoke napkins was not the right place for them. Then she suggested boiling an enormous pot of pho for the girls to try.

"No, Mum, no one drinks soup at a party!"

"But it's not just soup—there are rice noodles too."

"Mum, I think they want finger food."

"Since when do sixteen-year-olds get to demand what food their guests bring to their birthdays?" my mother muttered, but she spent two hours wrapping the rolls anyway, making sure all the prawns were lined up on their beds of mint and lettuce, so they would show through the transparent pastry skin.

"Don't you think you've made too many?" I asked.

"We don't want to come across as stingy."

"Hey, Mum, these look just like the ones at the restaurants," I said, because I knew it would make her happy. It was pretty easy to make my mother happy, whereas with the girls at Laurinda and their mothers, you had no idea.

"Do you want to take a jar of nuoc mam too?" she asked.

I imagined opening up the jar of fish sauce in front of all those girls and their finger sandwiches, and it spilling right on their white linen and blush floor rugs. "No, Mum. It's okay."

"Don't forget this." She handed me the present I had asked her to make for Amber: a Coast & Co. skirt from their upcoming catalog. My mother was a one-person birthday party dynamo, but unlike Amber and her mother, she had done it all so quietly.

When we arrived, my father got out of the car to help me carry the second tray of rolls. In the middle of the bright day, the Leslies' house looked more majestic than ever.

I noticed Chelsea coming up the driveway, holding a small plate with a dozen cupcakes. She was dressed in a frock that had little blue and green flowers all over it, and a cardigan made of a soft material that I somehow knew wasn't rayon or polyester.

"Dad, this is Chelsea," I said.

"How do you do, Mr. Lam?"

My father smiled at her and rang the doorbell.

Amber appeared. In her blue dress and sandals, she looked like a woman from a Botticelli painting. Her hair was washed and shiny, and the mascara on her eyelashes made her eyes look larger than ever, like a cat's. "Hello, Mr. Lam," she said. Then she squealed, "Chelsea! Lucy!" and gave each of us a fake hug, one of those ones where you loosely grab the other person's shoulders and lean close.

The house was filled with fifteen- and sixteen-year-old girls and a handful of boys, standing or sitting, eating sandwiches or out on the lawn drinking sparkling water. The scene reminded me a little of *The Great Gatsby*—Daisy Buchanan and her afternoon teas.

My father was taking it all in. I hoped now he would understand why his McDonald's party would not have made the cut. But the moment I thought this, I also felt sad and guilty to see my father standing there like a prewar Southeast Asian man, watching the colonizers sip French champagne in their villas. There was a heartbreaking innocence about the way he believed these girls had taken his daughter under their wing.

He found Mrs. Leslie and thanked her for having me over.

"Our pleasure," she enthused. "We love Lucy. She's a darling. She's almost become part of our family!" Then she noticed our rice-paper rolls and made such a noise about them that you'd think they had become new members of the family too.

When my father left, I stood there awkwardly for a long while as the other girls chatted about each other's frocks, about how beautiful Amber was, and about the girls who weren't at the party. Aside from politely saying how nice I looked, they didn't know what to do with me. I was a charity invite.

I noticed the little organza bags on a table. They were now filled with coconut cookies half-dipped in chocolate. A few bags had already been opened, and I saw cookies with half-hearted bites taken out of them. The Lamb would love these, I thought, wishing I could collect them for him.

"Their food looks beautiful and takes a long time to prepare," my mother had told me once, seeing a Hollywood wedding on television, "but it doesn't taste so good. It's the sort of thing you can only eat a little bit of before you are full." She was right, I thought as I looked at the sandwiches without crusts, the refrigerated hedgehogs and the cherry slices cut into smaller-than-normal portions and arranged on three-tier platters. The chocolate cups filled with champagne cream were sickly sweet when you bit into them.

Suddenly I had an ingenious idea. I picked up one of my mother's huge white plastic trays, fleetingly wishing that she had used black platters instead, so that they would seem less like conference catering trays. (Linh, sometimes I can understand why you found me so insufferable.) But at least the plate in my hands gave me the ability to go up to anyone at this party, and it got me out of having to make painful, polite conversation. I could be useful, which was better than being stuck.

"Would you like a rice-paper roll, sir?" I asked an elderly man in a navy suit who was talking to Amber's father. The man turned toward me, his gray eyebrows gathering in the middle of his forehead like two dueling moths.

"No, thanks," he muttered, and turned back to Mr. Leslie. "I didn't know our Amber had Jap friends."

Brodie arrived. She wore a green hat that matched her dress exactly because it was cut from the same cloth, an elegant kind of half cloche thing. She noticed an object Mrs. Leslie had on display. "Is this new, Dianne?" she asked.

"Oh, yes," Mrs. Leslie replied. "Tell your mother I finally found it! This Toby jug I'd been awaiting for ages. Apparently only two hundred were made with the face of Anne of Cleves."

For the first time, I felt resentment toward Mrs. Leslie. When I'd been interested in the jugs in that cabinet, all she had said to me was, "Oh, Lucy, that's my William Shakespeare cup, and the one behind him is my Charles Dickens mug, and the one next to him is Emily Dickinson. I just collect them for a bit of fun."

I held my plate of rolls out to them.

"Lucy," Mrs. Leslie exclaimed, "you shouldn't be doing this! Walking around at Amber's party serving the guests."

"I don't mind, Mrs. Leslie."

"These look beautiful, Lucy. Your mother is an excellent cook."

That plate gave me the freedom to walk around in areas of the house I never would have dared go alone, because I would have looked like a snoop. So wherever I heard voices or laughter, I wandered.

I came across a room with casement windows, and about seven little kids running around. This looks like the heart of the party, I thought. The Lamb would fit in here for sure, if his nose wasn't so runny. I wished that I had brought him along now. That room was where I spent the remainder of the afternoon.

"Where are my trays?" Mum asked when I arrived back home. She was sitting at the kitchen table, which was covered with white cotton shirts.

"They were still using them," I replied.

"You'd better make sure that they come back," Mum told me. "They cost me three dollars each."

I picked up the Lamb. "Look what I have for you!" I dangled the bag of macaroons in front of him, and he made a grab for them.

"Put him down," Mum ordered, "and help me finish this batch." She was carefully opening up buttonholes with a seam ripper. After doing the buttonholes, we had to attach the cardboard labels: *COAST & CO. CLOTHING, Size 10, Designed and made in Australia, $119.95.* Mum had already stapled the small bags with the spare buttons onto the backs of some of the cards, to be hand-fastened to the inside label of each shirt with cotton.

I sat in a vinyl chair next to her and picked up a shirt.

"Why didn't you tell me that Robina wanted to hire you as a tutor?" Mum asked me.

"What?"

"I saw Robina today and she asked why you haven't gone over to visit Tully and help her with her English."

156

"Mum, that was months ago!"

"I was so embarrassed. You never told us!"

"Come on, Mum, it's not like Tully needs my help!"

"You never tell us anything now," Mum said. "I don't know what that rich school is teaching you, but you've become secretive."

We sat in silence for a minute, doing our work. Inwardly, I seethed. Ever since I won the scholarship, my mother had been watching me to see if I would pick up all the vices that accompany wealthy private schools. My worst fear was that my mother's suspicions would be proven correct.

"You're forgetting your old friends," my mother added—but when she said this I felt my guilt lift somewhat. She was totally wrong about Tully, so wrong that I knew I shouldn't trust her judgment about my friendships ever again.

"You don't even like Tully yourself," I retorted.

Although Tully was always polite to adults, my mother was of the view that school had not made Tully any brighter, only more sycophantic and lost.

"What if Ivy tells Tully about the time that she came around for help with her English and word gets back to Tully's mother?" Mum asked. "How unfair would that seem to Robina, like I was trying to ignore her daughter while letting you help everyone else's?"

The one big thing I respected about my mother, the thing that set her apart from almost anyone else I knew, was that she was always level and fair. Currying favor with anyone was not on. If I had been invited to Yvonne's party instead of Amber's, she would have prepared me for it in exactly the same way. She always made me buy meat from Mrs. Cho's butchery, and never considered other places that might be cheaper.

But she was so stuck in her ways, so worried about being unfair, that she'd sacrifice my time to do all the things she couldn't. I began to see things from my father's perspective, and began to feel that I had a right to be annoyed.

"Hell!" I had been stabbing at the buttonhole too hard in my fury. Instead of opening it up so a button could fit through, I had made a nasty gash in the fabric that extended to the edge of the shirt.

"What have you done?" cried my mother, as if I had stabbed the Lamb. Grabbing the shirt and shaking it at me, she yelled, "Do you know how long it took to make this? Do you? Two weeks ago, you were putting buttons into the bags when I was hemming the cuffs. Last week you were ironing the interfacing on the collars. And this week, just when I'd finished all the pockets, you've gone and wrecked one! This is coming out of my pay! You've wrecked everything!"

She was almost in tears. "What am I going to say to Sokkha? He comes tonight after dinner. I can't make an entire shirt before then. You might not think this is important, because you have a different life now, but this shirt buys your bowl of rice every night." Now she really was crying.

After a while, she picked up the phone and dialed Sokkha. "I have some bad news," she told him. "Our baby got hold of some scissors and cut one of the shirts. I know. I'm sorry. No, no. I know I should have been looking out for him. Yes, I know, I know. But there's only enough to make new sleeves. Please. Please, if you have some to spare, just about a yard. Just the front panel. I know I won't be paid for it, but I don't mind. It was my fault anyway. . . . Thank you, thank you, brother. I just need a yard. I promise it won't happen again."

I felt so ashamed that my mother was groveling to Uncle Sokkha.

I used to have more time for Mum when I was at Christ Our Savior. I could easily finish my homework and help her with the sewing. But it seemed now that I never had time for anything except Laurinda.

I woke up around one in the morning. Somehow I knew Mum was not in bed. I went into our kitchen. The kettle was still warm. I knew she was in the garage.

"Argh!" she yelped when I came in. "You scared me! What are you doing up? You should be in bed. You have school tomorrow."

"Do you need some help, Mum?"

"No, I'm almost done."

And she was. I handed her a Coast & Co. label.

On the Monday after Amber's birthday, I was sitting in the library again, reading E. H. Gombrich's *The Story of Art*. *It is infinitely better not to know anything about art than to have the kind of half-knowledge which makes for snobbishness,* I read. *The danger is very real.*

I was staring intently at a photo of a statue, *Hermes and the Infant Dionysus,* when Mrs. Leslie interrupted me. "Lucy! What are you doing here by yourself?"

I wanted to be by myself, and this was what I preferred to do in my spare time. Was she going to drag me outside to where the Cabinet sat and tell them, "Girls, this is Lucy. You may remember her from the weekend and most of your classes. She will be playing with you"?

"This is a good book," I told her.

"Indeed it is." There was a long pause. She was probably thinking that a book is not a friend. "Those rice-paper rolls your mother made were delicious, Lucy."

"Thank you, Mrs. Leslie."

"She is a superb Vietnamese cook."

"Thank you, Mrs. Leslie, but we're not really Vietnamese. We are Chinese born in Vietnam."

"Oh, is that right?" She wanted me to tell her more.

"We're Teochew. Our ancestry is from Guangdong, in the south of China."

All these place names barely meant anything to me—all I knew was that we spoke a dialect that several million people across China and Southeast Asia spoke, a language that sounded both medieval and childish.

"Really? How fascinating. I've never heard of that language. Can you teach me a few words? How would I say 'eye'?"

"*Muck.*"

"Pardon?"

"'Eye' is *muck*."

She looked confounded, and a little worried that I was making it up, until I pointed to my eye.

"I mean *'me.'* How do I say 'I'?"

"Oh. *Wah.*"

"*Wah?*"

"Yes, miss. That's how you say 'I' in our language."

"Okay," she said tentatively, not knowing whether I was giving her pidgin shit. "What about 'he' or 'she'?"

"*Eee.*"

"Is that right, Lucy?"

"Yes." Those were the words. *Miao* was "cat." *Him* was "bear." *Ka* was "leg"—and she thought I was pulling hers.

"Well, I've never heard anything like it." Then she looked down at my book. "You know, Lucy, our library has an extensive collection of East Asian art books."

"Thanks, Mrs. Leslie."

"We also have a wide range of Chinese history books.

Perhaps you could find out a little more about your heritage in one of those."

I liked Mrs. Leslie—at times I even loved her—but really, how would she like it if I suggested to her that she should read books about the Irish Potato Famine?

The next day she found me again in the same spot. I had to bid farewell to Professor Gombrich and his lesson on the Ghent Altarpiece.

"Lucy, a few friends and I were talking," she said, "and I was telling them about your mother's wonderful cooking. Do you think there is a chance that we could get the recipe from her?"

"Sure, Mrs. Leslie. I'll ask Mum for it tonight."

"Better yet, why don't we invite you and your mother over for afternoon tea and a cooking lesson? I would love to meet her. Then she could show us how it's done! Perhaps this Saturday? Does that sound like a fun afternoon to you, Lucy?"

It would have been a fun afternoon for Mum, if she believed in fun. But she believed in work. I assured Mrs. Leslie I would ask my mother that night.

"Oh, this will be too exciting!" she said. "I'll ask along two other friends who'd absolutely love it." She already considered it a done deal.

Of course, I did not ask my mother that evening. I could easily imagine her response: "What? They want me to leave my work and show them how to *cook* something? And then will they come home with me and help me iron my inter-facing?"

My mother didn't really have any friends, only a handful of other ladies in the same line of work. Whenever there was a large order, Aunt Ngo and Aunt Tee would get together to do the non-sewing tasks: putting buttons and spare threads in plastic envelopes, opening buttonholes, installing zippers. It depended on who had the right machine. They would cook together, but definitely not in a champagne-sipping way. "Ngo, while we finish this batch of buttons, can you check on the beef stock?" my mother would ask, or Aunty Tee, with pins in her mouth, would rush to the kitchen to turn over the roast pork. Then they'd all get back to work.

Professor Gombrich was getting mighty irritated with Mrs. Leslie, because the following day she interrupted his lesson on the architecture of King's College Chapel in Cambridge to let me know that her friends could make it and to ask whether Saturday was still good for my mother and me.

"Mum can't make it," I told her. I didn't enjoy disappointing someone I liked so much, so I quickly added, "But I would be happy to show you how to make rice-paper rolls, Mrs. Leslie."

She smiled with relief, and when I saw her smile I suddenly realized the singular flaw in Amber's face. Mrs. Leslie was a warm Audrey Hepburn in her older, golden years, while Amber was a morgue-faced model who thought that smiling might give her premature wrinkles.

"That's wonderful, Lucy! Now, what ingredients do you think we'll need? Perhaps you and I could go to your local grocery store to get them after school on Friday. I've always wanted to know how to use the authentic things in an Asian grocery store."

I could just see Mrs. Leslie parking her BMW in the Sunray Station parking lot, next to the two-toned old trucks and the other cars with their paint peeling like eczema and their side mirrors duct-taped in place. I could imagine her stepping out in her clothes the color of soil and sand, among the housewives with their red-and-gold lace-edged nylon tops, purple polyester pants and twenty-dollar perms. We would walk past Second Life Academic Books, where the books were kept behind rope barriers due to the recent spate of thefts.

I could just see her at the market, Linh, marveling at the beauty of it all, extolling the parsimony of ethnic women and their ability to select ripe avocados and mangoes, bitter gourds and rambutans. Then we'd go back to her house to cook and she would tell her lady friends what a fascinating place I lived in, "so full of color and life, just like Ho Chi Minh marketplace!" and they would probably be envious that they hadn't had the special tour.

And here is the question I would have wanted to ask all of them, but especially Mrs. Leslie: "Would you want to live here? Or would you want to do this only once before you went back to your 'purveyor of fine foods'?"

I snapped out of my reverie. "No, that's fine, Mrs. Leslie. My mother can buy the ingredients. We're going shopping in the morning." And then, to stop her from offering to accompany my mother, I added, "After her appointment with the Chinese herbal medicine doctor."

"But what can I do to help?" Mrs. Leslie asked.

"Well, you can decide what sort of meat you would like to put in the rice-paper rolls."

"Great! I'll get the meat, then."

Linh, I knew it was wrong and sneaky of me to suggest the meat, because it was the most expensive ingredient, but

I didn't know how else I was going to get it. Mum and Dad never gave me pocket money—I just asked them for things I needed and they bought them for me. How would I explain that I had roped myself into an afternoon of cooking instead of doing homework, or minding the Lamb, or sewing?

"Dad, can I have twenty dollars to go on an excursion?" I felt bad asking him so soon after he had returned from his shift at work that evening, smelling like carpet chemicals.

"What? I thought your school covered all those things."

Not the chartered school bus, I thought to myself. Not the trip to Adelaide for choir camp. Not the field trips to Japan or France.

"No, this is an excursion to the special *Secrets of Ancient China* exhibition at the museum." Two things my father loved—education and our heritage. He pulled out his wallet and handed me thirty dollars. "I only need twenty," I said.

"Keep it for lunch."

"I'll bring lunch."

"Just keep it."

On Saturday morning, I caught the bus to Stanley. At the market, I bought Vietnamese and hot Thai mint, spring onions, cucumbers and bean sprouts. At the Asian grocery store, I bought vermicelli and rice paper. And then I went to Safeway.

As much as Mrs. Leslie wanted me to, I could not give them the "authentic" stuff. I could just imagine them *spooning* their fish sauce *over* their rolls, saying, "Ooh, this is very sharp and interesting," while trying not to twitch their noses because the smell was as sharp and interesting as a lash on the bum from a whip soaked in vinegar. In the condiments aisle at Safeway, there were not the two-liter glass bottles of fish sauce we had at home that we mixed with carrots and garlic, but there was a tiny six-ounce bottle made by a company called Ding's Delight. The logo was a pointy triangle field hat with two chopsticks sticking out of it. It was $4.25. What the hell? I wondered. How could something so small, artificial and crappy cost so much?

When I arrived at Canningvale Railway Station, Mrs. Leslie was waiting. She opened the trunk of her car and we loaded the bags. We drove past Canningvale Village with its strip of artisanal shops, past the streets with rising old Georgian and Queen Anne houses, until we reached her gate.

As I unpacked the groceries, Mrs. Leslie reacted as I imagined a new mother would when opening gifts at a baby shower. "Ooh, what do you call this herb?" she would ask, bringing it to her nose to sniff. She was particularly taken with the rice paper. "It's stiff!" she remarked. "I imagined it would have the texture of spring roll pastry." Then she noticed the Ding's Delight. Picking it up, she asked, almost accusingly, "Is this what you use at home, Lucy?"

"No," I confessed, "but real fish sauce takes ages to make." One truth and one half lie.

She told me that her friends Gloria and Margaret were coming with their daughters. It was then that I noticed the table had been set with dips and a cheese platter. "You know them from school," she said. "Brodie and Chelsea."

Of course, I thought. Of course their mothers were all friends.

It was eleven-thirty but Amber was nowhere in sight.

"Amber's probably still in bed," explained Mrs. Leslie. "I'd better go and wake her. She shouldn't be sleeping in this late. I bet you got up at a very early hour, Lucy, to go to the market and get all these things!"

Amber came out in her pajamas—small shorts and a white tank top—rubbing one eye. If I could capture this image and beam it into the brain of the loneliest and meekest Auburn boy, I thought, he would be a happy soul indeed.

"You're here early," she murmured. "Why?"

"You slept in late," corrected Mrs. Leslie. "Come and help us set up."

"I'm going to get some breakfast first." Amber wandered to the cupboard and pulled out the Special K. "Want some?" she asked me.

"No, thanks."

"Mum, Brodie, Chelsea and I are going out afterward."

"Where to?"

"Just out. Maybe some shopping."

Mrs. Leslie looked in my direction, and Amber realized her mistake in mentioning this in front of me. "You can come too, Lucy. If you want."

"No, thanks, I have to get home and help my mother with some things."

I really didn't want to hang out with them, Linh. Firstly, Amber had invited me but her tone implied the opposite, and secondly, I imagined they'd only go to shops where you'd emerge with stiff cardboard bags lined with tissue paper.

The other two mothers arrived at noon, with champagne and flowers and chocolate truffles wrapped in fine tissue paper. Around their necks were rose gold chains as thick as fingers, and silky scarves that smelled of perfume.

Brodie's mother was Brodie in thirty years' time. Her hair was cut into a bob as even as the blade of a cleaver. She had deep-set black-currant eyes, a long nose and large Julia Roberts lips. She was what Jane Austen would call a handsome woman.

Chelsea's mother, on the other hand, was a surprise. She looked like a version of Chelsea that had been taken out of the fridge and left to thaw for too long. Where Chelsea had bronze-brown hair, her mother's was copper, and Mrs. White's paler skin was flecked with freckles. With a big, friendly slab of a face, powdered like a doughnut, she was also the fattest of the three.

"Oh, this is delightful!" she laughed, seeing the ingredients set out on the counter. "What can I do, Lucy? Would you like me to wash these herbs? You are the head chef here!" I soon realized that Mrs. White found most things delightful, and the more she found them delightful, the more Chelsea found her unbearable.

Chelsea and Brodie had headed straight for Amber. They stood to one side of the granite island that floated in the middle of the large kitchen, while the mothers stood on the other side. I stood at the end.

"So, we get to meet your little Pygmalion project at last," Brodie's mum, Mrs. Newberry, said to Mrs. Leslie. I had no idea what a Pygmalion was, but it had the word *pig* in it so I was sure it was not flattering. She turned to me. "How do you do, Dianne's fair lady?" She extended her hand, heavy with rings, expecting me to shake it, so I did.

"Dianne, she is just as darling as you said she would be," proclaimed Chelsea's mum.

"Do you know who clamored to be Lucy's mentor at the start of the year, Gloria?" Mrs. Leslie asked Brodie's mum.

"Who?"

"Gracey Gladrock's daughter."

"Oh my God!"

"Deliver us from evil, and forgive us our trespasses," muttered Chelsea's mum, snorting with laughter.

Before I arrived, Mrs. Leslie had cooked some prawns and stir-fried some beef with sesame seeds, garlic and oyster sauce. Now she set everything out like a production line, and we were ready to roll.

I had no idea how Brodie's mother was going to do anything, because she had long fingernails with white tips. So I got her to dip the rice paper into the plate of boiling water; I figured it would not hurt her fingers as much as it would any of ours. As I showed her how it was done, she remarked, "Well, would you look at those dexterous Asian fingers. So fast!"

"Yes, Asians do seem to have more nimble fingers," said Mrs. Leslie. "When I was in Suzhou"—she pronounced it *Shoo-zhoo,* trying to make it sound more exotic, I suppose—"I visited a silk factory, and there were girls around Lucy's age, all with such small and delicate hands, embroidering silks. The owner told me that it was a four-thousand-year-old tradition, that sort of handicraft."

"How delightful!" exclaimed Mrs. White. "We've never been to China."

"You know which other people have nimble fingers?" asked Chelsea. "South Americans."

"Oh?" Mrs. Leslie loved stories about different cultures.

"Yeah, when we went to Venezuela two years ago, they stole my camera! Remember that, Mum? Those filthy, uni-browed pickpockets . . ."

Chelsea's mother's laughter stopped like the last sputters from a faulty tap.

"Oh, yeah, I remember you telling us about that, Chelsea!" piped Amber. "And how that hot waiter, Javier, was actually so gay on his day off, wearing a black tank and cut-off jeans."

"Don't you remember, Mum?" Chelsea insisted. "And how you said—"

"Well, I have to say, this is a real treat, Lucy," said her mother, cutting her off.

We finally sat down to lunch one and a half hours later.

"When Don was returning from Europe, something quite funny happened," Mrs. Newberry said to the other mothers when she had poured herself a glass of wine. "Would you like to hear it?"

"Oh, yes, please!" said Mrs. White. She clapped her hands twice. "Is Don back from Europe already?"

"Yes. He came back last week. Anyhow, on the flight, he was put next to this garrulous, obese loudmouth in a navy polyester suit, who just wouldn't shut up."

"Oh, I can see Don loving that," commented Mrs. Leslie.

"The man kept talking about how he was doing international business and opening up an import and export business in Asia, *that* kind of man."

What kind of man? I wondered. A businessman was a businessman, someone who owned his own business. According to my parents, they were all to be respected—unless they were in a crooked business like dealing drugs.

"I can just imagine the poor man," commented Mrs. Leslie. "From somewhere in Queensland. Ipswich, most probably."

"Yes, yes, yes!" Mrs. Newberry was stabbing the air with her rice-paper roll, but miraculously no prawn fell out. "Then the flight attendants come with drinks, and Don thinks, thank God, I do *not* want to hear about shoe manufacturing for the entire flight. Jesus!"

"Naturally, the good Lord did not come and save Dad," said Brodie wryly; she knew how this tale ended.

"Anyhow, Don was leaning back in his chair, enjoying the wine—as much as you can enjoy the abysmal wine they serve in business class these days—when all of a sudden the man next to him started to cough and clutch his arm—"

"Oh, I know where this is going," said Chelsea.

"Yes, and would you believe it, in less than two minutes the first-time business class flier next to him had a heart attack and died!"

"Oh. Oh, how dreadful." Mrs. Leslie put her roll down on her plate.

"But there were absolutely no spare seats on the flight," Mrs. Newberry went on. "So Don had to sit next to this guy until they reached the Hong Kong stopover and four flight attendants took him away!"

"How horrible!" exclaimed Mrs. White, but she couldn't help laughing.

"How hilarious, you mean!" exclaimed Mrs. Newberry. "And this is the funny part—can you imagine Don next to a paunchy dead man in a cheap acrylic suit for that stretch of time? 'Well, thank God he finally shut up' was what Don told me when he got home."

"Your man has a black sense of humor!" roared Chelsea's mum.

"Doesn't he!"

It dawned on me, as I watched the three older women together, that they had known each other since they were at Laurinda—and that perhaps they had even been the Cabinet of their day. There was the uneasy way Mrs. Leslie laughed at Brodie's mum's jokes, and Chelsea's mum's sidekick role—she would turn from one woman to the other, watching their faces very closely, so she could always align herself correctly.

Mrs. Leslie must have noticed the look on my face, because she quickly became sensitive and apologetic. "Oh, we should have known better than to talk about such dark things in front of you, Lucy."

"What the hell, Mum? I doubt Lucy from Stanley is going to be put off by that lame story."

How did Amber know I was from Stanley? Perhaps mother and daughter talked more than I thought.

"Yes, but Lucy came here *on a boat*."

"So?"

Mrs. Leslie sighed. "Forgive their ignorance."

"I get it," said Chelsea. "Those boats are rickety, so you're implying that Lucy must have seen people die and crap, huh?"

"Chelsea White, watch your language!"

"I am sure people crapped, but I was too young to remember anyone actually biting it," I replied.

Mrs. White's outrage turned into an enormous, shoulder-shuddering fit of hilarity. "Oh, oh, you! You are just too funny, Lucy."

It felt good that someone was laughing at my joke in a

mouth-agape-with-enjoyment way. The other two mothers just tittered uncomfortably.

Mrs. Leslie looked at me with her enormous brown eyes. She put a hand on one of mine. "You. Are. Such. A. Courageous. Young. Girl." I was afraid she might burst into tears.

Oh, come off it, I wanted to say, I just taught you all to cook a fake Asian fusion dish that didn't even involve a flame. But now the other mothers also started to insist politely but firmly that I was brave.

Suddenly all the attention was on me, which I did not like one bit. Yet I knew that their attention had never fully left me: I had been the presence in the room that cut short their frank and funny discussions of culture and criminals.

Out of the blue, Brodie's mum scoffed, "Ha! Gracey Gladrock's daughter! Of course she would. Of course."

"Would what?" I asked.

"Oh, Lucy, dear," cut in Mrs. Leslie. "It's just that you're so quiet and Katie could talk the ear off an elephant!"

"Lucy, there is something you must understand about the Gladrocks," began Mrs. White. "It's not that we mean to be cruel to poor Katie, but there's something *not quite right* about that family."

"It's also hereditary, my darlings, like misshapen heirloom squashes that only a farmer could love." That was Brodie's mum.

"Remember when we were at school, how poor gappy-toothed Gracey was always copying us?"

"'Oh, Gloria, how do you get your hair so straight and perfectly parted in the middle? Do you iron it?'" Mrs. White was mimicking Katie's mum. "That was her in Year Three."

Mrs. Newberry continued, turning toward me now, as if imparting sage advice. "No, I told her, ironing ruins the hair. It leeches the moisture out of it. It is very bad for the ends. I told her that as a filamentous biomaterial primarily composed of keratin protein, the best way to make her long, curly hair straight was to give it a reverse perm, a treatment that would relax the protein structure. Two parts conditioner, one part baking soda, one part methylated spirits."

"Mum, you are such a bullshit artist," said Brodie affectionately.

"It's perfectly safe, I told her, if you can do the limbo. Preheat your oven to three hundred degrees," Mrs. Newberry continued. "Lay your hair out on a baking tray. . . ."

My heart started to beat faster.

"Get down on your knees and tilt your head back, then shove the tray into the oven. Have a bowl of water nearby to cool your face. Remember, Gracey, I told her, it is very important to have that bowl of water nearby."

"Ha! Especially if your hair catches fire!" laughed Mrs. White.

"I can't believe the girl was stupid enough to try it," concluded Mrs. Newberry, as Chelsea's mum was almost crying from the hilarity of the story. Even Mrs. Leslie was laughing.

"Was she okay?" I asked.

"What?" The women seemed to have forgotten about me, and Mrs. Leslie turned my way. "Yes, yes, she was fine. She just got her hair singed at the ends. Her hair was so long that the grill was nowhere near her face. We knew she had attempted it because the next day at school her waist-length hair was gone. She had a Little Orphan Annie perm instead. Very cute."

But I could tell she meant the opposite.

"If someone tells you to jump off a bridge, Lucy," asked Mrs. Newberry, seeing the look on my face, "do you do it? Do you understand what we mean by that family being not quite right?"

"You're just saying that because she ended up with Lachie," laughed Mrs. White, but she stopped laughing when Mrs. Newberry swiveled and gave her a searing look.

"I thank my lucky stars every day I did not end up with that bastard," she said, "and I would prefer you never mentioned him again. The only reason she got Lachie was she dropped her pants and I didn't."

"No way!" exclaimed Amber with glee. "*Katie's* mother was a skank?"

"Queen slut of them all," said Mrs. Newberry, "eventually."

"Unfortunate indeed," said Mrs. Leslie. "But you must never, ever mention this to Katie, because her mother passed away when she was just a toddler."

"That prank was almost as good as the one we pulled on Mrs. May!" laughed Mrs. White. "Oh, that was classic. Do you remember that, ladies? Do you know about this one, girls?"

I watched the eager eyes of Amber, Brodie and Chelsea, who were like cats hearing the blade of a can opener.

"You mean when you hid the oven timers, Mrs. Leslie?" I asked.

"Oven timers?" Mrs. Newberry turned toward Mrs. Leslie. "What did you tell June Moon?"

"Lucy," Mrs. Leslie corrected her.

"Yes, yes," she murmured. Then she turned to me. "What exactly did Dianne tell you about Mrs. May?"

"That, umm . . . that all of you hid your oven timers in different parts of the home ec classroom, and that they went off at different times."

"What? Lame! Lame! You didn't even tell her the *good* part!" accused Mrs. White.

Mrs. Leslie shook her head, mortified.

Mrs. Newberry turned toward the other girls. "We greased the floor with Vaseline," she said slowly. "We greased it nice and thick, and we worked our way backward out of the room. Then we greased the door handle. When it was class time, we said to the old bat, 'You go in first, Mrs. May.'

"'As I should,' she retorted, and marched in, expecting us to follow. We hadn't greased the entrance, so it was only when she was halfway into the room and we heard her slip that we shut the door on her. Bang!" Mrs. Newberry clapped her hands together like a gunshot. "The oven timers were a sweet enhancement Dianne thought up," she explained. "Because cowardly Dianne here thought we shouldn't go through with our Vaseline plan."

Amber looked at her mother reproachfully, as if her killjoy ways were still evident.

"But you will be pleased to know that we incorporated your mother's little embellishment as well, so while the old bat was down on the floor, the oven timers were going off, one every two minutes, until they reached a deafening crescendo."

"Didn't you all get into deep trouble?" Chelsea asked in awe.

"Of course not. We had a fall girl: Gracey Gladrock!"

Of course, I thought. Who else?

176

"Fortunately, she was also rather poor at home economics, which meant that, more often than not, her pies were the ones dropped on the floor. So she had good reason to pull a prank like that. Also, she was going to have to leave the school at the end of the year anyway. We just helped hurry her along." Mrs. Newberry pondered. "As I recall, they were even both in the hospital at the same time—Gracey to have her first baby, and the old bat recovering from her hip surgery."

This was shocking to me. I thought that women like this, especially in houses like this, would sit and discuss art history or antiques or literature, Linh. Like my father, I had believed that educated people were gentler and kinder than the uncouth and unlearned masses—but now I wasn't so sure.

At two-thirty on the dot, the doorbell rang, and I knew it was my father. I followed Mrs. Leslie to the front door.

Dad was standing there in his work uniform, a frayed shirt and navy overalls with "Victory Carpet" printed across the pocket. "Thank you for letting Lucy come over to study," he told Mrs. Leslie. "We very much appreciate it."

"Study? Oh, no!" laughed Mrs. Leslie. "Oh, no, no, no! Lucy's been having a little fun. She's been teaching us how to make your wife's delicious rice-paper rolls. Come and join us, Mr. Lam?"

"No, thank you," replied my father, looking through to the dining area of the open-plan house, where everything was white and beige. "No, I have to be heading back to work."

"On a Saturday?" asked Mrs. Leslie, incredulous.

"Yes." My father did not explain that he was not heading back to the factory, but home to help my mother sew. He did not want to admit this because sewing was not a manly pursuit.

"We could drop Lucy off," said Mrs. Leslie. "She is welcome to stay here as long as she likes."

"No," I said. "It's very kind of you to invite me to stay, Mrs. Leslie, but I really have to get home."

"But wait—don't go yet. I have something for you!" She went back into the house. I thought she was going to pack me a Tupperware container of leftover rolls to take home, but instead she emerged with a monumental bunch of flowers, bigger than my torso, wrapped in tasteful bark and brown paper and tied with twine. All the flowers were native plants with furry, bulbous heads and pointy leaves.

"Wow, thank you, Mrs. Leslie—these are beautiful," I lied.

"All Australian stock," she laughed, as the others came to bid me goodbye.

In Dad's car, I had to sit in the back because the front seat did not fit both me and the flowers. I couldn't leave them in the back because they would roll around and smear yellow pollen all over the seats where my father sometimes placed completed rush orders for Sokkha.

"So, no study today, huh?" my father asked, and I was glad to be in the back where I could not see his face.

"No, Dad. She insisted I come over and teach them how to make rice-paper rolls."

"That's a good thing." My father still had the ability to surprise me. "Those girls like and respect you a lot. They probably also can't cook!"

The latter was true; definitely not the former. Oh, my father, he was still in love with the idea of me joining the Three

Graces, just as Mrs. Leslie was. It was as if they were trying to arrange a marriage.

"But what will we tell Mum?" I asked.

"Don't worry, we'll all work late tonight because tomorrow is Sunday. As if she will ask you about what you've been studying, eh!"

I looked down at the flowers and noticed a card. I pulled it out and opened it, and as I did, I saw fifty dollars nestled in the fold. I looked at the front mirror. Dad still had his eyes on the road. I put the note back in the envelope, and put it in my pocket. I would deal with it later.

I came home, and that was when we had our big fight, Linh. You and me, that evening, after my visit to Amber's house.

I needed to tell you all about Mrs. Leslie and Amber and my time at their tense estate.

So, that's what's been up with you, you muttered, sitting on the bed in my room. *I waited for you.* You had the Lamb in your lap.

I didn't know you were going to come, I replied, because really, I didn't. You had a habit of dropping in when I least expected. And every time you did this when my dad was around, he'd get pissed off. Luckily for you, Mum could stand you.

You write me these long, god-awful letters, but never see me anymore.

I've been busy lately. And my letters aren't awful.

For months your letters have been filled with wankery like "bulging arsenal of multilingual profanities," "sordid liaisons" and—my favorite—"flippantly audacious."

So that was what this was about.

I couldn't help it if I was trying to practice another language, I wanted to yell, because that was what this amounted to. You were just trying to mock my efforts because you thought it wasn't "me." And don't blame me for "flippantly audacious"—that was Brodie!

But you didn't even give me a chance to explain, to tell you about my terrible afternoon, to turn it into a funny anecdote, to show you what I thought of those ladies and their daughters. You just let loose.

Oh my God, you said, *those girls are worse than Katie. What are you doing with them? If they were at Christ Our Savior, we'd put them in their place. But you do nothing. I know you're avoiding me because you're ashamed of the ugliness inside you. So you just sit there sipping their little Italian soft drinks and enjoying their "culture" because they accept it.*

They don't accept me, I protested. The Cabinet puts up with me because of Mrs. Leslie.

I didn't say they accepted you, you told me in no uncertain terms. *I said they accepted the ugliness inside you.*

You always told me the truth. By now you were leaving, but before you did, you had to have one last stab: *By the way, your mother thinks those flowers are ugly.*

Get out now!

When you left, I wasn't sure I ever wanted to see you again.

A few days later, after school, I took the Lamb to the Sunray Shopping Center. We stayed away from the basement level, which was where all the people my age hung out, because I didn't want to run into you. I fed the Lamb a small tub of potatoes and gravy from KFC; a quarter of it spilled down the front of his overalls and got caught in the buttons. He chuckled with glee, the little snot, and stuck a finger in his buttonhole.

Then I took him to the Postman Pat carousel, which had three seats—one shaped like Pat's mailbag, one like his mail van and one like his black-and-white cat. You had to put a coin in a slot to make the seats move up and down for two minutes, but Mum would never let us operate it—she said you might as well throw away money. Luckily, the Lamb thought that sitting on one of the special seats *was* the ride.

I placed him on the black-and-white cat, even though he wanted to sit on the mailbag, because there was already another kid there, a little girl with a tutu and fairy wings over her pink tracksuit.

"Git lost—we was here first."

I looked up and saw a dinner-plate-sized version of the little girl's face, massive and scowling. Her mother.

"Have you got a dollar?" Before I had a chance to reply, she said, "Coz I'm not putting in a dollar for you too."

To her, people like us existed to supply people like her with the cheap and lurid-colored Chinese takeout food they loved so much, or the two-dollar T-shirts they bought from Kmart every few months. In fact, the Postman Pat carousel had probably been made by people who looked like me. Maybe that's why the seats were so small—to hold pert little bums like the Lamb's, not the wide load of her poor junk-food-fed pup.

And it was then that I understood my attachment to Laurinda. I was wearing my uniform, and this woman—who lived on welfare and fast food—would never be part of that world. She thought that people like us were going to steal her kid's job in the future, just as she thought we were trying to steal a free ride now.

It was cowardice that made me leave the carousel, not contempt—the contempt came later. In that moment there was only a flash of anger. I knew what you would have done, Linh, what you would have said. But you weren't there. So I could only do what I could do. I took the Lamb off the carousel, and he started to grizzle, and then cry.

In the past, stuff like this would have got me all wounded and teary, but now it didn't matter. Now I felt better than them, the whole lot of them in Stanley. You may not have minded being stuck there, but I was different. Now I could see a future where I didn't have to fight such petty battles all the time.

As I felt the woman's power over me shrink, I also felt something expanding in me—not empathy, but condescension. Before, I had accorded any adult automatic respect be-

182

cause that was the way I was brought up. But Laurinda had shown me that just because a person was an adult, it didn't necessarily mean you had to respect them.

Now I understood that these people were lower class, and being lower class was not a point of pride. It was disgusting, in a squint-faced, cement-mixer-voiced way, that a grown woman would buy herself cigarettes from Safeway and a moment later decide to deprive her child of a ride on a Postman Pat carousel just because another kid was also sitting on it. That was the kind of petty mentality they had, the sense that everyone else had it better.

"Don't worry, Mr. Lamby," I said. "We'll find you something more fun!"

I took him to Toys"R"Us and let him ride on all the scooters and three-wheeled tots' bikes they had. I bought him a Push Pop. I gave him a spin through the air as we walked toward the bus stop. He was so tired he rested his head on my shoulder, drooling on my blazer, but I didn't care.

On the train back, some blond girl was using her boyfriend's lap like an armchair and his chest like a pillow. Remember how we used to look down on girls like that, Linh? The skanks who got with the first St. Andrew's boy who looked at them?

This boy was all angles, and he had an Adam's apple like an origami corner, but his hair was dyed the color of salted caramel and he had warm brown eyes. The girl's hands were clutching the sleeves of his denim jacket, her face burrowed in his shirt the same way a sick person would burrow their face in their bedding.

From the back, you'd think she came from the warmest, sandiest beaches of Bondi. She lifted her face from her boyfriend's chest to get some air. Her eyes were swimming-pool blue and rimmed with black kohl. They layered down at my uniform and settled on my droopy socks with their overstretched cheap nylon hems, then quickly rose up again. Then she flashed me a smile.

She had spotted me straightaway, but it took me a while to recognize her beneath the peroxide and contacts. "Tully?" I tentatively asked.

"Hi!" she exclaimed, and introduced me to her boyfriend. "This is Alonzo."

"Hi," I said to him.

"Hi."

She smiled up at Alonzo. "This is my friend I was telling you about—the really smart one who got into Laurinda."

"Oh, Tully, don't be stupid. You're the really smart one." I was aware of how ridiculous that sentence sounded only after it came out.

"But you're the one who got in! Alonzo, I swear this girl was one of the smartest girls in our school."

"Tully is going to be valedictorian of her school," I told Alonzo. "I'm mediocre. I'm just going to fade away."

"Dux of a shitty school," murmured Tully. "And only get into a crappy uni through a financial aid scholarship where they bump up your score out of charity."

"Aw, come on, Tully."

"You know it's true!"

Since Alonzo was there, I couldn't offer Tully any polite consolation, or express my guilt about getting the scholarship, or even praise her Filipino boyfriend's cuteness. I wasn't sure how much she had revealed about herself, or even what kind of person she wanted to be with him, and I didn't want to blow it for her by mentioning her studious ways if he thought she really was the bad girl she was pretending to be.

But in the space of a few moments, we had assessed each other and understood just how different our lives were going to be. Tully had resigned herself to getting her diploma at Christ Our Savior, with the Spanish girls whose parents would cheer at their beauty school hairdressing graduations and the Vietnamese girls whose mums and dads wanted them to marry the young accountants in Sunray. The moment she didn't get the Laurinda scholarship was the moment Tully felt her chance had passed. Smart people won things, and went places, and got out of Sunray. And she was still here.

Everyone thought that I was headed for bigger things, but I wasn't trying to make Tully feel better when I told her that I was mediocre. At Laurinda I was average, at best. I had no outstanding talents.

She shifted about on Alonzo's knee so that she would be more comfortable, although she was so thin that she was probably sitting on bone. Tully had always been skinny, but now she looked like she'd just stepped off the boat. And I could not stop staring at her creepy electric-blue eyes.

"How are Yvonne and Ivy?" I asked.

"Good. Ming's out on parole and trying to stay clean. I think the family sent him back to Vietnam so he could be away from the wrong crowd."

"I heard that."

She looked a little surprised. "So you still keep in touch?"

185

"Yes," I lied.

The truth was, I didn't know much about how my old friends were doing, beyond the occasional talk with you, Linh. And I wasn't sure whether those talks would be happening anymore. This conversation was making me feel very uncomfortable, and there was still twenty minutes to go before we reached Stanley.

"Hey, nice trousers," I said to her, and meant it.

That was one of my greatest achievements at Christ Our Savior. I had a real connection to that uniform, even though the crest on the blazer pocket was just Velcroed on. In my Laurinda blazer, with its embroidered and immutable crest, I felt like an imposter.

At lunchtime the next Monday I was in my usual corner of the library, having a look at a Caravaggio book. Chelsea came bounding up to me like a deranged filly. "Hey, Lucy, Lucy, hey! What are you doing?"

I held the book close to my chest. "Just looking at something." It was a painting called *The Incredulity of Saint Thomas,* which showed some guy poking his finger into the rib cage of Jesus.

"Why don't you come and join us for lunch?"

"Oh, okay." What else could I do? Admittedly, I was curious about the Cabinet. I wanted to know whether Katie was right about them. I'd seen Amber at home and she hadn't seemed that impressive. In fact, all three Cabinet members, from my limited interactions with them, seemed petty and kind of boring—but maybe that was because they were with their parents. They were the sort of girls who acted one way toward adults and another toward people their own age.

I walked with Chelsea to the Cabinet's bench. When Amber and Brodie saw us coming, they patted the seat next to them. They wanted me to take Chelsea's usual spot.

This was even more awkward than being in Mrs. Grey's

office, or that afternoon with their mothers. It was some little game, I guessed, and I wanted nothing to do with it. "It's okay, I'll sit on the grass." I didn't want to stay for long.

"Well, then, we'll all sit on the grass," decided Brodie.

I knew that it was not my mum's rice-paper rolls that had got me into their secret society, but something else. I was interested to find out what they talked about among themselves, and how it was that they had the whole school in their thrall. What I was most curious about, though, was why they had suddenly decided to take an interest in me.

First we talked about Amber's party, but it was as if we had gone to two separate parties. Amber and Chelsea and Brodie had been to an outdoor one where there was finger food and attractive boys and a swimming pool, and I'd gone to a party where there were seven little kids who wanted me to fold them origami things and watch *Dorothy the Dinosaur* for the fifth time.

Mr. Sinclair walked past. "Look at that," muttered Chelsea. "Dressing like a peacock to impress the girls."

To be honest, Linh, I didn't understand how a navy suit and maroon tie were peacock-like.

"Now, Chelsea, be nice," warned Brodie. "We do, after all, have a nice girl with us. Wouldn't want to corrupt her."

"Hey, Lucy, you gave me such a cool present," Amber said.

"You'd left by the time presents were opened," said Brodie, "but you should have seen the look on her mum's face."

"What do you mean?" I asked, worried.

"Don't worry," reassured Amber, "my mother thinks anything above the knee is slut clothing. I can't believe you got me that skirt. I didn't even know they were in Coast & Co. stores yet."

I couldn't keep from smiling. They weren't, I wanted to tell her, but stopped myself. Let them think that I was the coolest girl in the history of Laurinda. It occurred to me then that even though I didn't like the Cabinet very much, for some reason I wanted them to like me.

In a little over a week, I discovered that Amber and Brodie had almost as much contempt for Chelsea as I did, except that instead of keeping quiet about it, they made fun of her.

"Hey, Chelsea, we heard that Jason from Auburn has the hots for Aminah."

And Chelsea would go off like a firework, because she had the hots for Jason herself.

It took me another week to work out why they let her hang around with them. They'd been at this school together since kindergarten. They'd been friends for too long, and had spent too much time in each other's houses, which meant they could not detach from her without their parents getting involved. It wasn't even that Chelsea was a rebel or a bad girl, though I guess that would have made her more interesting. It was just that she was so resentful and cynical.

She was also a buffer. Brodie and Amber kept her around because without her they would kill each other. With her there, they could be friends. They could pretend that they were not constantly competing. Not having hung around with boys had heightened their femininity and bitchiness in equal measure.

And now the Cabinet didn't mind having me around. This was unexpected and strange. It wasn't as if my Saturday afternoon culinary skills had suddenly made me indispensable to their operations. They never picked on me the way they did Chelsea. They never paid me much attention, come to think of it, but when they did, they were nice enough.

"Hey, Lucy," Chelsea would ask, "what do you think of Mrs. Goninan's shoes?"

"They keep her feet dry and warm," I'd say, deadpan.

"You're a crack-up."

From that time on, the Cabinet took good care of me. They became my *benefactors*.

I started to rethink things. So this was what Katie saw in them—they could be so helpful, and accommodating, and accepting. They even made sure I sat at the front with them during assembly, even though I wasn't a prefect. Of course we would never be equals, but the more I hung around them, the more I realized how much I didn't mind. They were like three big albino rats in a cage full of brown mice. You wanted to be close to the glorious creatures, not only because they were so compelling, but also because you hoped that if they smelled your familiar scent often enough, they would not eat you.

At the next assembly, Trisha MacMahon played the piano for a second time, which was unheard of at Laurinda, because there were heaps of gifted students. But Trisha really was something else. When she finished and the girls again gave their polite hand pats, I couldn't help myself, and I clapped loud and hard in the front row. I wanted her to know that at least one person appreciated her passion. Brodie and Amber looked at me, startled, and then Amber flashed me a wry sideways smile.

Then, surprise of surprises, Brodie, Amber and Chelsea began to clap like crazy as well. "Woo-hoo!" Amber hooted.

"Woo!" whooped Chelsea. "Good on you, Trisha!"

And because the Cabinet made it okay, suddenly the whole school began to applaud like mad, stamping their feet and hollering their support. Trisha stood up, bewildered. A smile spread across her face and she took a bow. She must have felt like a rock star. As she walked offstage, I even detected a tiny skip in her step.

"You are so cute, Lucy," said Amber as we walked out of the auditorium. "Isn't she just adorable?" she said to Brodie.

I waited for Mrs. Leslie at the front door of the classroom we'd used for my sessions.

"Lucy!" she exclaimed. "What can I do for you?"

I made sure the coast was clear, then tried to give back her fifty dollars.

"No, Lucy, stop this nonsense!"

"But the food didn't cost that much, Mrs. Leslie."

"I can't take a gift back. You also gave us your time."

"I can't accept money," I said, and I must have said it with some severity, Linh, because she looked taken aback. I realized she was worried it would seem she was trying to buy my time and effort, which I knew was not her intention. But there was nothing I could say that would not make her feel even guiltier, so I just looked at the floor.

At last she replied, "Then, Lucy, at least let me know how much you spent so I can reimburse you."

"It wasn't really that much."

"How much, Lucy? Forty dollars?"

"Seventeen sixty-five."

"Really?" She didn't believe me.

"I'm not lying."

She put the fifty back in her purse and pulled out a twenty. "Please take this." She shoved it in my hands. "No ifs, no buts! We had a wonderful afternoon, Lucy, and we are grateful to you."

"No worries, Mrs. Leslie."

I returned the money to my father. What was I going to do with it? Buy Coast & Co. fashions? Go clubbing? Buy Smirnoff Ices?

"What's this?" Dad asked when I gave it back to him.

"That excursion got canceled."

"Oh, that's a shame. But don't give this back to me. Just save it for next week's groceries."

In the second-to-last week of Term Two, I went with the Cabinet to the Year Ten Auburn-Laurinda social. Amber had called up my father a week before to ask in her sweetest voice if I could go to a dinner dance with her and a few other girls from school. Ordinarily, my father would rather break my legs than let me go dancing, but after she called, he almost commanded me to go. "You'll meet new people there," he said.

The day of the social, I went straight to Amber's house after school because I didn't want Mrs. Leslie driving by to pick me up from Stanley. Imagine my mum staring, mouth agape, at their fancy car, and the snot-nosed Lamb wailing as I walked out the door—it would have tinged the whole evening with futility and guilt. I knew I should have been in the garage helping Mum with her latest order, but instead I would be standing against a wall, watching crowds of strangers jerk about.

The theme was (PARTY) ANIMALS, as our tasteful black-and-white zebra-patterned invitations put it, but the Cabinet did not seem to take that very seriously. "Lame," Chelsea remarked, and a week before the social she handed each of us a headband with furry animal ears attached. Amber was a rabbit (the ears were suspiciously like a Playboy Bunny's), Chelsea was a bear (but not a grizzly one, more a fluffy bedside creature) and Brodie was Minnie Mouse. Predictably, I got lamb's ears.

My mother had made me a new cotton floral dress with buttons down the front, but I had my old jeans in my bag as well as a black shirt, because I wasn't sure how dressed up we were meant to be. All I had to do was change from my school uniform into my dress, so I was ready in five minutes. But Amber and Mrs. Leslie spent almost two hours in the master bathroom doing God knows what. They invited me in too, but after a few minutes of watching Amber get sprayed all over with a can of tan, I decided to go and sit on the sofa and read a book. Amber eventually emerged in a surprisingly modest floral dress a lot like mine.

Some of the Auburn boys were dressed casually in T-shirts and denim pants. Others were in neatly ironed navy, black or maroon shirts and khakis. One boy came as a circus ringmaster, armed with a plastic whip, while a few others wore khaki safari outfits with fake guns (hunters, ha). The majority, though, had plastic masks of gorillas, grizzly bears, tigers, sharks or other meat-eating fauna. It was creepy, the girls being so exposed (bare legs, bare arms, some tasteful cleavage) while the boys were so *masked*.

As soon as we arrived at the venue, Amber, Brodie and Chelsea snuck into the bathroom. Amber emerged in two satin slips, pale pink and black, one on top of the other, and her pretty Mary Jane shoes had transformed into heavy black lace-up boots. She looked like she'd been punched in the face, but I think that was the smoky-eye look popularized in whatever fashion magazine they all read.

Brodie had on a floor-length, strappy slip thing that was the shade of a three-day-old bruise—it shimmered purple, green and black. And Chelsea—well, Chelsea wore a black catsuit with high military boots, and an olive silk teddy over the top of that. And they all put on their animal ears.

I thought they had reached the pinnacle of grunge sophistication, while I was still stuck in my stupid green-and-white daisy frock because I had expected it to be like Amber's birthday party. My jeans and shirt were back at her house, so I couldn't change. And to top it all off, I had to wear the lamb's ears.

Since I was dressed for the part, I took the position of wallflower, planting my roots on one side of the room and clinging to the bags I was meant to mind for Amber and Chelsea while they giggled and sashayed their way to the center of the dance floor. As they gyrated, a photographer took pictures of them for the yearbook.

After a while I was aware I wasn't alone, but I stared straight ahead, in case my neighbor didn't want to talk to me. If I turned my head around to look, that would seem too eager, as though I was desperate for company—which I was.

"Hey, Lucy, you look like you're having fun."

It was Mr. Sinclair. Most girls would have been mortified to hang out with a teacher at a social. Not me. I was relieved someone was speaking to me. Mind you, if this had been a couple of months earlier, he would have had a tight band of girls crowding around him, springy and giggly.

Thankfully, he did not ask me to dance with him. That

would have been a pity dance, terrible and awkward. He just said, "Ah, dancing. I've never been good at that sort of thing."

Of course, I didn't believe him.

"Music," he began, "music should mean something. It is the stuff that gets angry young men and women believing in causes, or feeling like someone equally angry and insightful understands them. But what is this?" He quoted the cheesy lyrics of the song playing. "What does that even mean?"

"I don't know, sir. Maybe no one taught him not to mix metaphors. Or maybe it's a Zen koan."

"Ha!"

I smiled. I asked him what he thought of our new prime minister. I asked him whether he preferred Socrates or Seneca. Would he have drunk the hemlock, or stayed alive and not been a troublemaker in Athenian society? You see, Linh, when I wasn't feeling intimidated, I could carry on a conversation well enough.

There was a sudden flash as someone took a photo of me and Mr. Sinclair talking, and we both looked around to see who had taken it. No one was there, so it must have been the girl compiling the yearbook.

"Yo, I'll tell you what I want, what I really, really want," blared the music, an old song. *"So tell me what you want, what you really, really want. . . ."*

"What exactly does she want?" asked Mr. Sinclair.

"Don't you understand? What she really, really wants is to zigazig ah." Standing in front of us was a boy dressed in jeans and a button-up shirt. My heart rate increased—but then, my heart rate increased in the presence of *any* boy, because I had so few encounters with them. I wanted to flee.

"Ah!" laughed Mr. Sinclair. "Thank you for enlighten-
ing me, Richard. But now I'm curious about something else.
Why do you have a lion attached to your shirt pocket?"

"A clue," said the boy. "What vital organ beats beneath my
shirt?" He turned to me and smiled—and I swear, Linh, he
might have winked as well, but I was too shy to look him in
the eye.

"Your heart," said Mr. Sinclair. "Oh, I see. Very clever,
Richard the Lionheart."

I didn't know whether that was actually very clever or just
plain embarrassing, so I said nothing and turned my head
toward the dance floor. I watched the Cabinet dancing, hair
all shook up, their slip dresses flashes of color in the center
of the room. When the song ended, Amber headed straight
toward me, cheeks pink and warm, eyes shining. "Oh, there
you are! Come and dance the next one with us, Lucy!"

Now, let me tell you, Linh, lest you think I am a cliché, a
living, walking example of a high schooler's desperate desire
for popularity gone wrong, that *there is nothing more powerful
than the feeling of belonging to a group.* She dragged me to the
center of the room, and I had no choice but to do the best I
could. It was conscription, this, and I hated every moment of
it, but I learned to creatively convulse like the rest of them,
until time was up and we could go home.

Going to the social was tolerable, then, if not exactly fun. I
appreciated that the Cabinet had invited me to go with them.
I wasn't sure whether this had changed our friendship or
whether I would still be treated like the perpetual exchange
student in their little group. I soon found out.

Brodie stared at me with her scary dark eyes. "We like you, Lucy. You're loyal, and you keep quiet about things."

"Not like Katie," said Chelsea. "Tattling bitch."

I think they were waiting for me to bag Katie or Ms. Vanderwerp and pledge allegiance to them. But I remained silent, and I suppose after a while my silence became unnerving.

"We know your former friend dobbed on us, Lucy," spat Chelsea. "We know she went to the Growler and told her who it was that pulled the prank on Ms. V."

"We also know she dobbed on Gina too."

The Cabinet had got only one out of two correct. Katie might have ratted on Gina, but she would never touch the Cabinet. "I don't think Katie would tell on you," I said.

"Aww, Lucy, you're too sweet, but terribly naïve. You think that just because you wouldn't, others wouldn't as well." That was Brodie. "But what you don't understand yet is that the Growler *depends* on us to keep the others in check. You think the administration can just yell out orders from above and get all the students to comply? Not on your life. We have a crucial role. We tread gently, my friend. We play harmless pranks, but our pranks have serious consequences.

"Listen, Lucy. When my dad went to Auburn Academy in the eighties, there was a teacher named Mr. Hadley. He was this old, drooling man, close to retirement, but still clinging on to teaching shitty math. He was probably the sole reason why the school was always beaten by Forbes College in university acceptance for ten years straight. The boys hated him. He couldn't explain anything properly, and when the boys didn't understand he would just speak more loudly and slowly, as if they were deaf."

"Maybe *he* was deaf!" interrupted Chelsea.

"So one day they went to the butcher and got a pig's head. They put a wig on it and some makeup, and glued on some fake eyelashes. They put the head in the teacher's drawer in the classroom so that it lay on one cheek, and they arranged the hair to cover its piggy snout. When Mr. Hadley came to class that day, all the boys had their heads on their desks, shoulders shaking, except for one boy, whose hands and desk were all smeared with red ink from a pen. 'What's going on?' Mr. Hadley kept saying, but no one moved, and that one boy was just staring at the teacher's desk. When Mr. Hadley noticed droplets of blood on the floor, leaking in small plops from his desk, he finally opened the drawer.

"And he pissed himself. He literally pissed his pants. There was a spreading dark patch on the front of his pants, and the front of the room started to smell. He had to leave, walking out with his legs all funny. Needless to say, he went into early retirement."

I had no idea why they were telling me their stories.

"When Mr. Wang came to teach us Chinese in Year Seven," Chelsea said, "he was probably, like, only eight years older than us. He had a really thick accent, so thick it was kind of hopeless trying to understand him. And he'd picked a stupid first name: Carmen. What the hell? Didn't he know it was a girl's name? When he told us that the Chinese put their surnames before their first names, from that day on we called him Wanker Man. *Wang Carmen*—get it? And there was nothing he could do because it was his name!"

"Yeah, I remember in Year Seven," Amber began, "some girls filled a condom with water and put it on my seat just before I sat down. My dress was wet for ages. I laughed about it at school, then cried for hours when I got home. But I didn't go off and have a nervous breakdown."

"An insecure person here is like a loose nut," said Chelsea. "You just have to screw them up properly."

"We really got rid of Ms. V," breathed Amber, slightly incredulously, as if she was David after he'd felled Goliath.

"We purified the school," said Brodie, but by now it was hard to tell whether she was being ironic or deadly serious. Her laugh sounded like a machine gun, and her braces glinted like a steel trap. Sometimes Brodie said the most ridiculous things in dead seriousness, and sometimes she said the most serious things with deadpan mirth.

And that, I learned, was how you blurred the lines between good and bad.

TERM THREE

Dear Linh,

I was beginning to notice things that I should not have noticed, and to take an unhealthy interest in things that had never before interested me. Of course, back at Christ Our Savior we noticed girls who had stuff. On casual day, we all knew that Lisa's white peacoat cost $79.95, because we went to the mall after school and tried it on for ourselves. We crowded around Lisa and told her how good it looked and how jealous we all were. And that was it, Linh. We didn't lie awake at night burning with bitterness. But something new was happening to me. Now I felt a desire for things that I could not voice.

If houses were faces, then the houses in Stanley would be middle-aged men with most of their teeth knocked out or rotted to the core, surviving on welfare and reeking of beer, with a few vehicular misdemeanors to their names. Everything was so cheap and tacky here, I now saw. All the trees looked like shrubs. The great big concrete slabs of the Corinthian Hotel made it look more like a mausoleum than the classical Roman establishment it was modeled on. Even the Donaldsons' gnomes looked gauche; it occurred to me that they must have got them from the Reject Shop.

At the Sunray market I saw an old Laotian woman sitting

on a faded plastic chair, eating a banana and scratching her right big toe. I saw Filipino ladies carrying their fake Louis Vuitton and Chanel handbags to buy fish at the wet market. The dollar store that I loved so much, the place that brought such endless cheap joy to the Lamb, seemed like a roomful of junk. All the things that I had once loved so much now seemed sad.

Back at Christ Our Savior, most of us lived in the same dumpy houses, so we didn't see them as cluttered with boxes of fabric or cheap imported knickknacks. We were too busy doing things—jumping on our mums' sewing machines to make tote bags and summer shorts with the scraps left over from the floor, concocting seven different ways to use up a sack of potatoes, and even trying to arrange for our baby siblings to be betrothed to each other when they grew up. Silly, daydreamy girl stuff.

None of us at Christ Our Savior thought it was unusual that the Lamb came everywhere with me. They did not treat him like a specimen from another planet, existing solely to give them their daily dose of cute. Nor did they secretly shudder if he sneezed and snot popped out of his nose like two green worms. They would just hand me a box of tissues, or wait patiently for me to change his nappy. They did not mind if he sat on the floor with us while we were doing our homework, and they would grab some used paper and a pen for him too.

Now that my life had shrunk down to homework, and the Lamb, and sewing after school, my mind started wandering to places I had no business being in.

★ ★ ★

"Are you going to masturbate?" Gina asked me one morning, and I thought that I must have heard incorrectly, or that she was speaking to someone else, or that she was revealing her true sexual orientation by coming on to me.

"Yes, she's coming with us," Chelsea said, seeing the bewilderment on my face, and laughed. "That's what we call this illustrious event in the Laurinda-Auburn calendar: the Mass Debate. And we get to wrestle the boys for the top position."

When we arrived at the boys' school, I soon found out the reason for the name, Linh—the Auburn boys used language that had played with itself so much it had gone blind. I lost track of what they were supposed to be arguing. I should have felt smug accompanying the Cabinet to their debating finals, but instead I felt as though I was watching it all from a great distance.

Brodie, Amber and Chelsea were on the negative team. None of them had jobs, but they all had very strong opinions. The final speaker for Auburn, a boxy boy named Aaron, was almost apoplectic in his insistence that young people deserved as much pay as your minimum-wage working adult because they worked just as hard and learned twice as fast. His hands moved about like those of a mime artist on speed, so confident was he in the power of his words.

All those Laurinda girls and Auburn boys, in love with their own voices and ideas, so certain of going to university and winning internships, of moving to Canberra and maybe becoming politicians, so they could make decisions that affected people like my mum, and decisions for the grown-up versions of our Christ Our Savior friends, girls who believed that if they lived decent, small lives of community service,

205

their worlds would be safe. Our poor ignorant mates, Linh—they had no idea that beliefs which would affect their lives were germinating at these little debates, forming in the minds of these girls and boys who were practicing to rule in two decades' time. I wish I could say I admired their intellects, but I knew that intellect was not the be-all and end-all. I wish I could say I didn't have a chip on my shoulder, but I knew I had a whole Pringles factory up there.

The girls won the debate by a narrow margin. Afterward, the boys' team milled around the Cabinet.

"Hey, Brodie, you were good."

These Auburn boys and Brodie understood each other. They were on the same plane, while I was far below, paddling furiously on a life raft.

I didn't recognize anyone. The boys seemed handsome-forgettable, but of course I couldn't look directly at their faces. They all looked desirably good, because they all looked decent, neat and clean. I could understand why some people fell in love with a uniform. These boys' school uniforms were like suits, not only suggesting their future careers, but also preventing them from getting up to no good, like the boys of Stanley did.

I saw how Samuel, Aaron and Raymond ignored Amber altogether: they either didn't look at her while they were talking, or didn't talk to her while they were looking. Of course, they paid me no attention either. Yellow fever had not reached here, and I doubted it ever would. Girls like me were just not considered hot.

The Cabinet girls hadn't acknowledged or introduced me, so it was hard to be part of their conversation. I'd never been much good at finding openings in conversations here. I treated having conversations like stuffing envelopes—the moment a gap appeared, I was worried I'd insert the wrong thing, and it would be sealed and delivered. Or I'd insert something too large to fit through the post, and it would not be accepted. Most people were happy to send off junk mail, though, which was what small talk was sort of about. I stood around awkwardly while they talked. When there was a long silence, Raymond turned my way.

"Guys, this is Lucy," explained Chelsea. "She's new at Laurinda."

"Oh, really? Are you on exchange?" asked Raymond.

"No, I'm local."

"What part of Asia are you from?" he asked, as if he had not heard me.

Why couldn't we talk about books or politics, or even movies we'd seen recently (he at the cinema, me on illegally copied DVDs)? Amber could stand there thinking about taking a dump and the boys would presume the faraway look in her eyes signified deep thoughts and ineffable longings. When my face was passive, I was inscrutable and sullen.

I must have stayed silent for a moment too long, because Chelsea replied, "She's Chinese." Then she said to me, "You know, Aaron went on the China trip last year."

I turned toward Aaron. "How was it?" I asked. "Were the people really friendly despite being so poor? And was the food really great?"

He didn't detect my sarcasm. "Oh, yes. It's a remarkable culture."

What fifteen-year-old uses the word *remarkable*?

Raymond nudged Aaron. "Aaron went to Chongqing," he said. Maybe I was imagining it, but he seemed to take great pleasure in pronouncing the word like a racist chant. "Chong Ching," he repeated, and snickered.

"What part of China are you from?" Aaron asked me, in the way you would ask a four-year-old to hold up a handful of fingers to show their age.

"I was born in Vietnam."

"Hmm, how does that work?"

"Well, my mum went into labor and I popped out."

There was an awkward silence; my joke was hanging there like a tightrope walker without a net.

"I mean," he patiently explained, as if talking to someone who had just clambered off a boat and had to fill in an immigration form in a language they couldn't read, "why was a Chinese girl born in Vietnam?"

Linh, you would have retorted with "What's a white guy like you doing being born in an Aboriginal country?" but I didn't. "My grandparents migrated to Vietnam," I said. It sounded like I was apologizing for getting his question wrong, when he was the one who hadn't understood me. "Because of the famine. In China."

Don't get me wrong, Linh, these boys did try. The Laurinda girls too, because they were "nice girls." But they all began from a distant and inoffensive place of extreme politeness, and the first thing they noticed was our differences. They didn't understand that we were teenagers *in the exact same way they were.* I wasn't suddenly an expert on the Moon Festival or the My Lai Massacre, just as they didn't know about the history of the national anthem or the early Dutch discovery of Australia before Captain Cook.

208

"I see," said Aaron, even though he didn't.

Suddenly the boys spotted another Laurindan they recognized. As Trisha walked past, Aaron called out, "Hey! It's Trisha 'Maestro' MacMahon!"

And then, Linh, Trisha turned toward the boys, *as if the Cabinet was not standing there,* and replied, "Do you want aural pleasures, boys?" She had a surprisingly husky voice. I'd only ever really seen her from a distance, but up close Trisha was quite gorgeous: raven-haired with sharp cheekbones.

"How do you know each other?" asked Chelsea.

"Trisha has been playing for us," replied Raymond. "She played last week at our assembly."

"Really?" asked Brodie.

"Really," replied Trisha.

"She was damn good too," enthused Aaron.

I stood a little to the left while they continued talking, and then a bit farther apart, until I saw a wall of old oil paintings in which I could pretend to be engrossed.

"Why weren't you debating?"

This was a new voice.

You know, Linh, it really doesn't take long for a fifteen-year-old girl to fall in love. A boy only needs to look at her in the right way or talk to her in the right way. To see her in the right way. I had been pretending to carefully examine a portrait of an old man with a monumental mustache, while trying to block out the praise fest going on behind me. I turned around and came face to face with Richard the Lionheart. He was standing close enough that I could see the freckles on his nose. He looked at the painting.

"Ah, the old hat."

"What?" I knew it was rude, but "I beg your pardon" sounded like a middle-aged person's reprimand.

"H.A.T.," he explained. "Hugh Auburn the Third, founder of our august institution. His eyes are popping out because of the strain of holding his bladder in. It was a six-hour sitting. They had to capture every strand of his facial hair."

Against my will, I smiled. I didn't laugh, because it wasn't that funny, and I didn't want to sound like a bimbo. You had to be very careful when you talked with boys in public: every sound and movement was magnified, blown out of proportion like a grotesque foil character balloon. One little prick and you were deflated.

"Our debate finished early, so a few of us came to see the Division A teams."

Earlier, I'd heard debates going on in other rooms that sounded far more fun than ours. One room in particular sounded like one of the parliamentary question time sessions that they showed on television at three in the morning.

I didn't know how to talk to boys who were past the nappy-wearing stage of life. "What did you think?" I asked. "The boys were pretty good, weren't they?"

"No," said Richard. "They were tools."

Then I did something that I had not done too often this year. I laughed. I had not expected such honesty—or such audacity. You could never, ever say something like that with the Cabinet so close by; they had sonar hearing like bats. Fortunately, Aaron and co. were too engrossed in their conversation to hear.

That was another difference between girls and boys: boys

were insulted only if you yelled it in their faces. Otherwise, they were oblivious.

Amber was telling them about some old Italian men who had tried to pick her up at the Amalfi Coast last summer. Richard turned his head around to look. I felt a little miffed, but the fact was, everyone noticed Amber. She was like the sun: you could pretend it wasn't there, but you'd still feel its heat.

"Those boys—what kind of tools were they?" I asked. "Screwdrivers or hand drills?"

Aaron would probably have tried to explain the double meaning of *tool* to me, but Richard just smiled. He put his hand on his chin and pretended to muse on this.

"Screwdrivers," he decided. "Or maybe even sharpeners."

"Sharpeners?"

"They were so anally retentive that if you shoved a pencil up Aaron's arse, it would be filed to a lethal point."

"Hee hee. You could sharpen a few of them and use them as darts," I suggested. "It would bring new meaning to the term *backstab*. You could throw them at people and they'd get a visit from *E. coli* and friends."

Richard laughed. His laugh was both awesome and embarrassing in its loudness and enjoyment. Someone had found me funny at last. It wasn't as if I'd been hankering to be the class clown, but I felt like I'd lacked a personality for more than half a year. Finally someone had seen a small glimmer of what I once was—it was a blissful feeling.

"Colon and buddies."

"Salmon Ella and the Fecal Crew."

"Hey, that's a great name for a band," Richard said.

We were playing a game, and it was very different from the one being played beside us by Brodie and Trisha and Aaron, or by Amber and her fawning young men. Our game was not about demonstrating our intellect or sex appeal, or making mission statements. Our game had started off with having a laugh at another's expense and had now become a *Simpsons* episode—random and unexpected. This was the first time— the first time!—since arriving at Laurinda that I had felt anything like the spontaneity and fun that I had felt back at Christ Our Savior with you, Yvonne and Ivy.

"Were you that noisy group in Room 109?" I asked.

"Uh, yes, unfortunately."

"Well, you sounded like you had more fun than we did."

"Heh, heh." He had been in the other room debating minimum wages too, but in Division B, against other Auburn boys. He told me how he knew a little bit about junior wages because his father hired young workers for his footwear shop. Junior wages were the only way that young people in his town got any sort of employment, he had argued, and they made it possible for his dad to keep the business going.

But a boy named Eamon had declared that Richard's dad was too tight to pay proper legal wages and was exploiting the kids. Then the third speaker for the affirmative had concluded with "Richard here is as mincing in his words as he is with the shoes he tries on in his dad's shop when no one is watching!" The room had exploded in laughter, although a couple of boys—Richard's mates—had yelled, "Low! Low!" and "His store sells sneakers, you morons."

"Such idiots," laughed Richard, with genuine amusement. "That's private schools for you. My dad thought he was sending me to *Dead Poets Society*. 'O captain! My captain!'—my arse. Look at these ferals. Here come some more now."

Harshan and an Asian boy named Anton approached—the same boy Amber had thought would make a good boyfriend for me. This was Richard's gang, I realized.

"We have to go now, Lucy," Chelsea was saying to me. Then she saw Harshan and gave him a glare.

"See you," Richard called after me. "Pass on my regards to Ella the Salmon."

"Dork," muttered Chelsea.

I loved Richard the Lionheart, I decided. I loved all his little trio.

"I thought today was delivery day?" I asked Mum when I arrived home, eyeing the boxes of folded and ironed shorts in our living room.

There was something comfortingly chaotic about home. Things didn't necessarily make more sense than the crazy order at school, but they were at least so random as to be reassuring. For example, after spending an afternoon trying to do quadratic equations, I might come home to see our phone iced with toothpaste, or find a sock stuffed with crushed cupcake. In the Lamb's world, all sorts of combinations were possible.

"No, Sokkha didn't come today," my mother replied. "There's a letter for you. I think it's from the school."

It was another reminder about participation in Saturday sports.

"Can you watch the Lamb?" my mother asked. "I'm going to chop up some hunks of bony meat on the kitchen floor. I don't want him coming near the cleaver. Give him a banana."

I picked him up and patted his back. In more than half a year, he did not seem to have got any heavier. I sat him down on the sofa and peeled a banana. Then I cut slices off for him. In the center of each slice was a sort of face, the features formed by the black seeds. Each slice had a different expression. "Look, Lamby! Look at this!" He squealed with delight.

While he was eating his banana pieces, I took out the letter from the school and cut it in half. Then I folded two leaping frogs. I put one on the floor and pressed its back. It sprang forward. The Lamb thought it was magical. I gave him one and we had a paper frog race, though after a while his frog was all sticky with banana mush.

Dad returned from work and took the Lamb to the park, leaving me to finish cooking dinner with Mum. We laid out newspaper on the floor in front of the television. We had never used a dining table. When we had guests, they were usually the type to sit on the floor as well. At the end of the meal, we just scrunched up the newspaper and chucked it in the bin. It had never bothered me before, but now I understood just how uncivilized we were. We were like animals in a kennel, except that we cleaned up our own litter.

Things like this had begun to appall me, things that had never bothered me before, like the way my parents slurped their soup. When I say *slurped,* imagine the loudest and most obscene sucking sounds you can think of, sloppy chewing and gulping like cartoon characters. That sort of eating. But of course, even though it frustrated me no end, I could never tell them this.

I remembered that a few years ago, a friend of Dad's from the factory, Jimmy Macintyre, had invited our family over to his house for dinner. I could see that Mum and Dad were trying to do their best, in unfamiliar surroundings, to behave with a different sort of decorum. Even holding a knife and fork properly took a lot of effort. It was not that they couldn't do it—my parents were not clumsy imbeciles—but there was a graceful technique to scooping food into your mouth that was different from simple eating. And there was one thing they did glaringly wrong—they always ate with their mouths open. Chewing like cows.

It was a very uncharitable thought to have about your parents, but there it was, and once I thought it I could not undo what it was doing to my face. I was ashamed not of them but of myself, because their kind of rudeness was not deliberate and had the same unself-conscious quality as children picking their noses. Their rudeness was not directed at anyone, unlike the way Amber spoke to her mother.

But now, sitting on the floor, watching my parents became almost intolerable. I readied myself to make a simple request, to ask them to be less uncouth even though they would not see the point because we were at home, but still. As I opened my mouth to speak, my mother suddenly said, "The fabric cutter sliced the top of Sokkha's middle finger right off. That's why he didn't turn up today. His wife just called to tell me."

In a different household, this might have been met with exclamations of "Oh, how awful" and "I hope he's okay." But my father simply asked, "Would you like me to do the delivery, then? Do you think he will be able to work again?"

"He'll be back at it in a week. It's only the first joint of his middle finger."

"That's good. Good for him, and good for us."

"You have the hots for Richard Marr," declared Brodie the next day. So that was his surname. She had saved me from having to look it up in the Auburn yearbook.

"Aww, how sweet, Lucy has a crush!" mooned Amber.

Richard and I were private, I thought, but I knew I had no right to think this. Nothing at this school was private. They had seen us talking together.

"He's all right," conceded Chelsea, "but his friends are really offensive."

"What did he say to you?" asked Amber. "We heard you guys laughing about something."

"Bacteria," I said.

"Excuse me?"

"We were telling jokes about bacteria."

"Oh, wow, he's perfect for you, Lucy!"

It was the first time that the attention of the Cabinet had focused on me alone. It was a nice feeling, actually. It was as if my "crush"—which I had neither confirmed nor denied—was showing them that I was a little like them, that I too could feel this way toward a boy. But my glory was short-lived.

"You know what?" added Chelsea. "That's exactly the sort of pickup line I can imagine a geek like Richard using. To an Asian girl, no less."

"Yeah, some people love Asian girls—and I'm not just talking about bacteria boys either," Amber declared bitterly. "My mum has a thing for Asian kids. She reckons they all listen to their parents and finish their homework and do whatever their mums and dads say without whinging."

That wasn't fair! I thought. As if we wanted to go home to open buttonholes or iron collars or prepare stinking pig's hocks for dinner, or boil eggs or wash floors or wipe the bums of babies or do any of the other dozen jobs we had to do. It had nothing to do with us feeling self-righteous or better than anyone else.

"Well, well, well, Lucy, what can we tell you about Richard Marr?" asked Brodie. "We keep a mental file on him, as we do most of the Auburn boys. He sure comes from some bad blood."

"What, he has AIDS?" I asked.

"No! No, no, no!" replied Brodie, taking me literally as usual. "Oh, dear. No. Just bad relations, bad *associations*."

The Cabinet exchanged a look. They didn't tell me what was so wrong with Richard, but they'd let it be known that they would not deign to be around such a person, and that there was something wrong with me if I chose to. I did not know what their look meant, but I knew that I wasn't their friend after all. I was their prop.

When Term Three began, Trisha was back on the piano at assembly. She was becoming a regular—it was her third performance this year.

A fortnight later, when Trisha walked offstage once more, Brodie turned to Amber and shook her head slowly. Amber understood and nodded. It was just too much. "She's getting way up herself," muttered Chelsea, who was always their ventriloquist's doll. "Stage hog."

The fifth time we saw Trisha MacMahon at the piano, the Cabinet decided it was time to deal with her.

"Now, Trisha, we understand that you are monumentally talented," said Brodie one morning, "but maybe at assembly we could hear something other than Beethoven or Tchaikovsky?"

They formed a tight circle around Trisha so that the teachers would think we were just having a little chat as we walked to class.

"Oh, yes, of course," said Trisha, nodding enthusiastically. "I'll tell Mrs. Grey I'll play Rachmaninoff next week."

What was worse than Trisha not picking up on Brodie's polite cease-and-desist was the Cabinet finding out that Trisha herself was organizing all these performances. She had probably volunteered for the Auburn assembly too.

"Geez, I'd hate to be up myself," muttered Chelsea.

"Pardon me?" asked Trisha.

"Nothing."

"Come on, I heard you."

"Don't you think that the opportunities at Laurinda should be shared?" queried Amber.

"But everyone likes my performances!" protested Trisha.

"Stop it, please, Trisha," Brodie said quietly. Her quiet voice could stop arguments in their tracks. "Stop it before you embarrass yourself."

At recess that day I could not join the Cabinet because Mrs. Grey wanted to see me. I sat on the bench outside her office, next to a tiny girl with a face too small for her large features. Even though she had beautiful big eyes and lips like pillows, the disparity made her look a little clownish. She was picking miserably at the hem of her blazer.

After a few moments of silence, I tried to make her feel more at ease. "What are you here for?"

She looked down, and at first I thought she was extremely shy, until I saw that she was pointing to her feet. Then I noticed that her socks were not the regulation anklet length, but long and white, even though they were now pooling at her ankles. Like her face, her legs seemed to be covered with scaly acne.

"I forgot to get a uniform pass," she whispered. "I didn't think I needed one because of my psoriasis, but Mr. Abraham noticed them and sent me here."

"Don't worry," I reassured her, "it's not a big deal." Secretly, I knew better.

"Nadia Pinto," called Mrs. Grey's secretary, and the girl stood up and disappeared behind the door.

Ten minutes later she came back out with red-rimmed eyes. Nadia Pinto didn't look at me as she walked back to class.

It was my turn.

Mrs. Grey's eyes were the color of pickled onions, shot through with hair-width strands of red. Her cheeks were etched with lines to match. The girls were saying she was a closet alcoholic.

"I'm concerned about your performance, Miss Lam," she said as soon as I sat down.

"But I'm working hard, Mrs. Grey." I racked my brain to see where I had gone wrong. I'd had good results on my midyear exams. "Maybe I could go back to remedial English with Mrs. Leslie?" I offered disingenuously.

It turned out she wasn't talking about my academic performance.

"It seems to me, Miss Lam, that you've become uninterested in what Laurinda has to offer. You've become lackluster. Insipid."

"I'm sorry, Mrs. Grey, I don't know what you mean."

"Not taking advantage of all the remarkable opportunities here for you. You have not attended any Saturday morning sports."

"I thought they were voluntary . . . ," I began, and trailed off, immediately realizing it was the wrong thing to say.

"You did not come to our Constitutional Convention in Term Two."

Of course not, I wanted to tell her. I'd have had to stick toothpicks in my eyes to prop them open.

"You did not get involved in drama or music."

"But I did some debating," I protested feebly.

"You attended the debating finals. That is not the same thing. The truth of the matter is that you are not becoming the well-rounded individual that we envisioned when we accepted you into this college. Do you think that is a fair assessment?"

No, I wanted to say. It's crap.

"The letter from your former principal said that you were involved in the school choir and Tournament of Minds, and that you started a book club."

Ah, the halcyon days of youth, I wanted to say to her. Alas, my mind is not as sharp as it once was. Actually, this would not have been far from the truth, because I was feeling exhausted all the time now, and I didn't do half as much as before.

I forced myself to look Mrs. Grey in the eye in case she thought I was being evasive. I didn't see myself reflected back. She seemed to see me solely as a human doing instead of a human being, and all my doings had to add to the prestige of Laurinda. At that moment I felt nothing but repulsion as

I looked at the white orbs of pearl hovering above her neck-line. Someone who wore the remains of sea mollusks strung around her neck and would make a thirteen-year-old cry over wearing the wrong socks was not someone I respected.

"We may need to have a word with your parents," she said. "The letters we sent home don't appear to have been read."

Good luck with that, I thought. Maybe you can courier them to my father at the carpet factory.

"I understand you have become friends with Brodie New-berry and Amber Leslie." For some reason she left out Chel-sea. "These girls demonstrate the Laurinda spirit," she said. "Particularly Brodie."

Brodie's a dickhead, I thought.

The truth was, Linh, this school sucked you in. It de-manded every part of your life and mind. In order to be a Laurinda girl, you had to dedicate every waking minute to doing its bidding. I had to make myself "deserving" of the scholarship; at the moment I was blocking its march Forward in Harmony. I had to be one of those girls in the brochures: holding a test tube in the science lab, or laughing with manic glee on the sporting field. I had to be the well-adjusted stu-dent whom the school could tout as its Equal Access success. That was why I was allowed to be so close to the Cabinet, when everyone else had to orbit like distant planets. They were the sun bringing life to my barren earth; they were civilizing the beast in me.

"I'm afraid that if you don't get your act together," Mrs. Grey was saying, "you might not be an appropriate cultural fit for this college."

She knew exactly how to get to me. The only way I could

be that girl was if I gave up my family—if I stopped working in the garage with Mum, and stopped looking after the Lamb.

"Academic results aren't everything, you know, Miss Lam."

We sat in silence. Then Mrs. Grey reached into her desk drawer and pulled out a brochure.

"There's a conference in a month's time, at the University of Melbourne," she said. "Dr. Markus will be presenting on behalf of our school."

Dr. Markus was the Latin teacher and history coordinator. He had got his PhD for research into the use of the comma in contemporary English translations of traditional Italian children's books circa 1965–85. Some girls claimed he was an even worse teacher than Ms. Vanderwerp, but the school board thought Laurinda was lucky to have enticed such a learned scholar to publish papers and represent it at conferences.

She pushed the document at me. "'Equity in Education,'" I read, "'in the Twenty-First Century.'"

"Some schools will also have student participants," she continued. "For instance, Meredith Grammar is sending three of its Indigenous Access students along to do a dance."

I waited for Mrs. Grey to continue.

"We want you to give a short speech on behalf of the school," she concluded. "So get your act together. We are trying our best to be inclusive, Lucy, but we need you to cooperate."

Now I understood what all this was about. I suppose I should have shown more gratitude, or jumped at the opportunity to speak at the conference. But I felt like a puppet, and I didn't want to have my strings pulled.

Nothing escaped the Cabinet. At lunchtime, when we found our usual spot near the rose garden and sat down, they started in on me.

"I hear you've been asked to speak at the Equity in Education conference next term," enthused Brodie.

How did she know about this?

"How exciting. How lucky for you, Lucy! You get to put yourself out there."

"It's only for ten minutes," I said.

"But there'll be university staff there, and professors, and lots of important people. Wow, what an honor."

"What do you think you'll talk about?" asked Amber.

"Well, since it's about equity, I might talk about fairness."

"Oh, you mean equal access, and getting into this school on a scholarship because you're so smart, that kind of thing?" asked Brodie.

I did not fall for her flattery.

"No," I said slowly. "Maybe how different schools cultivate different cultures of fairness. For instance, at my old school we had a student representative council—"

"But you're not meant to be talking about your old school,"

interrupted Chelsea. "You're representing Laurinda, remember?"

"Hmm," mused Brodie. "How about you focus on the two schools' different academic standards and extracurricular activities? Do you think that would be a good approach?"

"I'm not sure about that," said Amber. "The last time I spoke outside of school was at Poppy King's Red Lipstick Luncheon. Those ladies liked hearing personal stories of motivation and success."

"I think what Lucy is doing is very different," said Brodie.

"You're right," I said. "Maybe I will talk about how broke my old school was and how it's a hundred times better here."

"We didn't mean it like that!" protested Chelsea, with her sensitive-offended look. She paused and pouted so that I could apologize, but I ignored her.

I hadn't meant to blurt any of this out. I wanted to keep my cards close to my chest, but once I got started I couldn't contain myself. "I suppose I'll also mention our culture of fairness and respect toward teachers."

I watched a vein in Brodie's temple throb as she tried to work out the best way to deal with this unexpected revelation: that while I was sitting there with them, silent and smiling, I was thinking all the time, and I was judging them.

Chelsea looked incensed; two red patches appeared on her cheeks, like sunburn.

But Brodie simply turned to me and said, "Lucy, you're just going to be wasting your time, when you could really be impressing the audience with the story of your own achievements."

They thought I was like them, and that I would want to use every opportunity to show off.

I did not reply. Usually my silence rendered me invisible, but this time the quiet was ominous because it was a silence I had caused deliberately.

"The teachers must think you're so innocent, Lucy Lam, with your sad, big brown eyes," hissed Chelsea. "But we know. We know what you're like. You may look timid, but you're devious."

Then I knew. I knew that the Cabinet did not want me messing things up for them. Next year we would be at the senior campus, and they wanted to maintain their unassailable Unholy Trinity, their position at the top. Because it appeared to the teachers, and especially to Mrs. Grey, that they had taken me under their wing, whatever I said would be a reflection of their work.

They had to keep me in line. They were the ones who would be held responsible for me, the ones whose duty it was to infuse me with the Laurinda spirit. Being a Laurinda young lady was all about controlling your impulses when it was beneficial to you. You moved by stealth, and maintained clean nails.

I stood up. "Excuse me," I said. "I've got to go."

"Where?" demanded Brodie.

"To the bathroom."

"No!" shouted Chelsea.

If they weren't deadly serious, this would have been hilarious—just like the time they tormented Ms. Vanderwerp and then told me to wet my pants rather than leave the room.

"You've got to be kidding," I said, and this time I really did leave.

★　★　★

Most of the bathrooms at Laurinda were disgusting. There was a visitors' bathroom in the main building that had gleaming white tiles and lavender hand soap in a pump, but the ones we used had stone walls, concrete floors, 1950s stainless steel sinks, and mirrors so old that they were dark at the edges.

There were four toilets in the Year Ten bathroom, but the lock of the last stall didn't work. Often that was the cleanest toilet, if you didn't mind leaning forward to hold the door closed with your fingertips while sitting down to do your business. If there was no one else in the room, I always used that stall.

When I walked in and saw that it was occupied, I peered into each of the other three stalls. Two of the toilets were coated with thick, smeary dark brown crap on the sides of the bowls, and the third had a disgusting coiled floater on top of the water. This was a new low even for Laurinda.

Trisha MacMahon was standing at the sink, washing her hands, so I told her how much I enjoyed her music.

"Thanks," she replied. "Can't believe how often they want me back! Can't believe how disgusting these toilets are either. I've come in twice in half an hour but the last one's never free." She bounced out of the bathroom but I decided to wait.

About three minutes later, who should skulk in but the Cabinet. I opened my mouth to say something but Brodie put a finger to her lips. She and Amber glanced at the occupied stall and exchanged a look, then Amber nodded.

Chelsea watched this wordless communication. There was glee in her eyes as she readied herself at the sink in front of the closed stall's door. Then she swung her body around and gave he broken door a swift and sharp and forceful kick—

a very hard one—and then came a sound I would never forget, a sound like when you snap apart a cooked chicken wing.

It all happened so fast and so silently that I had no time to warn whoever was in there. I expected a snap like that would be accompanied by a monstrous howl, but all we heard was one "Ahhhhhhh," one long weeping "Eeeeee," and very shallow and fast breathing followed by more whimpering.

Inside the stall, with her green cotton underpants still around her knees, was Nadia Pinto—Nadia of the wrong socks and severe psoriasis. She was clutching her left hand with her right, and mewing like a cat hit by a car, her eyes and nose and mouth leaking.

Although there was no blood, I could see that there was something very, very wrong with Nadia's fingers and wrist.

"Oh my God," cried Brodie in genuine dismay. "Oh my God!"

"What the—?" Chelsea was also incredulous, but I didn't know that she had any right to be. She knew someone was behind that door, she also knew the door had a broken lock, and she was the one who had kicked it in.

Brodie dashed over to Nadia. "Oh, oh. Oh, we're sooo sorry," she cried. "Oh, no. Oh, no. Can you get up?"

Tearfully and obediently, Nadia stood up. I watched as Brodie pulled up Nadia's green cotton underpants for her, all the while murmuring, "Oh, we're so sorry. We need to get you to the hospital." I watched as Brodie walked Nadia out of the bathroom, a hand on her shoulder holding her close, leading her to the school office.

News like this travels fast, and soon gawkers were milling outside the office, so much so that they were later told off for obstructing the ambulance. When it arrived, Brodie was still by Nadia's side, her protector, hissing at anyone who got too near. She climbed in the back with Nadia.

As it drove off, I saw Brodie peering at us from the back window. Tears were streaming down her face.

Less than a week later, all four of us—Brodie, Chelsea, Amber and me—were summoned to the school conference room. We sat on one side of the table, while on the other side sat Nadia Pinto, her mum and dad, and Mrs. Grey.

"We need to understand why this happened," explained Mr. Pinto, a rotund man with a patient air about him. He looked accustomed to rooms such as this one, with its antique carpet, oval mahogany table and glass cabinets.

"We just didn't know," began Amber. "Sometimes the stall doors swing shut by themselves when there's no one inside."

"Yes," conceded Mrs. Grey. "They're all designed like that."

"We had all come in at the same time," explained Chelsea. "All the doors were closed, and the only way you can tell whether a stall is occupied or not is by the little green VACANT sign. Well, all the signs said VACANT. We had no idea that the lock was broken, or that Nadia was inside."

Brodie put her head in her hands. "We're so sorry. I pushed the door open—I didn't know Nadia's hand was there." She started to weep softly. "It wasn't even that hard a push, but the door jerks open so violently, and Year Eights have such little hands and . . . oh God . . ." Brodie couldn't continue because she was so devastated. "I'm so sorry. I wish it had been my hand."

The Pintos looked at each other. "Don't be like that," offered Mr. Pinto gently, "it wasn't your fault."

Mrs. Pinto reached over and patted Brodie's hand. "You stayed with our daughter for hours, and then came back to visit her the next day too."

Mrs. Grey made no interjections, but her eyes bored into us the whole time.

Only Nadia seemed unfussed by the whole thing. Her hand was bandaged up. She had two broken fingers and a broken wrist, but they would heal just fine, the doctors had assured her. In fact, she seemed positively *happy* about the whole experience. "Brodie was so kind to me," Nadia said. "She held my other hand all the way in the ambulance."

"Mrs. Grey, thank you for meeting with us," concluded Mr. Pinto. "We were worried that perhaps there was something Nadia was not telling us. You know, like bullying or some such thing. She's such a quiet girl, and sometimes we can't tell these things. But it appears this was all an accident. We're sorry for taking up so much of your time."

Then he turned to us. "We know it was an accident," he said. "We're glad that you responsible older girls have explained what happened and are taking such good care of our daughter."

Nadia looked at me and smiled. I supposed she recognized me from our meeting outside Mrs. Grey's office, when I'd offered her vague words of comfort. I knew she trusted me. She felt like we were on her side, and that this fortunate "accident" had aligned her stars with those of the glorious Cabinet.

I smiled back, tight-lipped, guilt-ridden.

At lunchtime, the Cabinet got the keys to one of the sound-proof music rooms, and we met there. When the door was closed, Brodie let rip. "Damn it, Amber! I can't believe we had to talk to the Growler about this. We weren't meant to get the Indian girl!" she shouted. "I thought you said she was still in there!"

"But I saw her go in!" cried Amber. "I saw her walk into the bathroom!"

Suddenly it all made sense. I'd been a bit slow on the up-take, but it struck me exactly *who* they had intended to get.

"Trisha MacMahon walked straight back out again," I told them. "She was put off by the crap you smeared all over the toilets, so she just washed her hands and left."

"Why didn't you bloody *tell us* that?" cried Chelsea.

"Because you didn't tell me what you were going to do!" I retorted, and that shut them up.

"Lucy," said Brodie in an even voice—she had calmed down now—"we did not want to get you involved in this, you understand."

"Yeah, even though *she* started the whole thing," muttered Chelsea.

"Oh yeah?" I was mad now. "How did I start it? By clapping loudly?"

"Yes, you created a megalomaniac who thinks she's top shit," spat Chelsea.

"People like her music at assembly! Where is the crime in that?"

"There are quotas," explained Brodie. "In a place like this, there must be quotas. And Trisha is demonstrating that it's okay to hog the quotas. You of all people, Lucy, should understand that there are finite places, and we believe in equal access. It's the very reason you're here at Laurinda."

"You make no sense," I said. "What is this crap?"

"Those girls," sighed Amber, talking to me as though I was really, really slow, "those girls are like dumb animals. Did you see the way that stupid Indian girl looked at us?"

I didn't bother to correct her about Nadia's ethnicity, because there was no point.

"They are like dumb animals who will stomp their feet at any bull, and with enough stomping you get a stampede." Chelsea's metaphors were getting even stranger. "Now, tiny Lucy Lamby, do you want to be crushed in this wild stampede?"

There was nothing more to say, but Chelsea took my silence as assent and turned toward Brodie. "Good one today, Brode. That weeping shit really got us out of trouble with the popadam's parents."

"Screw you, Chelsea!" Brodie suddenly shouted, livid with rage that her tears might be seen as fake. "Don't you understand anything?"

Chelsea's mouth was open wide. She had no idea what was going on.

"Damn it, Chelsea, we're not *racist*!"

"I'm not made for this school," I told my father that evening after dinner, when Mum went back into the garage. "I want to go back to Christ Our Savior."

"What do you mean?" he asked, alarmed. "Are you failing?"

"No!"

"Are you being bullied?"

"No."

"Then what's wrong? Are they going to cut your scholarship?"

Here was my trump card. "Maybe," I answered, in a tone that implied it was the school's decision and no fault of mine.

Now my father was really alarmed. "But why?"

"I'm not involved enough. I don't do any sports or drama or play an instrument."

"Ridiculous. You are involved academically, and that's what counts."

I could not tell my father I was no longer one of the top students. "They feel I am not part of the community."

"What can we do to fix that?" my father asked. "What sport would you like to play? What activities can you join? Do you want to learn an extra hobby?"

"No."

"You're not doing much to help yourself." He shook his head sadly.

He wasn't one of those fathers who didn't mind if their daughters didn't care about school as long as they knew how to boil a good pot of rice. No, he wanted me to make something of myself. I remembered how once, when I was in elementary school, one of his factory friends had come over and accidentally spilled a cup of coffee on my homework. That evening my father copied out all three pages of the handout in his best calligraphy so I could fill in the blanks.

I also remembered how he used to make me work through my school readers with him not once but three times every evening.

"I'm not fitting in," I confessed.

"Nonsense. What about that friend of yours, Amber? You're always going to her house after school. It looks like you're making friends very well."

"Those girls only like me because I don't talk that much."

It was true. I was tolerable to them because I never expressed my opinions, so I always seemed to reflect their best selves back to them. I suppose I made them feel magnanimous, kind and tolerant.

"Why do you care so much about your classmates anyway?" Dad asked. "It's not like you will see most of these people again once you finish school. When you are successful, they will be the ones at your doorstep."

I almost laughed, imagining the Cabinet sitting on the stoop of my future house, waiting for me as I returned from my work as a bank relationships adviser or something like that, which only my parents and the good people of Stanley would think was impressive.

I cared because I saw the Cabinet every single day, and when you are fifteen, a year is longer than when you are twenty-five or thirty-five, and the future is stretched out like an unknowable measuring tape.

"You have a scholarship here," railed my father, as I knew he would. "There is no opting out of it. The reason you feel like you're not doing so well is because the standard is a lot higher at this school. But that's not a bad thing—it's a good thing, an excellent thing."

Yeah, yeah, I thought. Confucius says, hang around those better than you because you will better yourself.

I knew I was being ungrateful for my good fortune, and I was sorry I had ever mentioned my dissatisfaction to my father. The truth was that I could not escape my circumstances, nor did I really expect him to allow me to change them.

I decided I wasn't going to hang around with the Cabinet anymore.

It wasn't a difficult decision, Linh, because if I continued to spend time with them I knew I would go mad. Also, although I knew you were still angry with me, I had the feeling you might come around. My worst fear was that I might lose you entirely. The school was driving me insane, and it had nothing to do with the difficulty of the work. It was the other stuff I couldn't bear—the way the place could swallow you whole if you let it.

The Cabinet fascinated me in the way that movie characters did. Their lives didn't seem quite real—*they* didn't seem quite real. I often felt as though I was on the set of a TV show, where the grouting on the tiles was still ivory because no one actually lived there. The grout around Amber's bathroom floor tiles was perfectly white, I recalled as I was cleaning ours at home with a toothbrush. A few days later it would be gray again, and in a few weeks it would be black. It was as if grime attached itself only to certain types of people, and once you were marked, you were marked for life.

I had become self-conscious about things that never

bothered me before. The way my teeth were slightly yellow. How my nylon socks lost their elasticity at the top after a term of washing. And just my general grossness, the way I must have smelled. It got to the point where if I needed to go to the bathroom at school, I would wait until the whole room was empty, then I would wet two paper towels in the sink with warm water and soap, and take them to the stall to clean myself. I knew that if I hung around these girls for much longer, I would also start worrying about getting fat. There was already enough wrong with me that I didn't have room for any more insecurities.

In the end, leaving the Cabinet was easier than I had expected it to be. I just stopped going to their corner of the school yard and went to the library instead. Never big on confrontation or closure, I did to them exactly what I had done to Katie.

Katie and Siobhan were close now, the sort of closeness where they whacked each other playfully with their books, shared lunches and made plans to visit Katie's farm in Mallah over the holidays. I saw them and felt a familiar ache in my chest, Linh, an ache the exact shape of you.

I wasn't afraid of being alone, but I was afraid of what people would think about my solitary state. People, even well-intentioned people, were always trying to take away our quiet little successes and joys and replace them with big, overarching fears. At this school, the worst thing was trying to rise above the limits set for you by the minds of others. Each girl was an island of her own dreams and insecurities, thoughts that made us different in a deeper way than the differences of musical tastes, clothes or even culture. Thoughts about the best way to be stoic, how to live with very little control in life, how to make the most of a miserable time doing something that you were supposed to love. And if people thought that fifteen-year-old girls never thought about these sorts of things, it was only because we didn't have the words to express them.

We talked all the time, but we hadn't yet learned the words to link thoughts and ideas with any depth of feeling, because we didn't really talk to adults. We talked only to each other. And within this little world, we imprisoned one another. You could be anyone you wanted, Linh—until you were judged and held captive by everyone else's thoughts. Nothing has a stronger hold over a girl than the fear of the thoughts of her peers—thoughts that change five times in a day. No wonder things are so complicated with teenagers.

So I went back to the library and to flicking through old yearbooks. This time I started at the end of each book, because that's where all the extracurricular activities were—the photos of Laurinda girls and Auburn boys engaged in debating, drama, sports and music. I was searching for one specific face.

And there he was, in a photo from Year Seven, in the junior orchestra. He played the trumpet. He had the same gap between his front teeth, and the same straw-colored hair. He was chubby and looked like the awkward twelve-year-old he was. He looked exactly the same in the next photo in Year Eight, but things had changed by Year Nine. He'd grown vertically and lost his festive plumpness. He looked dignified with his trumpet against his chest and the school colors sewn on his blazer pocket.

Knowing that Richard the Lionheart—and presumably his allies—understood the undercurrents of our schools as I did made me feel less alone. I imagined the two of us standing strong against the slings and arrows of outrageous wealth. I imagined us forming a secret pact, a duo that wrote about the bizarre things we witnessed at school. We would meet up once a week at the Sunray Public Library to exchange notes. We would fall in love as we wrote a great satirical novel together about private colleges, won over by each other's wit.

We would get married; Harshan and Anton could be his groomsmen, and Yvonne and Ivy would be my bridesmaids. The Lamb could be the ring bearer. We'd have our reception at the Mirabella Center in Sunray because they served crab claws. He would sell his dad's shoe store when his dad retired, and we would use the money to start a French café in a posh suburb, filling the walls with shelves of books.

Then I stopped, realizing how stupid my fantasies were.

I remembered something Richard had said: "My dad thought he was sending me to *Dead Poets Society.*"

Richard had a group of friends. He talked to everyone. He was like Katie—not popular, but he probably had a happy home life and a close-knit community in the outer suburbs of Melbourne near the farming properties. He didn't need school to validate him. That's why he could laugh when the boys made fun of his dad's shoe shop. He was lower middle class, but he wasn't ashamed of it, as much as the other boys ridiculed him.

I wasn't going to do anything about this crush. I wasn't going to find him and ask him out to a movie, or do any of the things that seemed so simple and easy on TV. I wasn't even sure how to pursue a friendship with a boy. But Richard and his allies had reminded me I was funny and daring, and could even be all the things you were, Linh. So that evening, after I'd put the Lamb to bed, I sat down in the garage to write my conference speech, calmed by the familiar hammering of my mother's sewing machine.

When helping me with my first politics essay, Mr. Sinclair had advised me to get to the heart of the matter and talk about what was important. I began writing.

Laurinda has taught me that if something is not right, then you have the power to change it.

Laurinda has taught me that you should be nice to everyone.

Laurinda has given me opportunities to be discerning.

Those three lines were a good start.

That first day back in the library, I'd kept thinking the Cabinet would be looking for me—that they would catch me in the act of searching for the Lionheart. I felt like a fugitive and collected a couple of heavy history books as an alibi. On the second day, there was still no sign of them. By the third day, I knew they had given up on me.

I was no great loss, after all. The strangest thing was that we had both English, history and politics together. They could have asked me then why I was no longer joining them, but they didn't. They had tried their best, they could say to Mrs. Grey. And now they were free to talk about all the clandestine business they could not talk about in my presence.

I felt a great relief.

Then, on the fourth day, they came to get me.

"Lucy! So there you are!" said Brodie. "Have you been here for the past three days? What have you been doing?"

"Studying."

"Oh, you dweeb," said Amber playfully. "Come back and join us."

"It's okay. I've really got to catch up on some work."

"Did we say something to upset you?"

"No." Everything you do pisses me off, I wanted to tell her.

"We've been so worried that we've done something to upset you. We thought you might be mad at us."

I was furious at them, but I just wanted to be left alone. "I'm studying," I said. "I don't want to fall behind."

They knew I was lying. "We could help you," suggested Amber.

Girls don't have to say nasty things to convey them. Even two simple, benign words—words generally reserved for reassurance—can be flung low and hard like dried-up cow dung. "I'm fine."

There was a silence. "Well, we're hurt that you won't open up to us about what's wrong," said Brodie. "And something is clearly the matter. But we're always here if you need our help. We're still your friends, Lucy."

And with this magnanimity, and a pat on my shoulder, they walked out of the library. But that didn't mean they left me alone. In the next few days they became an overzealous pastoral care tag team, bugging me at every turn and corner.

As a general rule, teenage girls never, ever see solitude as a choice. Katie and Gina were prime examples. They might clutch copies of *The Bell Jar* to their hearts, but they could not imagine that a girl could be by herself and truly *not care* about being by herself. They saw this *not caring* as the sign of a deep sickness. This was why, a week later, Mrs. Leslie came looking for me. "Lucy," she said, "could we perhaps have a little chat?"

I knew the Cabinet had set her up. She led me to the pastoral care room, which to me sounded like a place for sick farmyard animals. When we were both seated, she told me that Amber had said she was concerned for my welfare. "Amber tells me that you no longer want to be her friend."

What was this, kindergarten? "That's not true," I said. I felt sorry for Mrs. Leslie.

"She says that you've been sitting by yourself all week in the library. Is that true?"

I didn't say anything.

"I understand that you might be depressed, Lucy."

"What do you mean, depressed?"

"Perhaps something is the matter at home and you are not telling anyone about it?"

"No." I knew I sounded defensive.

"What is happening at home, Lucy?"

"What did Amber say was happening at home with me, miss?"

"Nothing. She's just worried that there might be concerning things going on at home."

"Like what?"

"We don't know!" cried Mrs. Leslie. "That's for you to tell us, because nothing seems to be the matter at school and yet you've suddenly decided to leave your friends and spend all your lunchtimes in the library again."

"I'm sorry, miss." I really was, because Mrs. Leslie cared

243

about me, and she genuinely believed my absence was a great loss to her daughter.

I began to cry—but not because I had upset Mrs. Leslie, or because I was sad about anything. I was crying out of frustration, frustration that I could not be left alone, that no girl at this school could possibly be allowed some space to breathe and sort out her own thoughts. Not all groups were created equal; I knew that. But I had been stupid enough to believe that my presence or absence would not make any difference.

I was also crying because I understood now that no one ever left the Cabinet of her own volition, and that the three of them weren't going to let it go. There would be consequences.

"Child, the doorbell," my mother said to me over the machine-gun hammering of her sewing machine. It was a warm Monday afternoon, and I'd been home from school for an hour.

"I didn't hear anything."

"It rang." Despite being surrounded by noise all day, my mother had supersensitive hearing.

I only had time to grab the Lamb's sippy cup and hoist him onto my hip when the doorbell rang again. Stupid, impatient Sokkha, I sighed. I went back inside the house and opened the door.

Standing there was Brodie, still in her school uniform.

And standing behind her was Sokkha.

They must have arrived at the same time, and for a moment I wondered if he had offered her a lift in his white van. That would have been hilarious, Brodie's white face peering from the back, her hands outstretched to ward off cascading rolls of material as the van swerved down our street.

I saw a look of extreme nervousness in Brodie's eyes. Sokkha was frightening if you weren't used to him, and his finger was still bandaged up. He was finishing off a cigarette, and his eyes were bloodshot—he looked like he'd had a late night. Sokkha didn't just deliver. He worked too, when there was work to finish.

By this time my mother had come to the front door, running a hand through her uncombed hair. In a bright blue Esprit T-shirt and, to my embarrassment, fluorescent orange Target tracksuit pants, she looked as if she had just crawled out of bed in the middle of a long and lingering illness. The bags beneath her eyes were big enough to carry groceries in, and her skin was the color of uncooked pastry. She put a hand to her brow like a sailor looking out to sea. This was probably the first time today that my mother had seen sunlight.

She peered at Brodie, then noticed Sokkha. "Ah, there you are, brother."

He fished out of the breast pocket of his green-and-red batik shirt a crumpled white envelope. He handed it to her; a hundred-dollar note was showing through its plastic window.

"Take your friend inside," my mother instructed me. "I'm going to count the money."

Brodie had no idea what was going on. I had no idea why she was here, and I really didn't want her to see the inside of our house.

"Go!" my mother hissed, so I really had no choice.

Brodie followed me inside, taking in the peeling wallpaper, the boxes everywhere, our mismatched couches and the lingering smell of baby pee and mold.

"How did you get here?" I asked as she sat down on the couch.

"I caught a cab."

"You what? From the school?" The trip must have cost her seventy bucks.

What would Brodie have seen through the windows of the taxi? I wondered. The used car sale yards that had bunting around their perimeters, and signs declaring CHO THUE XUE CAR RENTAL $11 A DAY. The overgrown hedges, the shopping carts on lawns. Instead of a book library, Stanley had a tool library, for men to go and build things or smash things. "So they don't smash their wives," my father once joked.

The front yards of Stanley were hives of masculine activity—pieces of metal and scrap automobile parts, half-completed projects and rusty bits of machinery, like Thomas Edison's junk pile in an alternate universe where nothing would ever succeed despite a hundred thousand years of trial and error, mostly error. These rested in relative peace alongside faded plastic swing sets that had not been used for a decade.

"Who's that?" Brodie asked, pointing to a photograph on our wall.

"Oh, that's my great-uncle Hung. My mum's dad's older brother."

"He's hot."

At a time like this, and in a house like mine, she was still playing the we-are-connected game—and this time we were connected through our nonracist appraisal of the hotness of the male species. If Yvonne had come over and done the same thing, I wouldn't have minded, but this was Brodie. She'd fixed on the only thing she found redeemable, the only thing of beauty in our house, a photo of my handsome uncle.

"He died during the war," I added, expecting to see the expression on her face change, but it didn't.

"My great-grandfather died during the war too," she said. "World War II."

"Would you like a drink?" I asked, hoping that she would politely decline; all I could offer her was my mum's Nescafé.

"No, thanks."

"Want to hold the Lamb?"

"Pardon?"

I held the Lamb out in front of me.

"No, thanks." She didn't even make the characteristic oh-he's-so-cute murmurs most girls did when faced with a baby, no matter how ugly the kid was. She was beginning to freak me out.

"Lucy, we are concerned about you. You left without a word. You won't tell Mrs. Leslie what's wrong. You won't talk to anyone. You've withdrawn into yourself. You don't even want to be around your friends anymore."

So she had come all this way because she wanted me back in the Cabinet? It was hard to believe. "I'm sorry," I lied.

"We care about you, Lucy. If something is the matter, you should let us know. If you're depressed, don't lock us out."

"But I'm not depressed."

Brodie avoided my eyes and looked around the room. No wonder you're depressed, I bet she was thinking. You live here. You're looking after that runt of a baby.

"I just needed some time to myself."

"I understand," said Brodie. "But we're always here to help."

"Thanks."

"Gah!" yelled the Lamb out of the blue, and Brodie jumped. I could tell she didn't like the way he was watching her, and I knew that he would keep gazing at her in a squirm-inducing way. The Lamb didn't blink very often, and his eyes were

248

such a dark brown that in the dim light of our living room you could not tell where the iris ended and the pupil began.

He was staring at her teeth. He had never seen braces before.

My mother came back with her wad of money. She looked at us, me sunk into the back of the couch with the Lamb and Brodie perched on the edge. Brodie stood up when she saw my mother. She walked over and extended a hand, turning on her high-wattage smile. "Hello, Mrs. Lam, very pleased to meet you."

My mother looked bewildered. She transferred her crushed envelope from one hand to the other and took Brodie's hand limply. "'Allo." Then, "You eat?"

"Pardon?"

"My mum asked if you'd like to eat something."

"No, thank you, Mrs. Lam," Brodie said, still smiling. "I ate something before I came."

"Okay," said my mum. By then she had exhausted her store of English words, so she turned to me and said, "I'm going back to work. Don't let that girl get anywhere near the garage, you hear me?"

"Yes, Ma." It was funny, the hushed tones my mother used to speak about her work. She lived in constant fear of being reported to the authorities for the illegal sewing she was doing.

When my mother left, Brodie asked, "What was your mother whispering about?"

"Nothing." It was none of her business.

"What was that in her hand?" she asked.

"None of your business."

"Gah!" yelled the Lamb again, and this time he pointed at Brodie. I wanted to kiss his little marshmallow cheek, but then she would have thought that I had set him up. He just wanted to see the metal machinery in her mouth.

"Also, about the talk you are going to give at the University of Melbourne," Brodie began, and at last I understood why she was here. She wanted me safely locked away before I could do any damage to their reputation.

"So you came to talk to me about my speech?"

"No! I came because we are concerned about you."

I sighed. "I don't give a stuff about the stupid talk." At that moment I really wished that Tully had won the scholarship instead of me.

"Exactly," persisted Brodie. "That's the reason I'm here. Because you don't care enough, Lucy Lam."

I couldn't believe that Brodie—thin-nostriled, hawk-eyed Brodie, sitting there in the middle of my living room—was asking me to worry myself catatonic over a ten-minute appearance at a university. All the carefully cultivated politeness was gone from her face. She could not help herself.

"I appreciate your efforts, Brodie," I told her. "But I really don't need your help. I've got my conference talk under control."

"Do you?" she asked.

"Yes."

"Can I see it?"

"What?"

"Your talk."

"What are you, my teacher?"

"From day one we've taken you under our wing, Lucy Lam, and you throw it all back in our faces. We try to help

250

you fit in, and you refuse to cooperate. The Growler specifi-
cally asked Amber, Chelsea and me to look after you when
you were moved into our English class."

Liar, I thought; it was Mrs. Leslie who had plucked me
from solitude and established me in Amber's life. I had become their white ladies' burden. Now, whatever I did wrong
reflected badly on them. They'd offered help and I'd refused
it. But they did not realize that I did not need Laurinda. Everything I loved was in this house, in two rooms.

"This is impossible!" sighed Brodie, perhaps because I did
not seem to her to be feeling enough guilt. "I'm sorry we
even tried, Lucy." Even her sighs were exaggerated gestures
stolen straight from American TV.

Suddenly there was a splashing sound from our kitchen,
then an enormous thump that shook the floor of our house.

"What was that?"

"Mum just killed a fish."

"What the—"

"That's what we're having for dinner. She makes tasty fish
with ginger and coriander. Come and see, if you like. She'll
be gutting it now."

Brodie gave me a look, as if I was deliberately trying to disgust her—which, admittedly, I was. Yesterday, Mum and Dad
had driven to the Sunray market, and they'd returned with a
bucket containing the thrashing fish.

"Well, I'd better not interrupt your dinner, then." Brodie
stood up.

"How are you going to get home?"

"I'll call a taxi."

"Let me get our phone for you."

"No, it's all right." And from the front of her schoolbag she

251

pulled out her phone. The only people in Stanley I had seen with that brand were businessmen and builders.

My father arrived home and saw Brodie standing in the corner of our living room. After she hung up, she smiled at him and apologized for being on the phone.

"Lucy," Dad scolded, "why did you let your friend waste money calling from her father's phone? She could have used ours."

"That's all right, Mr. Lam," she said. "It was a short call. I was just booking a taxi."

"A taxi? Don't be ridiculous—we'll take you home."

My father was the one being ridiculous, I thought. He didn't even know where she lived.

"Lucy, how could you let your friend catch a taxi?" my father said accusingly, as if I had stolen the umbrella of a frail old lady on a day pummeling with hail.

"No, really, it's all right, Mr. Lam. You're having dinner soon. I don't want to disturb your family."

"Nonsense. Join us for dinner! Lucy, lay down the newspapers."

I prayed that Brodie would leave before she had time to realize our environmentally friendly choice of dining ware.

"No, really, Mr. Lam, that is very kind of you, but my parents expect me home for dinner." She probably thought we were going to eat her and that the newspapers were to line the floor to clean up the evidence.

After her taxi left, my father turned to me. *"Wah!"* he exclaimed. "Extraordinary! That friend of yours takes taxis by herself."

My encounter with Brodie showed me that there was something obscene about this school's idea that doing good somehow had to *feel* good too. I thought about the Laurindans and their charity events where they gained makeovers or lipsticks, and their afternoon teas with guest speakers who were missing arms or legs or who were of a color rare in these quarters. These events fostered a feeling of goodwill they could control, but Brodie had served herself a slice of our life and felt it too gritty to digest.

Meanwhile, in politics we were studying the maiden speech of a politician who'd announced that Australia was in danger of being "swamped" by Asians. "They have their own culture and religion, form ghettos and don't assimilate," she had declared, and I heard an echo of what was happening to me at Laurinda. I was regressing back to my ghetto of one and not assimilating, even though the Cabinet had extended such a gracious hand to me.

And Mr. Sinclair. Over the course of the year, Mr. Sinclair had changed. No longer did he wear his smart suit jackets. He came to school in a shirt and navy trousers, sometimes even an ugly green cardigan with wooden buttons. He was dressing like an old man. And he was teaching straight out of books. *Introduction to the Three Levels of Government. The Federal Judicial System. The Small Claims Tribunal.*

Admittedly, now that he was giving us the nuts and bolts, I was learning more about our political system. No longer could the Cabinet monopolize the class. But I was also saddened, because now Mr. Sinclair was teaching as if he were driving a car along a very narrow road, getting to the destination as quickly as possible. No more taking the scenic route.

One afternoon at school, Amber found me. "I need to talk to you, Lucy," she said.

"What about?"

"I need to talk to you in private."

"No, you can say it in front of other people." I crossed my arms in front of my chest. I was having none of this, and I knew the other girls were interested in what was happening. They were always interested when the Cabinet cornered someone.

"Please," pleaded Amber.

We walked toward the back of the bathroom.

"Lucy, I know Brodie came to your house to ask you not to do something."

I stayed silent.

"The truth is, Brodie's in a bit of trouble with Mrs. Grey."

Ooh, it was "Mrs. Grey" now, I thought. This was interesting news.

"It has to do with her chapel speech, and then Nadia Pinto. Mrs. Grey believes Brodie has crossed some sort of line."

Brodie has always crossed lines, I thought bitterly. The

only difference this time was that while the line was being sprayed, the paint had streaked across the pointy tips of Mrs. Grey's plum leather pumps. And for the first time, Mrs. Grey was worried.

"That's why Brodie came over to your house, Lucy. I told her it was a bad idea and that you were a very private person. But you know Brodie. She does what she wants. I know she came to shut you up, Lucy," she told me, "and I know you don't like her. And if you don't shut up, it makes her look bad."

"Look bad?" I asked in mock innocence.

"It will look like she orchestrated the whole thing to rub it in that the school has no control over anything that happens in the classrooms, bathrooms or . . . how the school is represented to others." Amber was trying to sound artless, but I knew she was choosing her words very carefully.

"I'm sorry, Amber. I don't understand what you're getting at."

"Brodie was the one who put your name forward for the Equity in Education conference," she confessed.

"Why would she do that?"

Brodie never gave anyone else an opportunity unless there was some direct benefit to the Cabinet. After her chapel talk, she had the students eating out of her hand, but that was precisely the problem: the administration could see that the Cabinet was now growing far too influential. Although Mrs. Grey was probably relieved that the unstable Ms. Vanderwerp was gone, Brodie's talk had been a direct demonstration of the Cabinet's power—and Brodie had relished it a little too much for Mrs. Grey's liking.

The triangle—the most stable of geometric shapes, with

its wide support base and pointed tip—now needed one last element: the Cabinet needed to be seen as the *good* girls they thought they were. They wanted to show that not only were they mentoring the less fortunate girls here, but they were also concerned about sustaining the school's public image. At Christ Our Savior, you helped maintain the school's reputation by offering your seat on the bus to the elderly. Here at Laurinda, things were infinitely more complicated.

Amber took a deep breath and then blurted out, "I don't think you should listen to what Brodie says anyway."

I looked at Amber. Beautiful, cowardly Amber. It had taken all her courage to say that to me. But this was not the real revelation. The real revelation was that Brodie had believed I was malleable enough to do her bidding—and that she thought my appearance at the university conference would change Mrs. Grey's belief that the Cabinet was becoming a threat to the school's unity.

"Amber," I said, "do you really think I would get up in front of the academics and professors and principals of high schools and read a speech about how fifteen-year-old girls torment teachers with tampons and break little girls' hands? What kind of idiot do you think I am? I'm on a scholarship here."

"Lucy, I know you wouldn't do that," Amber said, although I knew this was news to her. "But if you'd like, my mum could help you. I know you've never done this sort of thing before."

"Do you expect me to thank you?"

"Pardon?"

"To thank you, Amber," I repeated like a speech pathologist. "Should I be thanking you for telling me to be myself?"

"What?"

"Would you like me to bow, like Harshan did?"

Her eyes became unfriendly. "Don't forget what my mum's done for you, Lucy Lam."

"What does that mean, Amber Leslie?"

"It means be careful what you say."

"You wanted me to hang around with you because I make you look better," I blurted out. This had never occurred to me before because it was a colossally immodest idea, but the moment I said it, I knew it was true.

Amber laughed. No one had ever said anything like that to a Cabinet member before.

"I make you guys look like you're not vicious. I make you look charitable. I'm like your pet, and you want me to be forever grateful for whatever scraps you throw my way." Well, Emma Woodhouse, handsome, clever and rich, I was thinking, I'm not going to be your Harriet Smith anymore. "It's the truth," I told her, and walked away.

Still the Cabinet would not leave me alone.

Since Brodie's visit to my home, my life had suddenly become very interesting to them. It was as if an innocuous and uninteresting girl suddenly turned out to be an orphan, or to have cancer, or to have a secret life as an underage escort. For others, there was the vicarious thrill of being associated with her, but also the need to be careful, to make sure they didn't get too close, lest her sadness or sickness or depression rub off on them.

"What exactly does your mum do?" Brodie asked me the next day when I was pulling my bag out of my locker, getting ready to go home. The rest of the Cabinet was with her.

I had stayed behind to photocopy a couple of pages out of the yearbook without anyone seeing. I quickly shoved the pages into my bag.

"You were at my house—you could have asked her yourself."

"She doesn't speak English."

"Why does it matter what my mother does, Brodie? That's a personal question. What if I asked you what your mum does?" I retorted.

"She's a professor of management at Monash University. If you asked, I'd tell you," she explained reasonably. "That's what friends do. They talk openly about things like this because it's no big deal. Unless, of course, it is for *you*."

That was unfair. None of the trio had been remotely interested in what my parents did until now.

"Mum works."

"Yes, but doing what exactly?"

"She sews."

"Well, why wasn't she at work when I came over?"

"She works from home."

"Yeah?"

"Yes."

"Amber told us that yesterday you were being evasive with her. We just want to make sure we don't end up associating with shady people."

"What does that mean?"

"You should know."

Rage was building up in me. And suddenly I felt as if you, Linh, were standing behind me, pushing me to be who I was before.

"What the hell are you talking about?"

"You know what I'm talking about. Who was that pimp guy I saw outside your house?"

She knew how to get to me. It was the most insidious, vilest thing anyone had said about my family. I hated these slutty virgins who knew how to aim prurience like a poisoned arrow, directly where it hurt most.

My hands were shaking. I wanted to spit in her face, pull her hair. I wanted to slap her senseless.

Instead, I replied, "He's the heroin dealer, you moron. He was giving my mother money for the shit. His name is Sokkha, and if you insult my mum again he'll kick you so far that by the time you stop rolling, your clothes will be out of fashion."

I didn't need to punch her in the face. This girl, who calculated the effect of every word she uttered, finally understood that there was nothing random about either my speech or my silence.

"I wasn't saying anything!" Brodie protested. "I was just asking what your mum did."

"But you think I'm dodgy."

To reply in the most barbed way she could, Brodie said nothing.

I doubted that the Cabinet really believed we dealt drugs, but now they were looking at me as if I were rabid. I walked out of the locker room and toward the oval, to the back entrance of the school, where my bus stop was. I could feel them creeping up from behind like a cheap and ill-fitting pair of underwear.

"How dare you!" railed Chelsea. "How dare you!"

I turned around. "You think I'm feral, but you broke a girl's hand!" I said. At least three dozen students were milling near the back gate of the school, waiting for their buses, but I didn't care. "You bullied a teacher out of the school! You do evil things and get away with it because you think you're untouchable!"

"No student can bully a teacher, Lucy," Brodie explained gently, as if I were a child. "She wasn't doing her job. She couldn't teach. If she could, none of that would have happened."

"She was nice!" I retorted—but I might as well have said, "She wears organic cotton socks!" or "She was clean!" for all the relevance it had.

"You're such a suck-up."

Then, as I neared the fence, I thought I was imagining things. But there you were, Linh, standing among the kilts and blazers of glory. Soon we were standing on the same side. I could barely believe it. I had not seen you for so long, but there you were: an ally in the face of adversity! My heart rose. I did not have to battle these bitches by myself. There was no time for introductions.

We turned to face the Cabinet.

These girls knew that bad words were only truly bad if saved for special occasions. If you used them often, they lost their power and became like any other word that expressed annoyance or surprise, the two expressions that now pinched Brodie's face—although, in her carefully controlled decorum, only her mouth twitched at the corners. Girls like her were always going to judge girls like you, and judge anything you said not by its content but by your Stanley accent—so you gave it to them, as loudly as you could.

"Fuck youse!"

Heads turned. Girls' jaws dropped. A few parents who were walking toward the gate looked on in horror. The after-school teacher, the poor soul vested with the task of delivering these girls safely to their buses, was Mr. Sinclair, and he was striding toward us.

"Excuse me?" Brodie sounded like an English teacher, and for a moment I thought that her shock was at your bad grammar.

"Youse are all sick. The whole fucking lot of youse."

Mr. Sinclair was now standing directly in front of us. "Young lady, we do not tolerate that kind of language here at this school!"

"I don't give a shit," you told him. "I'm not part of this school."

I did not go to school the next day.

I woke up and decided I didn't even want to get out of bed. My peripheral vision had shrunk, like the picture on our old television. When you switched off the black-and-white box, the image grew darker around the edges, and was then sucked into a little black hole at the center. I spent some time examining my own hands and fingernails, intrigued that such things belonged to me. Pink and brown and many-pronged, they looked like creatures of the sea, like tentacles without a head or body attached.

"What's wrong?" Mum asked when she realized I wasn't in the kitchen making myself a sandwich to take for lunch. "Are you sick?"

I didn't have a fever, I didn't have a headache, but my hands felt like they had turned to anemones, my feet to coral.

All year I had tried to keep a low profile, to just get on with things, and you'd ruined it in a few minutes. But you know what? I didn't care. I didn't care, because that day was the last time I would ever see you. I hadn't realized it then, in the excitement of the moment, but now it was sinking in.

I wish I could have told you how much talking and writing

to you meant to me all year. How you were my bullshit detector. How you listened and kept me true, even when I wanted to block my ears, because you had no filter between your thoughts and your mouth. How you were my best friend, and how it was only because of you that I never felt isolated or desperate to attach myself to anyone at Laurinda. But after our moment of triumph, you fled without even looking back, and I knew that even if I chased after you I would never catch up.

You were gone.

What had happened in the span of less than a year? I had gone from being the girl most likely to succeed, the well-liked all-rounder, the one who was smart but helpful and not crazy-competitive like Tully, the one who would make the factory workers of Stanley proud, the one with conviction, to the girl least likely to achieve, the one who would never join any club ever again, who withdrew into herself, who got herself kicked out of remedial English.

"Look at you beautiful girls," Sister Clarke used to say to us before every parent-teacher interview at Christ Our Savior. "Look at you all. So strong and full of life, despite the suffering your folks went through. Look at how smart you are, look at how creative you are, look at how kind you are. You are going to make your parents so proud." And then she would ask us to come along in the evening so we could translate for our parents.

Mr. Galloway had once said, half jokingly, to another teacher, "Watch this one! She's going to be prime minister one day," and I had believed him—not that I wanted to become prime minister, but he gave me the faith that if I harbored such a dream and worked hard enough, it would come true. I had believed that hard work would make anything a certainty.

Now I wasn't so sure.

I knew that the kind of life my father dreamed for me was small, so small, in comparison to the life of culture and art and politics and power that the Cabinet had ahead of them. There was a reason Stephanie Phoung had ended up working as an accountant above her parents' jewelry store in Sunray. It had probably started when she'd arrived at her new school and quickly learned to keep her head down and do her work, and to block out everything else.

I was as hardworking as ever, but it seemed that the other girls were playing a game whose rules they all knew—rules that they couldn't even explain to me, because they were born into them, which left me in the lurch. Not that I was ever a threat, because now I was a creature that slunk against walls, the ghost that walked through corridors, so invisible that I could not even make anyone else feel good. I lacked something in myself.

I lacked you, Linh. And you were never coming back.

It was not like losing my best friend. It was like losing my soul. You would have known what to say if you'd seen girls treat a teacher as badly as the Cabinet had treated Ms. Vanderwerp. You would have put them in their place. Yet the triumph of seeing the shock on the Cabinet's faces had quickly withdrawn into a snail-like shame. In the past, I would never have felt ashamed of you. I would have chased after you.

I felt as if someone was sitting on my neck, and it suddenly became hard to breathe. I knew now without a doubt that you were disgusted by my cowardice. I thrashed about in bed, and the feeling moved down to my chest. It was like someone was opening and closing a fist in there.

Oh, I'm a goner, I thought. I'm gone. I can't even get air in my lungs.

I sat up in bed, clamped my mouth shut and breathed through my nose. I waited until my hands stopped shaking and my breathing slowed. I had to get out of bed. I had to stop being so useless. I had to put my no-good, useless self to good use.

I called up the school to tell them I was sick.

"I'm sorry," said Mrs. Muscat in reception, "but we need your parents to confirm that."

I stood by the doorway of the garage, still in the old T-shirt and tracksuit pants I'd worn to bed, with the phone in my hand. "Hey, Mum, can you tell the school I'm sick?"

"You know I don't speak English."

"Just tell them I'm sick."

My mother released her foot from the pedal of the Singer and took the phone. "My dawtah she seek," she called into the phone, then handed it back to me.

"We need a note and medical certificate verifying this, Lucy," said a very suspicious Mrs. Muscat.

I hung up. "Hey, Mum, do you need any help?"

"I thought you were sick?"

"Not *that* sick."

I pulled up a chair and took up a small pair of snipping scissors to cut the loose threads from the shirtsleeves she was sewing. We worked silently for a long while. The Lamb was still asleep in my parents' bed, squeezing a rubber toy shaped like a rabbit.

"Don't you get sad?" I finally asked my mother, not knowing the word for "depressed" in our language, or if such a word even existed. Our word for "sad" literally meant "pressured heart." "Being inside this dark garage all day, doing exactly the same thing every day?"

"The garage keeps me out of the sun," she replied. "Look how white my skin is. I don't even have to use that Oil of Olay stuff!"

"Mum."

"And sewing isn't the same as picking fruit or planting rice or working on machines. Feel how smooth my hands are. These are hands of leisure."

"Answer me seriously, Mum."

"Do I seem sad?" she said. Then she looked at me, as if she had not seen me for a long time. "I think you're the one who might be sad."

"Nah."

"Sometimes I get anxious, especially when we have to finish an order. But I know that one day we'll move. It's going to happen, you know. Look at Robina. She did it in less than eight years. And we are all working very hard in this family."

My mother's absolute faith in achieving success in her world made me feel even more miserable. She was content with simple comforts because she had lacked them for most of her life. My mother didn't know the names of things—red cedar, art deco, Edwardian. Unlike my father, she had never seen the Leslies' house. To her, a table was just a table; the only accompanying adjectives would be *ugly* or *beautiful*. A 1940s vintage oak table would be "old and ugly" to her, and a plastic white Italian table with gold curlicues would be "new and beautiful."

266

Brodie would have called the things in our home "tacky," the term used by wealthy people to describe the most beautiful things poor people could afford—machine-embroidered bedspreads and plastic flowers in plastic vases molded to look like crystal. Blouses with multilayered ruffles. Enormous stuffed toys from Kmart. A plastic fluorescent print of Jesus Christ with a heart that lit up. How could I joke about tacky things without also laughing at my own mother and the way she cared for these possessions more carefully than Amber cared for the Leslies' Moulinex blender? How could I buy a three-dollar chocolate croissant without feeling like I had wasted half an hour of her labor?

To be a part of the Cabinet, I'd had to keep my true self apart. And there's only so much of yourself you can hide, Linh, before you start to fall apart.

"Why did your friend come over the other day?" my mother suddenly asked.

"She just wanted to give me some homework I left at school."

"And she took a taxi out here just to do that?"

What could I tell her? That Brodie had come to suss out where I lived and what my mother did?

"Yes. She'll probably get a new car when she turns sixteen."

My mother looked at me as if I was trying to rub it in that she and my father were *not* going to get me a new car when I came of age.

"She's spoiled," I said, and I could see my mother's face sag with relief.

"You don't have to be the best at this new school," she told me. "You don't have to be the smartest. You don't have to be like that girl. All you have to be is a good person. I see everyone around me getting the things they want in life. Robina and her husband with their business, Tee with her son at university, Ngo with her new house at Ambient Estates. And every time I go over to one of their houses, they always talk about it. But that proud talk soon turns into a list of complaints. The local butchering business is being seized by supermarkets these days, Tee's son comes home really late at night and she has no idea where he's been, Ngo's builder cheated them out of seven thousand dollars."

My mother sighed. "And I have to sit there and tell them, well, sister, at least you're rich. At least you're successful. At least your boy is in university now. But do you know what I *never* do? I never tell them about us. I never tell them that your father often works in the garage with me after his shift and we talk. That we made a tent out of netting for the Lamb. That I sometimes let you stay home with me when you're not sick."

I couldn't look at my mother, but I could sense her looking at me. She always figured my excuses out.

"I never tell them about our lives. You know why? It is not because I am ashamed. It is because some things are just *good,* too good to be judged."

I knew my mother was telling the truth, because she never lied. She didn't even understand white lies. She just stayed silent if she didn't agree with someone. And I understood now why I had been so enraged when Brodie came over to our house uninvited. I could cope when I kept my two worlds separate, but Brodie had seen the most precious part of me, and she'd trashed it.

★ ★ ★

268

I didn't go to school for the last three days of Term Three. There seemed no point. I woke up haggard, my eyes circled by darker and darker rings. At night I couldn't get to sleep, even though I was working all day with Mum in the garage. My mind was infected with a kind of virus, and I felt a sickly miasma hover around me. The Lamb began sleeping in my bed. Only with him there could I get some rest, next to his sweet, milk-scented face.

But something was happening to the Lamb too. No longer did he have his eureka moments. He would sit for long stretches of time in his box, just looking out the window or listlessly tearing scraps of paper. Perhaps he was missing Dad, who had been working the late shift for the past couple of days.

I sliced bananas for the Lamb. I even let him hold each one in his hand and see the little expressive face made by the black seeds in the center. But he didn't put the pieces in his mouth anymore; he didn't even hold up each banana segment to look at it. He just held it in his fist until it got mushed up. Just as well, I thought, when I realized that each seedy face looked more worried and anxious the deeper I cut into the banana.

"Give him his bottle," my mother told me. But the Lamb kept turning his head away.

"Hey, Mum," I called. "Mum, the Lamb is not well. He's not drinking from his bottle. He's coughing too."

"Oh, no," said my mother. "Try to pat him to sleep."

Every time I tried to put him down in bed, he kept grizzling and sitting up. He wanted to be upright; when he was lying down, his nose was blocked and he found it hard to breathe. There was also a strange rasping sound coming from his chest, which scared me.

I propped up some pillows so he could have a rest sitting up, holding on to the pillows like a koala to a tree. I patted his back until he fell asleep. Then I had a little nap next to him. Even though I was anxious, I was also exhausted.

The Lamb woke me up with a massive gasp that shook his whole torso, as if his chest were a maraca filled with rice grains. "Lamby," I cooed. "Sweet Lamb. Did you have a bad dream? Did you give yourself a fright?"

That evening my mother suggested she take Lamb to bed with her because he was sick. I reluctantly handed him over after dinner. The Lamb had been making noises all evening, as if he was whistling under his breath very softly, even though he wasn't even old enough to whistle yet, and his mouth was closed.

He woke up whistling at two a.m, my mother later told me. He refused to lie down again, even when Mum held him in her arms to make him go back to sleep. There was something wrong. When the skin of his neck started to look like a vacuum cleaner was inside his throat, sucking it in each time he inhaled, she panicked and shook me awake.

"Call your father at work!" my mother cried. I looked at the Lamb in her arms; his lips and nose were a strange bruisey color.

Picking up the phone, I rang the factory. "This is an emergency," I said. "Please put Warwick Lam on the phone."

I heard the man at the other end yell out, "Oi, Warwick!"

By now my mother was wailing in the kitchen, clutching the Lamb.

"Why are you calling me at work? What's wrong?" my father asked when he reached the phone.

"The Lamb is not breathing," I told him. Dad didn't even say anything—he just dropped the phone. I went into the kitchen.

The Lamb's breaths were coming out short and grunting. His nostrils flared and his eyes were open with panic. I called 911 and asked for an ambulance. Then I ran to the Donaldsons' house, ignoring the barking of their Dalmatian, and knocked on their front door. No one answered. I knocked until the porch light came on, but still the door remained shut. I stood at the center of the front step so they could see through the peephole that I wasn't some crazy hooligan come to mug them, and at last the door opened.

It was Mrs. Donaldson, groggy with sleep, in blue-and-yellow pajamas. "Who is this?"

"It's Lucy Lam from next door," I told her. "Please help us! My baby brother is not breathing!"

"Do you know why he's not breathing?" she asked me.

"No!" I cried.

She then went inside her house, and I was so angry and panicked that I wanted to charge in there and drag her back out. But soon she emerged with an asthma inhaler. She and I went back to our house, to my mother in the kitchen and to the rasping, gasping Lamb.

"For heaven's sake, sit him upright," commanded Mrs. Donaldson. "Sit him upright so air can get into his lungs."

I showed my mother what to do, with my hand supporting the Lamb's skinny back.

"What's that?" my mother asked me, as soon as she saw Mrs. Donaldson's inhaler.

Mrs. Donaldson shook it and then placed it at the Lamb's

271

lips. She pressed the top of the inhaler just as the Lamb took a breath in. He started to cough.

"It's killing him!" yelled my mother. "What is that stuff? It's going to choke him to death!"

I patted the Lamb on the back, hoping to help ease his cough. What if my mother was right? I thought in panic. What if this medication was only for adults?

"Don't pat his back, rub it," instructed Mrs. Donaldson. "It will calm him down." She rubbed the Lamb's back in circular motions, quietly telling him, "There, there, sweet pup. Just have a little rest. Just take it easy."

The ambulance arrived at the same time as my father. The paramedic took the Lamb into the back of the van and sat him up on the stretcher. They put a face mask on him, which was attached to a machine. "That's a nebulizer," explained the paramedic.

The color slowly came back to the Lamb's fingers, lips and nose.

"This little fella's had an asthma attack," said the paramedic. "You're very lucky he was given a dose of Ventolin to tide him over."

"Oh, I was so worried!" cried Mrs. Donaldson, peering in through the back of the ambulance. "It was Harold's inhaler, but I thought the baby might have been having an asthma attack. Harold has bad lungs, you know, from years of living behind these factories. But I didn't know whether you could give adult Ventolin to a small baby. I just had to give it a go."

"You're very lucky to have such good neighbors," the paramedic told us.

"What could have caused this, doctor?" asked my father.

"Well, hard to say, really. Has the little tacker had a bit of a cold recently? Or maybe something in the house triggered an attack."

"Like what?"

"Chemicals, maybe, cleaning products. Dust mites. That sort of thing."

To be on the safe side, the paramedic wanted to take the Lamb to the hospital. I wanted to go too, but Mum said I should get some sleep and that Dad would go. I gave the Lamb's fist one last squeeze and clambered out of the back of the vehicle.

Mrs. Donaldson was still standing there, waving them off.

"I'm very sorry to have woken you, Mrs. Donaldson," I told her.

"Nonsense, child. He'll be all right, the wee lamb." She turned and walked back to her house.

When the Lamb arrived home the next morning, he had some pink in his cheeks. "He'll be okay," my father told me. "He just needs to rest and recover and take his medicine."

The one thing I wanted to do was hold him again. I had to wait a long time, though, because Mum would not let go of him. She would not put him down, and she patted him until he fell asleep. When he woke up I made him a special treat of mashed apples, and spent all afternoon in the house with him. Mum kept checking on him every twenty minutes.

That afternoon, another letter from school arrived in the mail.

> *Dear Lucy,*
>   *Due to your unexplained absence from school and our inability to contact you, we regret to inform you that we must withdraw our invitation for you to address the Equity in Education conference.*

I didn't give a toss now—it was one less thing to worry about—but I thought of Ms. Vanderwerp, how the Cabinet had weeded her out. We were all equal at our harmonious school, but those who stumbled and fell face-first were just an embarrassment. How ghastly! Ladies, avert your eyes! How horrid, like the man who had the gall to die on an airplane midflight!

A few days later the council health-care nurse came over, and I translated for Mum. "This is his Ventolin inhaler, spacer and face mask," the woman explained. She was in her mid-forties, with hair dyed red and braided like licorice. She then asked to look around our house.

"What for?" Mum asked me warily.

"She just wants to make sure that the places the Lamb spends his time will not trigger any more attacks."

Mum was reluctant, but we showed her the bedrooms—my parents' and mine. She suggested we open the windows to let the dust mites out and the sunshine in. "Sunshine has anti-septic qualities," she told us. Then she pointed to a corner. "What are these boxes?"

Clothes, I told her.

"You can't have half a dozen boxes in each room like this. Clear these out into the garage!"

Finally she asked to see our garage.

"No!" said Mum. "She'll turn us in to the government!"

"Don't worry, Mum, it's okay."

I had the feeling that this nurse had probably looked in more garages than a mechanic; I think she already knew what she would find. The first thing that would hit her would be the smell, the smell of treated synthetic fibers, the urine-like odor of the fabric preservatives and sprays applied to keep bugs out when the rolls were being imported from China.

She showed no surprise when she entered the dark,

windowless space, a bare lightbulb hanging from the ceiling. She looked at the sewing machine and the overlocker, the stacks of fabric in loose piles. A blanket on the floor and a pillow, for times when Mum wanted to take a nap. And, in the corner, the Lamb's cardboard box, graffitied with scribbles and smeared with banana mash.

She raised an eyebrow at me. "Is this where he stays during the day?"

"Yes. But it has netting around it."

"Good grief! Don't you realize this room is filled with dust mites?"

No kidding, I wanted to retort. How I wished you were with me then, Linh.

"Let me be honest with you. If an animal were kept in a pen like this all day, we'd call the SPCA. This needs to be fixed immediately." She looked at my mother with unblinking disapproval. "I will be back in two weeks' time. This needs to be gone."

My mother cottoned on to what the nurse was saying, even though she couldn't understand the language. "Tell that demon head I want the Spanish nurse from the hospital," Mum whispered to me. "The Spanish nurse doesn't come into people's houses and judge them."

Poor Lamby. We had caged him and tried to keep him satisfied with sweets and scraps of paper, so that Mum could work on her machine and I could complete five-hundred-word essays about the Bolsheviks. We put him in his walker, even though he was probably too old for it, so he would not reach out and touch dangerous things. We were so distracted by getting ahead that we didn't think to make him happy, because he was already such a smiley baby who delighted in little things.

After the nurse left, Mum started crying. "They're going to take away my work."

"No, Mum, they won't. They're just a hospital. Anyway, we can live on Dad's salary."

"No! On that pittance? When they keep changing his shifts and not giving him a permanent position? If I don't work, what will be my purpose then?"

Mum could not read books to the Lamb. She could not entertain him. That was my job. Mum did love him, but she could not do "fun." Back in Vietnam, village kids were left to find their own fun. Kids like me started working for the family at eight. Kids like me sold paper fans at the marketplace with a baby balanced on one hip, or found factory work.

"I don't know how to be a mum," she told me.

"You're a good mum," I reassured her. It was true. She had helped raise her three younger siblings, who were now scattered across the world, and by the age of five she had known how to burp a baby.

"All I ever do is yell at you."

"That's not true."

"Your father thinks I should stop working and just look after the family," Mum said. "But besides cook and clean, what else can I do? I can't help you with your schoolwork. I won't be able to speak to any of the Lamb's teachers. I can't hang around the other parents at school. I've been sewing since I was thirteen years old."

We slowly started to change the patterns of our days. We let more light into our rooms. My father bought an air purifier.

My mother spent three days cleaning the house from inside out. Instead of having cardboard boxes around the house, we got plastic laundry tubs with lids from the Stanley gift shop. We got a big playpen so that we could put free-range Lamb in the backyard on sunny days and he could play in there in full view of Mum's open garage door while she worked.

I spent all my days with the Lamb, from the moment he woke up till we put him to bed in the evening. The terrible thing that had almost happened to him had jolted me out of my torpor. It was as if I had been drowsy at the wheel of a car, until a last-minute swerve from the road got my nerves and limbs working again, jump-starting my heart.

I dressed him, fed him his bottle and his breakfast, and carried him everywhere. I sat next to him reading books while he napped, and remembered the times he was meant to take his asthma medication. We baked small cakes with a packet mix and iced them with Nutella, sugar and butter. I mixed detergent with water and we blew bubbles through drinking straws.

As he recovered from his cold, I made sure I took the Lamb out of the house every day. Often we just roamed the streets of Stanley. Sometimes we stopped at the mini-mart and I bought him a treat.

I went to the Sunray library and, miraculously, they had Professor Gombrich. I sat in the park with the Lamb and *The Story of Art,* showing him the pictures. "This is Van Gogh's bedroom in Arles," I explained to him as he peeled a clementine. He glanced at the picture and went back to digging his thumb into the citrus. "Where is the red?" I asked him.

The Lamb pointed to the bedspread.

"Very good, sweet Lamb. What about the green?"

He pointed to the chair cushions.

"Now, what about the yellow?" *The wood of the bed and chairs is the yellow of fresh butter, the sheets and pillows very light greenish lemon,* Van Gogh had written in 1888. *There is nothing in this room with closed shutters. The broad lines of the furniture again must express absolute rest.*

As I gazed at the picture, I felt peace, peace I hadn't felt in a long time. "A waste of a mind," Chelsea had once scoffed when we saw a well-heeled woman wheeling her pram across the road. But this work brought me some peace, a peace that had been hard to come by since I'd been at Laurinda. Now I understood my mother's desire that every day would unfurl like the last, with no major dramas.

After my breakdown, and the Lamb's hospital visit, I did not yearn for excitement. I liked the quiet company of the Lamb and Professor Gombrich. I liked spending time with Mum at home, and doing things that made an immediate difference to our lives: cleaning dishes and doing laundry and cooking a huge pot of stock. There was nothing wrong with this, I thought.

"Vince said that his wife told him there was a job as a trimmer at the Stanley seafood plant," Dad told Mum one evening after we had put the Lamb to bed.

"But are you qualified to do that?" asked my mother.

"You don't need any qualifications to cut up seafood," my father said. "And it's not a job for me. It's for you. They're only hiring women. They want to pay the lowest wage."

"Me?" exclaimed my mother. "But I can't even speak English!"

"You don't need to. Anyhow, you'll learn on the job. It pays pretty well, especially the overtime and late shift."

"But what about the Lamb? He's just recovered—"

"He's the reason I think you should work in a factory," my father said. "No more dust mites and dirty chemicals to make him sick. We could clear up the garage. We could rid the house of all these boxes. And we'll never see that Sokkha again."

"Yes, but who will look after the Lamb, huh?"

"I have been thinking about this," said my father. "And—"

"I'll look after the Lamb!" I interrupted. "I will! If Mum works the late shifts, I can look after him when I come home from school."

"See?" said my father. "Your daughter is smart. That school is clearly doing good things to her brain."

"But what if she fails because of me?" Mum persisted. "What if she fails and loses her scholarship?"

"I won't fail," I promised. "I won't, Mum. The Lamb doesn't bother me. How is this any different from what I've already been doing? I'll work on my schoolwork inside, or in the backyard, in my bedroom, wherever. I'll keep a good eye on the Lamb."

My mother was still unsure. She didn't want to leave what she had been doing for so many years, but she knew she could not continue either. It was making us sick.

"Let me tell you something, Quyen," said my father. "Do you know how much the rates for working the late shift are per hour?"

"But nothing is going to be worth leaving the house, leaving Lucy with the Lamb—"

280

He told her.

I watched the amazement spread across my mother's face. How magical that number seemed, and those words, *per hour!* She would still be here during the day with the Lamb. Sure, she wouldn't get much sleep, but she had never slept much anyway. She was always up at daybreak and working late. "This is going to work out, Mum, this is really going to be a good thing!"

"Quyen, listen to your daughter," said Dad.

"How soon do they want someone to start?" Mum asked, scrunching the bottom of her shirt in her hands.

"As soon as possible."

And it was sooner than we thought. My mother had not worked in a factory before. She was scared on her first evening, Linh, but my father drove her to the factory early and spent her orientation shift with her as her translator. Then he went to his own shift at Victory.

When both my parents came home the next day, they didn't look tired at all. "I can't believe how kind they are," Mum kept saying to us. "I can't believe how easy the work is, how much slower the pace is than sewing." The most wonderful thing of all, of course, was how much she was getting paid for the overnight shift.

We began eating like kings, because Mum got an employee discount on seafood: calamari, prawns, flake, sometimes even salmon. I missed the live fish, though. The garage was shut, but we did not sell the sewing machine or the overlocker. We kept those for security, in case we needed to do some emergency work.

I was spending whole days with the Lamb because I was still on term break. They rolled by gently, as I did my holiday homework with him playing on a mat next to me. Or I'd sit in the bathroom reading *The Story of Art* while he splashed in the bath until his fingers looked like raisins.

Soon it was the last weekend of the holidays. I would be back at school in two days. Every time I thought about going back, I felt like I had live spiders in my stomach. Saturday was one of those unexpectedly hot days near the end of the year, a day of blue sky and acacia scent. "Maybe you should take the Lamb to the shopping center," Mum suggested. "It's clean and cool there."

We caught a bus to Sunray, and I parked the Lamb's stroller out in front of the plaza. I went into the supermarket, carrying him in my arms. I loved supermarkets. You didn't need to travel outside your suburb to see the world in one place, each state's and each country's produce stacked neatly on shelves and racks: bananas from Queensland, dates from the Middle East, sweet soy sauce from Indonesia, nougat from Italy, prawns from China, and frozen dinners from America.

The Lamb and I spent a long time in the candy aisle. "You can only have one, Lamby," I said to him. "Only one, so choose carefully."

At the checkout I balanced the Lamb on my hip. I decided I would take him to Wendy's to get a Funny Face cone. I didn't care that they cost $3.30. This would be a special treat. I knew I was behaving like a typical Stanley teen mother, but I now understood how their days would stretch on for ages and then suddenly snap back because of an emergency, and how much of this seemed beyond their control, so they could think only about the next thing to do to make their babies happy, and then the next thing after that.

The Lamb spotted more candy at the checkout counter, and he grinned with recognition and pointed. He was squirming on my hip and I was trying to stop him from grabbing at them when he lunged and almost fell out of my arms. For balance he grabbed the hair of the lady behind, who was leaning over to take a roll of cough drops.

"Ouch!"

When I turned back to apologize, the woman's head was down and she was rubbing her hair with both hands. I noticed her groceries on the conveyor belt: a small tub of strawberry ice cream, a single-serve gnocchi heat-and-eat meal, and a block of rum raisin chocolate. Small treats for a single older lady. How terrible that the Lamb had marred her day.

"I'm so sorry," I said, hoping that she would not be one of those horrible git-lost-we-was-here-first welfare women, the type to say, "Teach ya son to keep his paws to himself, whydoncha?"

But when I looked up from the groceries and saw the woman's face, I recognized her. Her cheeks were more con-cave, her hair was grayer and longer, but it was definitely, unmistakably her.

The last person I expected to see.

"Ms. Vanderwerp!"

She looked at me through eyes that squinted a little, as if trying to see through a thick fog. I bet she doesn't even re-member me, I thought. I bet she wants nothing to do with that school, that class, forever and ever.

Recognition lit up her goldfish-bowl glasses.

"Linh?" she asked me. "Linh Lam," she repeated. "Is that you?"

She could never get my name right.

And then, embarrassingly, in the middle of the checkout line, I started to cry.

After Ms. Vanderwerp had run her groceries through (and paid for mine as well), after we had collected the Lamb's stroller from the front of the plaza, after she'd taken the Lamb to the newspaper stand to get a stuffed wombat while I went to the bathroom to wipe the tears and snot from my face, she led me to the food court.

We sat on the white plastic benches. She had collected some hand wipes from KFC and gave the table a good wipe-down with three of them. Then we both sterilized our hands with the remaining wipes and shared an order of fries.

I told her how sorry I was to be part of the class that had tormented her. I began to sniff again, but knew I had no right to be such a crybaby. I was in the wrong, and I had been cowardly that day.

"You had nothing to do with it, sweetheart," she said.

She was trying to make me feel better, but this wasn't some historical moment she was teaching me about. This was stupid teenagers messing with her life. When she called me sweetheart, it made me even sadder. She told me that kids pulled pranks all the time, and that she had been in a vulnerable state back then.

"I shouldn't have reacted like that," she said. "I gave some of you poor girls a good scare, didn't I?" She tried to make light of it, though she could tell I wasn't convinced. "I've been a teacher for a while, Linh," she said. "I've taught in tough state schools, large Catholic colleges and one or two private girls' academies. In no other place have I encountered such disrespect and nastiness, from top to bottom. I'm not blind. I saw how those girls treated Katie, how they ignored you. I saw how they imposed their will on the other students. But they were clever about it."

It was like being bitten by a spider, I thought, with venom you couldn't squeeze out because you couldn't locate a raised red welt. No one would believe it if you told them, because the spider had left no evidence. Only when the toxicity spread through your body would anyone realize what was happening, and by then it would be too late. That was how it was at Laurinda with the Cabinet running the show.

Ms. Vanderwerp smiled a strange and sad half smile. "The funny thing, Linh, was that of the three girls, the prefect was the one who'd mostly been indifferent toward me. She never seemed to join in while the other two carried on and mucked about. But when I gave her that B-plus for their assignment . . . well, sometimes still waters have piranhas beneath."

She told me that Brodie's sleek, seething mother had gone straight to see the Head of High School. Ms. Vanderwerp had been called into the meeting. "Don't you think you are blowing things a little out of proportion?" she had asked. "Students get B grades all the time."

Mrs. Grey had opened up Brodie's school file and pointed

to the neat columns filled with identical alpha symbols. "Look, Martha. The mark you've given seems a little inconsistent with Brodie's other marks, don't you think?"

"But a B-plus hardly constitutes failure," replied Ms. Vanderwerp.

"Perhaps you might want to consider a . . . reevaluation?" suggested Mrs. Grey.

Ms. Vanderwerp then turned and spoke directly to Brodie's mother. "With all due respect, Mrs. Newberry, if Brodie believes a B-plus is tantamount to failure, perhaps Brodie needs to learn how to fail a little."

After Brodie's apoplectic mother left the meeting, Mrs. Grey shook her head. "That mark is going to cost us a fifty-thousand-dollar donation."

"It seems petty," Ms. Vanderwerp replied, not heeding the warning, "to withdraw a donation just because your daughter got a B-plus."

"Gloria Newberry will make it seem like you're the petty one, Martha." Yet Mrs. Grey had no choice but to let the lower mark remain.

"And then, a few weeks later, that incident in our classroom happened," Ms. Vanderwerp concluded. "So you see, Linh—it was between them and me."

Yet I knew the old Linh Lam would have spoken up in that classroom.

But the old Linh had allies, and the old Linh knew she had a place at her old school. It's so much easier to be a hero when you know you belong.

Now Linh was no more, because over the past three terms I had turned into a stranger named Lucy.

Ms. Vanderwerp had no idea how close I'd got to the Cabinet, or of the explosive end to our time together. I didn't want to tell her about any of that, so instead I told her all about the Lamb, while he dozed in his stroller and she patted my hand. She murmured kindly about what a hard time it must have been for all of us.

"You know, I understand how you feel, Linh. My father was in the hospital earlier this year."

No wonder she had been so anxious at school. When the Lamb was sick, it had consumed us: the checkups, visits to the pharmacy, the nurse looking over our house.

"I'm sorry," I told her. "Is he okay now?"

"No, dear. He passed away."

I didn't know what to say—it was too sad. I started to cry again, but she said, "It's all right, Linh. He was eighty-nine." She sighed. "Boy, but those last few years were really, really tough. Endless hospital visits and chemotherapy, and everything had to be sterile because his immune system was so weak."

Her eyes blurred behind the glasses, but they did not spill. Drawing her shoulders back and composing herself, she said, "Well, Lucy, what happened to me with those girls was a blessing in disguise. I got to spend the last weeks of my father's life by his bedside. It put me at ease to know he was not alone at the end."

When we parted, the kindest farewell I could give Ms. Vanderwerp was a wave. I had been crying into a tissue, and she probably did not want to be hugged.

★ ★ ★

The encounter left me disturbed and agitated. I could not stop thinking about the rottenness of Laurinda. The thought of going back for the final term made my heart palpitate the same way it had before the Lamb went to the hospital.

"Maybe it's a good idea for me to stay home for a few more days, to make sure the Lamb is fine," I said to my mother on the final Sunday of the holidays.

"He's already fine."

"But just for a few more days . . ."

"We have an air purifier now," Mum said. "I don't know what happened at that school to make you afraid to go back."

"Nothing!"

"Then you must return. Return and do your best. That's all I ask of you."

"You don't get it, Mum," I protested. "I'm trying my best in my studies. But this school isn't just about study. It's a hard place. Girls are judging me all the time."

"People have their own business to mind. I don't believe they are all watching you to see what you're doing."

My mother did not have the remotest understanding of high school.

"Take my new job," she said. "When I started, I was scared to death of the machines, and it smelled so bad. My fingers weren't used to the cold. I thought the foreman would surely fire me after the third day. But I plodded on."

"Yes, Mum, but you've never been around people like this. They're watching me, waiting for me to mess up. *All the time.*"

My mother sighed. "Why can't you just ignore it? Ignore it and keep your head down and work hard, like Tully did."

"I'm not Tully!" I shouted. "I'll never be Tully."

"But you'll also never be like that tall girl from your new school," Mum said. "The one who came over. I know this has something to do with her."

My mother, she didn't miss a thing.

"Keep your head down and soon she'll stop bothering you," she said.

"But, Mum," I protested. I had no idea how to make my mother, who'd spent the better part of a decade in the dark of the garage, understand this school, let alone how the Cabinet imposed their will. "You've never been around *groups of people like this*."

"You were too young to remember," she told me, "but one day when we were on the boat—I think it was the fourth day—some Thai pirates came. At first we thought they were fishermen, but then we saw the knives in their hands. Suddenly they were on our boat, yelling and waving those knives around. We couldn't understand them but we knew enough to get down on the deck and press our stomachs to the floor while they searched for any gold we might have.

"It seemed like the time went on forever. I had you flattened next to me, and prayed that you would not start crying. During that endless wait, even when there was silence, no one wanted to be the curious one. There was only one person killed that day, and he was the first to raise his head. After that, the pirates left without looking back."

My mother's point was this: be vigilant and be silent. It was almost our family motto. That was how we inched ahead, unthreatening and undetected. I had to go back to school, and Mum was saying that this was how I would get through the final term. I should lie low and let the perils pass over me.

After all, if the school could forget Ms. Vanderwerp so easily, then I could make myself invisible too, so that people would likewise forget my terrible last day of Term Three. Probably no one would even notice my return, I thought, because the Cabinet would have been doing their best to efface me.

I had no choice but to drag myself forward, softly plowing through time, moment by moment, until I pulled through to the other side of Year Ten.

TERM FOUR

With my backpack on, I shuffled through the school gates, hoping to blend in with the other girls. But for the second time that year, my uniform gave me away. Everyone else had remembered to wear the summer uniform of blue short-sleeved shirt and pleated light gray cotton skirt. I felt heavier than ever, inside and out, like a soldier from another battalion fighting a war I could never win.

Gina cornered me at my locker. "Lucy, how come you're in your winter uniform?"

"I'm cold," I replied tersely, my flushed cheeks revealing my lie.

"You know you're not allowed to wear that. You need to get a uniform pass."

Since when had Gina become a prefect? I opened my combination lock and began to unload my books.

"Don't ignore me," she threatened as I shoved my bag in. "Just because you got suspended last term doesn't mean you can avoid the Growler, you know."

"What?"

"Oh, yeah, act surprised."

"I wasn't suspended!"

"Huh!" scoffed Gina. "While Katie was waiting for her grandma to pick her up, she saw you going crazy at the Cabinet. And the scholarship girl does not miss the last three days of term for no reason. You've never been away all year. *We all know about it.*"

Maybe Mr. Sinclair had had a word with other staff members about my outburst. That seemed unlikely, I thought, because Mr. Sinclair didn't believe in punishment by committee. We had talked about Socrates at the social. Anyhow, if the school had suspended me, wouldn't they have sent a letter? Then it sank in: my absence had given the Cabinet the perfect opportunity to spread a rumor that Mrs. Grey had suspended me for misconduct.

"Sinclair was on after-school duty, wasn't he?" asked Gina.

"Yes."

"Katie said that after you left, he told off Amber, Brodie and Chelsea."

"What? Why would he tell *them* off?"

"I don't know," confessed Gina. "But what did you do?"

I stared at Gina so long and hard that she looked away.

Then she remembered another thing: "And, while you were away, they decided to swap you for that Year Eight girl Nadia. You know, for the Equity in Education conference." And then she left, swinging her summer skirt like a fan.

I'd vowed not to let myself get agitated, and yet already I was shaken. Even though I had not wanted to give the stupid talk, I felt robbed. They'd decided to replace me with thirteen-year-old Nadia Pinto? This was what they meant by *diversity,* just because she was *brown*? She was a sweet girl, but she could barely string a couple of sentences together.

Mrs. Grey called me to her office at recess. She glared at my uniform and told me off, but that was not the real reason she wanted to see me.

"You missed the crucial last week of term," she told me. "We gave your privilege to speak on behalf of the school to Nadia."

"I understand, Mrs. Grey. I'm sorry." I'd only missed three days!

"No, I don't think you fully understand these privileges. All year, Miss Lam, we have been waiting to see what you would offer the school. You came to us full of potential." She shook her head slowly and sadly, and closed her eyes. "Even after the girls kindly took you under their wing, you refused to participate." She opened her eyes again and lasered them onto me. "What's more, your behavior on your last day of Term Three was entirely unacceptable. I may need to have a serious talk with your parents, to renegotiate the terms of your being at this school." She sighed wearily. "We may even have to rescind our offer if this is not working out for you."

This news hit me like an unexpected blow, and it was all I could do to swallow the rising lump in my throat, to stop my eyes from welling with tears. I sat on my hands to stop their trembling. I did not know how to reply. I had spent so long lately thinking of a way to leave Laurinda, and now here it was, offered to me—yet somehow I felt even worse.

I left Mrs. Grey's office in a state of shock. I suppose, from the school's perspective, I had brought this all upon myself, by refusing to throw myself into the *rich social and cultural life of the college* while never explaining what was happening at home. Yet I could never tell Laurinda the truth of what had happened during that term break. It was bad enough that Brodie had visited—I definitely hadn't wanted the rest of the itchy-fingered, judgmental young ladies coming over to pinch the Lamb's cheeks. I did not want the school to send us a bouquet, because they would have got it all wrong. They'd probably have sent a classy white one, which would have scared the hell out of my mother because it would have reminded her of death.

Walking down the corridor, I saw through the window that the Cabinet was sitting on their bench again. They had always been a trio; my being around them had not really expanded them into a quartet. And now I understood why Gina had been so blunt with me. She was my replacement, but she was sitting on the grass like a loyal subject, gazing up at the seated Trinity. Through the glass, I watched Gina fling her head back and laugh at something. Her hair, I noticed, was back to its natural brown and tied in a ponytail.

There was still fifteen minutes of recess left, and I decided to spend them in the library. I retreated into the back corner and pulled out a book about Rodin. Staring blankly at the photos of marbled lovers and stone-cold thinkers, I worried about what my father would say.

Someone tapped me on my shoulder and I almost dropped the book.

"Hi, Lucy. How are you doing?" Standing in front of me, with her hair neatly parted in the middle and a wide smile on her oval face, was Siobhan. She and I had never spoken to each other before.

"Okay," I replied cautiously. I assumed she wanted something, maybe some tidbit of gossip from my meeting with Mrs. Grey.

But all she said was "It's good to see you back."

"Thanks."

"Yeah, great to see you back, Lucy," added Stella, coming up to join us. "We missed you."

I began to worry. These were the kinder girls in the class, and I suspected that the Cabinet might have put them up to this. "Make sure you keep an eye on poor Lucy," they would have told everyone. "She's not feeling herself. And these are her last days."

But then Katie appeared from behind the two girls and vehemently told me, "Lucy, you really put them in their place, those bitches!" Two patches of pink appeared on her cheeks.

This was a Katie I had never seen before. I didn't even know she could swear.

"I went off at Brodie because I was mentally ill," I replied flatly, still in shock.

"You're funny, Lucy," she said. "I never realized how funny you are."

"No, it's the truth."

Seeing the expression on my face, they had the decency to leave me alone.

In Mr. Sinclair's class there was now open hostility from the Cabinet. One of them had brought in a magazine, supposedly to moon over Mercury Stool, but just as Mr. Sinclair entered the classroom, Chelsea nudged Gina and exclaimed, "Oh my

God, look at the singer. Gingers are so not hot. Gross." It was juvenile, just like the chocolate heart incident, but again there was no way Mr. Sinclair could turn to these girls and say, "I'm a thirty-two-year-old man, I don't care what you kids think of me," without sounding like he actually did care. He ignored the taunt.

I felt awkward being in his class, and ashamed. I did not want him to single me out that first day back, and he didn't. He didn't pay any particular attention to me. He was just teaching, business as usual.

When the class ended I went up to his desk. "Can I talk to you, Mr. Sinclair?"

Mr. Sinclair was now very careful, and made sure the door remained open.

"I just wanted to apologize," I said. "About my language last term at the bus stop. And going crazy at those girls. And, yeah, doing it in front of all the parents and younger students."

"That was some very colorful language you had going on there that day, Lucy."

"I'm also sorry for swearing at you in particular."

Then Mr. Sinclair did something surprising and annoying: he started to laugh. I had been repentant and sincere, and he found it hilarious! So funny that no one nearby could have mistaken his deep, crazy laugh for flirtation of any sort.

But maybe he was scared that I would cry in front of him, so he started to apologize. "Lucy, I'm sorry for laughing at you. I went to a Catholic boys' school—no foul language could shock me. What you did reminded me of when I was a student at St. Martin de Porres. Whenever the boys had a problem with each other, they would wait outside the back gate until the last of the teachers had cleared off. We would gather our friends in two different groups—one for each boy. Then we'd have it out with each other. We'd fight. There would be a winner and a loser. And then the next week, whatever we'd been fighting about, whatever grudge we'd had, would generally be forgotten. There was respect for the winner. That was how we laid our issues to rest. Girls, on the other hand . . ."

I knew he was thinking of a way to tell me what I already knew. "Well, you know when you swore at Brodie and her friends?"

"Yes." He was going to say that I'd fought dirty, that I'd been feral and unfair and cowardly, I thought, and braced myself.

"Well, why didn't they yell back at you?" he asked.

"Maybe they were more decent," I said.

"Lucy, do you really believe that? That they are more decent than you?"

How could I answer that? Of course not. But that would make me sound self-righteous and prim—exactly like them. That was the reason they had refrained from yelling back. It was beneath their dignity, it would have made them look as bad as me. It would have been distasteful.

"I don't know, sir. Maybe I care less about decency than they do."

Mr. Sinclair laughed again. "You are a real character, Lucy Lam. I salute you. You don't talk very much, but when you do, you always tell the truth. You know, before Martha—Ms. Vanderwerp—left, she told me to keep a close eye on you. She said you were one to watch because you were full of promise."

"Thanks, Mr. Sinclair. Actually, I saw her recently."

"Did you?"

"At the supermarket. I didn't know she lived in Sunray."

"Ah, her father did. She's had a lot on this year, Ms. Vander-werp."

"Mr. Sinclair, I am very sorry about my role in what happened—"

"Lucy," he said, "I couldn't have found a sorrier student. I needed to instill a sense of shame in some of the girls that day, but I did not want to single them out. I had to involve the whole class, even though some of you didn't deserve it. I apologize for that."

I was not angry at him. He was a teacher, and he'd done what any decent teacher would do. I did not understand anything about his life. I didn't know whether he was well liked in the staff room, or whether he was being made into a scapegoat like Ms. Vanderwerp. I didn't know whether the other teachers took him seriously, or whether they mocked his Socratic classroom. I didn't know what he talked about when he went home to his family. But my encounter with Ms. Vanderwerp had shown me that not all teachers lived in blissful ignorance like Mrs. Leslie.

In a single morning, I had swung from dread, to anger, to despair, and just when depression was about to engulf me, I had been handed this small but rock-hard nugget of hope. Both Mr. Sinclair and Ms. Vanderwerp had seen something in me. Full of promise, they had said. Was that true? And if it was, was this a reason for me to stay at Laurinda?

★ ★ ★

When the bell rang for lunch, Katie followed me down the corridor. "Are you going to the library again?" she asked.

"I suppose."

"You can't lie this time, Lucy Lam. You don't have any homework to finish. It's the start of term."

"I like it there."

"You like being *alone*?"

I nodded.

"Seriously?"

"Yes."

"So . . . the Cabinet didn't push you out?"

"No." So *that* was what they were telling people.

"Then why did you go off at them last term?"

"You know why," I told Katie. "They're sick girls." I turned away, about to go through the glass doors of the library.

"Hang on," she said. "I know Mrs. Grey is thinking of kicking you out next year."

"How did you know that?"

"Lucy, haven't you worked it out already? Nothing is secret at this school. Mrs. Grey's office window opens onto the corridor, and when she calls students in during recess and lunchtime, the whole school watches and listens."

"Well, what happens to me is none of your business, Katie." I was sorry the moment I blurted this out. I liked Katie, but sometimes guilt can make you a little cruel, and I still felt guilty about abandoning her at the start of the year. But also, she had reminded me that the whole school was a crowd of eyes and ears, and the self-righteous passivity of all those rumormongers and scuttlebutts irked me.

"But it is my business," she told me, "if you choose to spend the rest of your time at this school hiding in the library, letting everyone else think that you've done something wrong. Your silence gives others the impression that you're ashamed of yelling at the Cabinet. Lucy, even if you're the strongest girl with the most independent mind, the sort of girl who doesn't mind being alone, the sort of person who would rather be by herself than with the most powerful clique in the school, *no one else sees it that way*."

"I couldn't care less how I am seen."

"Of course you don't," said Katie. "No one who cares about her social position would leave the Cabinet. Don't you get it, Lucy? No one understands where you're coming from. *You're not seen*. That's why it's been so easy for them to spread this story about how you've gone bonkers, how you're not coping."

I shrugged. "It's probably true."

"It's not true, and you know it, Lucy," Katie said. "The Cabinet wants you out of here because you told them where to go, so now other people are getting ideas. And Mrs. Grey wants you out because she thinks you don't give a stuff about the school."

If only Mrs. Grey knew how much mental energy I'd spent on Laurinda!

"We created the Cabinet but Mrs. Grey encourages them," Katie said bitterly. "That's why they've been allowed to run wild. She can't afford to lose them because their mothers run the alumnae association and make massive donations."

"No, Katie," I snapped. "Do you want to know why Mrs. Grey loves the Cabinet? Because they maintain the Laurinda myth. They keep the dissenters in line. Sometimes they even cull the weak. A little accident here or there, and a trouble-some girl or teacher is out. And they don't do it out of the goodness of their hearts, do they, Katie? The payoff is that they get status and credit. They give posturing speeches about how great they are, but they *steal* and they *maim*."

"I know, Lucy, I know," said Katie. "That's why I can't let you go back to the library. You can't retreat. You'll be gone by the end of the year if you do. You can't *choose* to be alone here with no one to back up your story."

And here was the bitter paradox of adolescence: alone, I was most myself, most true. But the self that really mattered was the self that was visible, the self that could be shown to other people. And here was Katie, proposing something radi-cal: that she would support whichever self I needed to be out in the world.

"I have a photo of Mr. Sinclair's bum!" Gina was waving around a printed photo in the classroom before politics.

"Where the hell did you manage to get a photo of his bum?" Chelsea asked.

"At the Year Ten social. See?" Gina held out the photo so Chelsea could see. It was too far away for me to get a close look. Then she added, "Lucy was a good decoy."

"What?" Brodie yanked the photo from Gina's hands. "Let me see that. Oh, my," she giggled coyly. I had never heard her giggle before. "That is a good angle. Look, there's Lucy, smiling away in the background."

"Yeah, she kept him talking so I could get a good shot."

"You're a liar!" I yelped.

The two glanced at each other, as if to confirm that, yes, Lucy Lam did have a habit of going off at the slightest provocation; Lucy was so unhinged that her door was practically falling off. Discipline, self-control—that was what eleven years at Laurinda had given these girls, and they were things I lacked.

"You don't even like him anymore!" I accused Gina, to tell her that I knew she was up to no good. But as soon as I'd uttered the words, they were taken to mean something entirely different.

"Ooh, this is very *interesting*," remarked Chelsea. "I didn't know Lucy had a crush on Mr. Sinclair. I thought she liked Richard Marr."

"That's not what I meant, and you know it!"

"I also have a photo of Lucy making eyes at Mr. Sinclair!" said Gina. "It's very sweet. Wanna see?"

Katie and Siobhan entered the room. "What's happening?" Katie asked.

"Grab the photo from Brodie!" I shouted.

But Brodie now had both hands behind her back and was smiling like a sunflower. "Touch me and it will be harassment, you lezzo," she sneered at Katie. She sat down in her seat just as Mr. Sinclair entered the room.

All through class the Cabinet and Gina smiled at me, challenging me to say something. Then Chelsea giggled.

"Got something to say?" Mr. Sinclair asked her.

"Yes, as a matter of fact, I do," she replied earnestly. "My sister's reading a book at uni called *The First Stone,* by Helen Garner. Have you heard of it, sir?"

"No," he said, but his response came so quickly that I wondered whether he was telling the truth. I'd never heard of the book—they were always citing sources I didn't know—but I knew Chelsea was getting at something.

"Chelsea, is this relevant to lawmaking by subordinate authorities, which is our topic today?" he asked.

"Well, it's about politics and power. It's about these two girls at a college—"

"I'm sure it's a fascinating book for you to discuss on your own time, but today we are focusing on delegated legislation, if you please, Chelsea."

The class continued, with Mr. Sinclair writing on the board and explaining things, and us distractedly taking notes. I had to find a way to get that photograph from Brodie, I kept thinking. I should have grabbed it and torn it up the moment Gina had dangled it in front of us.

A thought flashed through my mind: stand for something, or you'll fall for anything.

"Mr. Sinclair," I said. "They have a photo of you."

"Pardon, Lucy?"

"They have a photo of you from the social. They took it from behind you."

At first Mr. Sinclair didn't register what my last sentence meant. But then he did, and at the same time he realized my tone was not light or fun. "And where is this photograph?"

Brodie glared. Gina looked like she wanted to kill me. Amber kept her head down.

Katie spoke up. "Brodie has it."

"Come on, Brodie," Mr. Sinclair said, extending a palm. "Hand it over."

Brodie sat there, staring blankly at him. "Hand what over, sir?"

"The photograph. Now!"

"I'm sorry, I don't know what you're talking about, sir. I don't have any photograph."

Mr. Sinclair gave a great sigh of exasperation. "You know exactly what I'm talking about."

"No, I don't, sir, and I would appreciate it if you stopped looking at me like that. It's creeping me out." She then made a big show of turning over her folder, turning out all the plastic loose-leaf pockets and flipping through the pages of her exercise book. There was nothing there. She stood and emptied the pockets of her skirt. A handkerchief with lace edging, half a packet of fruit Mentos. That was it.

"No other pockets," she concluded, as if she were the one conducting the investigation, the head of the police force.

How could it have disappeared like that? I hadn't heard her tear it, I hadn't seen her eat it. Then I realized what she had said: no other pockets. She wasn't wearing a blazer! She didn't have hers with her, but Amber was wearing hers.

"Amber Leslie has it!" blurted Katie, just as Amber was giving Brodie a sideways curve of a smile.

"I do not!" declared Amber. "How dare you, Katie, you liar!"

"Amber Leslie, stand up and come over here now," Mr. Sinclair said. "With your things."

I had no idea where he was going with this and I hoped he knew what he was doing.

Amber stood and walked insouciantly toward Mr. Sinclair, until she was directly in front of him. "Yes, sir?"

"Give me the photograph."

She made the same display of turning out her books and folders and her skirt pockets, and the two side pockets of her blazer, which were piped with gold and maroon. "You see, sir? Nothing."

Of course, every girl in the class knew there was one pocket she had not turned out. Edmondsons was as expensive as hell, but they were definitely quality suppliers. Every girl's blazer had an inner pocket sewn into the lining.

"Sir, it's in the inside pocket of her blazer," Siobhan said.

Of course. Mr. Sinclair wasn't going to touch Amber's blazer.

"I don't understand why you're picking on Amber," muttered Chelsea. "It's not as if she's the type to go around taking pictures of people's bare behinds for kicks."

Mr. Sinclair paled. It was not just a cliché. One moment he was normal-toned, even a little red from frustration, and the next time I looked at his face I realized why redheads were more susceptible to skin cancer. I didn't know how to tell him that he was being had, that there was no nude photo.

"Search me," Amber said, her hands undoing the top button of her blazer. "Or, if you'd like, I can take it off for you. . . ."

"No!" yelled Mr. Sinclair. "You stay right where you are, Amber Leslie! All of you—stay exactly where you are until I come back."

When he'd left the room, Amber smiled coyly and took off her jacket. She whirled it above her head with one finger and threw it onto Mr. Sinclair's desk, to the whoops and hollers of her friends.

No one else was celebrating. This had gone on long enough, and it wasn't funny.

"Come on, everyone, give Amber a big round of applause!" shouted Brodie.

Only two other pairs of hands started clapping, steadily and slowly increasing in tempo, a three-person percussion dance track for Amber's performance.

"This isn't funny," I said.

Gina and Chelsea clapped louder, raising their hands above their heads and whooping, like some kind of tribal spirit-rousing routine. "Wooo! Woo! Woo!"

"Oh, for crying out loud," exclaimed Siobhan. "This is so pathetic."

Siobhan would never have said that earlier this year. Something was happening at last. Something had roused the soporific inhabitants of Laurinda, made them shake the dust from their hair. I finally understood—the Cabinet was now collapsing, the glass had fallen off the hatch and people were climbing out. Still, Brodie stood firm in her center position on the top shelf, using whatever charm she still had to keep the girls in their places, and entreating the others to close the damn door and replace the glass. Now I understood why the Cabinet had taken the extreme measure of bringing Gina into their group. It had been an act of desperation.

But now most of the eyes in the room were not focused on the Cabinet. Stella rolled hers at Katie. Katie sighed dramatically and raised her hands in the air. Even Trisha MacMahon gave me an elusive smile, as if to say, how ridiculous. Then she made her long pianist's fingers into a pistol and raised it to her temple. *Shoot me now.*

"Where do you think he's gone?" asked Amber, still believing she was the center of attention. "He's missing the show."

"The sexy, sexy show!" whooped Chelsea. "Amber, you sexy beast! Shove it down your skirt, Amber! He'll never find it."

"This is seriously not a joke," warned Katie.

"Shut up, Miss Tautology," sneered Brodie.

"Come on and show us what you've got, Amber!" Gina hollered.

Amber pulled the photograph out of her blazer pocket and slowly rotated her hips in time to the claps. Just as she was shoving the picture down her skirt, pushing down hard because she wore it extra-tight to accentuate her funnel waist, Mr. Sinclair came back into the room. And he had brought Mrs. Grey with him.

They both stared at the scene, the three girls cheering, Amber's jacket spread out on Mr. Sinclair's desk, thrown with perfect precision so its sleeves dangled over the edge as if hugging the wood, and Amber dancing around seedily and ramming something down her skirt.

"Give me that!" snapped Mrs. Grey, extending her arm.

Amber, who only a few moments ago had been so brave, so crazy, so wild and so full of her own power, stopped. Her hand was still wedged in her waistband.

"Now!"

Amber pulled out the creased photograph and handed it over.

Mrs. Grey looked at it. "Back to your seat, now! And take your blazer with you."

Amber picked up her blazer and went back to her seat.

"Unbelievable!" scoffed Mrs. Grey. Then she turned to Mr. Sinclair. "Well, Howard, I hope this has restored some order to your classroom." The unequivocal contempt in her tone turned up the corners of Brodie's mouth. Mrs. Grey had spoken to Mr. Sinclair not as a colleague, or even an adult, but as if he were a child who had tattled on another, younger kid for stealing his toy. "No more silly business," she said.

Before she was out of the room, Katie blurted out, "I think Gina has more! They're in her folder."

"Oh, for heaven's sake, Katie!" She turned toward Gina. "You have no reason to hold onto any more photos from that batch, Gina. Do you understand me?"

Gina looked at the woman she called the Growler, the woman she and the Cabinet thought they could outsmart, yet who could in an instant make her feel trivial and ridiculous and childish. "Yes."

Those photographs, in the span of half an hour, had become worthless currency. No one cared anymore. Even Mr. Sinclair was ashamed, ashamed that he had panicked over something so trite, ashamed that the photos didn't even come close to confirming his worst fears that, somehow, someone might have snapped a picture of him at the men's urinals, ashamed that when Amber had started to unbutton her blazer he had been so out of his mind with worry that he had run out for backup and dragged in the strongest and most powerful woman he knew, the Head of High School. The woman who could make anyone feel trivial and ridiculous and childish.

We all knew who ran this ship.

News always traveled fast at Laurinda. When Katie told Siobhan and Stella about how my days at the school were numbered, they too were furious. So I was surrounded by unexpected allies as I waited by the gate after school for my bus.

"Getting rid of the scholarship girl just because you spoke the truth," Siobhan declared. "How low can they get?"

Trisha MacMahon joined us. "I have rehearsal this evening, so I'm just hanging around," she said, by way of introduction. "Can't believe they're thinking of kicking you out." I knew she'd had a soft spot for me ever since she found out I had started the applause for her at assembly. "They were going

313

to break my hands, those bitches." Trisha flexed her beautiful fingers. "I really should think about getting these things insured."

The girls told me that the Cabinet had let Nadia Pinto join them for half a week last term while I was away, as they prepared her for the conference. Trisha had heard Amber yelling at the Year Eight girl. "No, Nadia, you can't just read off the page. You have to memorize the whole thing. Jesus, it's only ten minutes!" Nadia must have cried at least five times under the Cabinet's tutelage. The final straw had come from Chelsea. "Wear a maxi pad, in case you get nervous and piss yourself," she'd told her. Once the conference was done, Nadia steered clear of the Cabinet, and not even Brodie's velvet assurances could bring her back.

"But you were the first girl to leave them," Siobhan told me. "You set it all in motion."

I didn't think I should take credit for something I had done for my own self-preservation.

The four girls waited with me until my bus arrived. As we chatted, I sensed an invisible barrier had dissolved. Now there was no ominous force judging us for every decision we made, nor were we worried about how we seemed to each other. Trisha told us that she'd joined a band with two Auburn boys, and that the one she had the hots for, Spinky, was going to drive her home after rehearsal. Siobhan told us how she was going to quit French lessons next year because she had failed her last test. And I told them about my morning meeting with Mrs. Grey.

"They can't just kick you out," Katie declared. "I mean, come on, what grounds do they have?"

My bus arrived and I got on and looked out the window. The girls waved. The bus was heading back to Stanley, but I knew now with certainty that I did not want to stay there for the rest of my days. Something had shifted: maybe there was a future for me at Laurinda after all.

VALEDICTORY

Dear Linh,

The final day of term was "Celebration Day," a day for the Year Tens to celebrate their graduation to the senior campus. We filed out of our classes after lunch and walked down the Avenue of Alumnae behind the school. It was a paved path with little metal plaques set in the center of each stone tile. Each plaque had a past student's name on it, but the students were not chosen because of distinction or achievement. They were there because they or their parents had paid for the honor of letting future students walk all over them. Goodbye, *Grace Gladrock,* I thought. Goodbye, *Gloria Green.* Goodbye, *Dianne Archer.* Goodbye, *Margaret Thorpe.*

This past term, Katie, Siobhan, Trisha, Stella and I had formed our own loose group, but it was a group in which no member was in thrall to any other. I could spend a few days by myself in the library and not be ejected from the group, and Trisha had her separate life of musician friends. We felt a freedom to be ourselves—something we hadn't felt at school all year. It was surprising to discover that even though we'd been in classes together, we'd known so little about one another until now. How ordinary and comforting it was to know that others held the same feelings, fears and aspirations, even if we had different goals.

We each had to ring an old brass bell to symbolize how our voices had made a difference at the school. When Katie did it, her face was flushed, as if she was going to cry. She had spent four years here. I imagined the end of Year Ten at Christ Our Savior, and my friends going to Mass. There would be no bell for those girls to ring, even though it would be the last time— the very last day—some of them would be in high school. Even so, many of them would be more educated than their parents. There would be hugs and congratulations, but they'd never sign each other's uniforms with permanent markers, which was what some of the Laurinda girls were planning to do after school. They'd work out who had kid sisters who might need their clothes.

We filed into assembly, where the whole school was gathered, and offered an onstage farewell. *"Concordia prorsum, semper progrediens, semper sursum,"* we sang in Latin. Forward in harmony, always progressing, always aiming high . . .

I had once thought this way about my life—*before* I received the Laurinda scholarship. But I knew now that success had to mean something to *me,* not only to those around me. You could do all the right things and still feel as though you had failed. For example, at the start of the year Mr. Sinclair had thought he was an excellent teacher, and he was. But when students started disliking him and hinted that he possessed not only a busy mind but busy hands, everything went downhill. Now he was doubting his teaching instincts. What was worse, he felt threatened by a bunch of teenage girls, and he probably didn't know whether his paranoia was necessary for his survival or just irrational fear.

Onstage, I was closest to the curtain, hidden behind Gina's hair and Siobhan's shoulder. Still, I could see the front row of the audience. Mrs. Grey was sitting there, her large hands in her lap, watching us. Some of the teachers were singing along, but she wasn't.

I wondered what made her tick. I thought about how, a fortnight ago, for just the second time this year, I had gone to see her of my own volition. I had decided on a course of action and I needed her approval.

"Why are you here to see me?"

I handed her two typed sheets of paper.

"What is this? An English essay? I don't want to read your essay drafts."

"It's a speech."

"The education conference was months ago."

"It's not for that, Mrs. Grey. I would like to give a speech at Valedictory Dinner."

I knew the audacity of my request would shock her, and it did. "You can't volunteer for a thing like that, Miss Lam," she said. "You have to be nominated by a teacher."

"Mr. Sinclair has nominated me. His note is attached."

She looked down and, sure enough, saw that I wasn't lying.

Lucy Lam has shown extraordinary improvement in her one year at Laurinda, he had written. *I believe she would be the ideal candidate to deliver the closing address at Valedictory Dinner and give the vote of thanks.*

"The talk is two weeks away. This is very late notice."

I knew very well that once she wouldn't have hesitated to give one of the Cabinet permission to speak at assembly at short notice, but I also knew that things had changed for the Cabinet now. In class, when they tried to make their usual snide remarks, they were either quickly cut down with even snarkier comments—"Speak for yourself, Chelsea, you philistine"—or met with indifferent silence.

Brodie had mentioned loudly last week in homeroom how Dr. Markus had nominated her to give the closing address at Valedictory Dinner. "I had to say no," she said. "Seriously, three weeks is just not enough time to craft a good speech. What was he thinking?"

But we all knew the real reason. The Cabinet was now held in such contempt by the student body that if Brodie got up to speak, her reception might be worse than lukewarm, and she didn't want to be shamed in front of all the parents and teachers. She was a shrewd operator: with two more years at Laurinda, and reputations to repair, she had decided the Cabinet would lie low for a while.

But this was no longer about the Cabinet. It was about me.

I explained to Mrs. Grey how I felt that I'd let down the staff of the school (which was not entirely a lie, as I did not specify which staff), and that I should have been involved in more extracurricular activities. I lamented everything I had done to give offense to my fellow students and to the college. I told her how rewarding I had found the year to be for my personal growth. I pleaded to be given a chance to demonstrate the Laurinda spirit.

"I'm ready to join in," I said.

It had taken me close to a year to work out what this school wanted from me: I did not need to be particularly accomplished or successful, I only had to *appear* to be, and all would be forgiven. Once I realized how simple it would be to do this, I knew Mrs. Grey would not refuse my request.

I had seen how, initially, no one had really clapped for Trisha but they had all roared for Brodie, how the Cabinet had used me as an instrument for their own glorification, and what a big deal both the administration and the Cabinet had made of the Equity in Education conference. And I had learned one important thing: this was how leaders were created here. If you looked the part, you could play the part. So that was how I'd ended up with a speaking spot at Valedictory Dinner.

That evening I wore a red dress my mother had given me. She'd made it with the cloth I had badly wanted at the beginning of the year. She also handed me twenty-five dollars so I could go to Tran's garage salon down the road. I knew she was feeling guilty about not coming to the dinner because she had a shift at work. "Even if I went," she told me, "it would be a waste of sixty-five dollars. I wouldn't be able to understand the English. Why don't you use the money to get your hair done and buy some nice shoes?"

All I could think about was how horrible I had been all year to my mother, all those arguments about the kilt, the plastic trays, those moments of wondering what it would be like to have Mrs. Leslie as a mum. Yet Mrs. Leslie was refined but without resolve. If I swore at her, she would cry. If I swore at my mother, she'd slap me in the face. Mrs. Leslie tried to treat her daughter like a friend and equal, but my mother always maintained that distance in which respect blotted out any hypocrisy. Mrs. Leslie could gently encourage Amber to be a doctor instead of a nurse, gently nudge her into classical instead of jazz ballet, but to Amber it would feel like a shove.

My mother did not care if I studied to be a nurse instead of a doctor, or a teacher's aide instead of a lawyer. She didn't care if I wanted to be an artist or sell cell phones. I had been reading all her mail and translating for her since I was nine, even accompanying her to the clinic during her pregnancy with Lamb. She knew I was capable of navigating life in this new world, even though she could not provide me with any maps. She never sat me down to talk about respecting my decisions and choices. She just let me make my own, all through my life, without question.

"I'm afraid you'll have to go by yourself," my father had told me the evening before. He had hoped to come, but with Mum at work there would be no one to look after the Lamb, and Dad said this was not like the Teochew Chinese New Year celebrations at the May Hoa restaurant, where you could bring babies and let them yell at the top of their lungs.

I was disappointed, of course. But deep down inside I knew too that I did not have to prove anything to my mum and dad. This was not about winning awards or being the best at anything at school, but about proving to myself that I could cope with life, that I would be resilient and always survive. I didn't need to subject my family to my posturing.

I would do it alone. I would show the Cabinet that I was and would always be Linh Lam. I'd come to this school after an unexpected blessing, a full scholarship that felt pilfered from a more deserving girl. I'd come loose and curious and unattached, thinking that if I was principled enough and well liked enough, things would go my way.

When I learned that you couldn't penetrate a tightly packed place like this so easily, I'd tried to make myself paper-thin so I could squeeze through the gaps. Now it was time to be straight-spined and focused, to ignore all else but getting into university. University would mean freedom, from Stanley but also from Laurinda.

It was only two more years, and two years did not seem that long.

Dad took some photos of me before I left—"to show your mother how beautiful you are tonight," he said. He took lots with me standing in front of our brown curtains, a few with me sitting on the couch, and some with me holding the Lamb. He then handed me a small box. "Here," he said gruffly. It was a bottle of L'Air du Temps. "Last month, Quang was selling some merchandise from the trunk of his car after work. Don't tell your mum. She doesn't like this sort of stuff. She thinks it's fake—she won't even use the Calvin Klein bag I got her."

"Thanks, Dad."

I sprayed some on and expressed my delight so that my father's feelings would not be hurt. In all honesty, though, the scent reminded me of rich old ladies.

They had picked a beautiful venue for Valedictory Dinner, a historic mansion that was now an events center. The room had high, decorated ceilings, deep blue curtains tied with cream tassels, flocked brocade wallpaper and chandeliers. When I saw the paintings in the foyer of Lord Auburn and his ilk, it dawned on me that the school might once have owned this place.

Since my parents weren't coming, there were extra spots

at our table, and Katie had asked to bring her cousin along. I found my place and met Katie's grandparents and her older brother, who were exactly as I'd imagined: cheerful, kind and earnest. Then her cousin came back from the bathroom, and I almost fainted.

"Well, hello, Miss Salmon Ella," he greeted me. "Fancy seeing you here at this fancy dinner."

"Fancy that," I replied.

"You've met my cousin before?" Katie asked, bewildered.

Before I could reply, Richard said, "Oh, yes. Your friend and I have met exactly twice. Once at the Year Ten social, which you had decided would be too terrible to go to, and the second time at the debating finals, which you clearly didn't qualify for."

"Rub it in, why don't you?" Katie playfully retorted to her cousin. "You're such a dick."

The night began with a slide show of images from our cohort's four years at the middle school campus. There was Katie in Year Seven reading *Anne of Green Gables,* girls playing sports, Amber as Juliet in the school play, and the class cooking for International Food Week. Even the girls who had never really felt they belonged were getting nostalgic, I noticed, but I didn't feel very much until the photos of this year came onto the screen: the social and the girls dancing in outfits their mothers did not know about, the Cabinet's debate with the Auburn boys and, near the end, a shot of teachers sitting in the staff room with mugs of tea. Ms. Vanderwerp was there, smiling into the camera with her cup and eyebrows raised.

After the main course, Mrs. Grey made her farewell address. Then she introduced the guest speaker, who had been named Young Leader of the Year for her work teaching Bangladeshi street kids how to paint with oils. Her name was Markita White, and she was Chelsea's older sister.

Where Chelsea's passion was expressed as an angry adolescent tirade against authority, Markita's was like a hot geyser spraying goodwill on one and all. "It is a great gift to bring creativity to the lives of the most disadvantaged young people in the world," she enthused. "And to take them seriously as artists by letting them use the materials and learn the techniques of the old masters." She flicked through a slide show and talked about the poor kids with their pleading eyes, distended stomachs and reaching hands—hands outstretched for paintbrushes. People in the audience were calmly tucking in to their salmon. The last slide flashed an image of Markita White in sunglasses and safari clothes, her arms around two small brown children. Everyone applauded.

Then, while dessert was being served, Mr. Sinclair stood up to introduce me. "I nominated Lucy Lam to speak tonight," he said. "Not only is she an insightful student of politics, she also espouses the values of honesty and humility that make for a lifelong learner."

It must have been a baffling introduction for anyone used to the way Laurinda unfurled a list of achievements like a long banner. Mr. Sinclair had even left out the thing the school considered most important: that I was the inaugural recipient of the Equal Access scholarship.

Now I was standing onstage.

"Thank you, Mr. Sinclair, and thank you, Mrs. Grey, for

giving me the opportunity to speak this evening," I began. "My mum and dad are not here tonight, but their names are Warwick and Quyen Lam. We came to Australia on a boat from Vietnam when I was two. We are Teochew Chinese. I come from Stanley, one of the most socioeconomically disadvantaged suburbs in Victoria. According to the Australian Bureau of Statistics . . ."

I was speaking the truth, and rattling off some impressively grim numbers, but my heart wasn't in it. My figures stacked up on top of one another like worthless currency, as I looked out at the audience and they smiled back at me. A desire to please started to rise up in my throat like sick, but I suppressed it.

It was really awful to speak after Markita White! Damn it, her tale of slum-dwelling South Asian kids had trumped my carefully crafted script, because now people were listening to me as if I were just another poor child with outstretched hands, to be helped by Laurinda.

Was this why Mrs. Grey had let me stand here tonight—to bring diversity, to demonstrate that the school was charitable and I was deserving of its charity through my stoicism and spirit? To give a talk that would stir a few warm feelings before everyone went back to stabbing their raspberry chocolate tortes with their little silver forks? To be "that impressive Asian scholarship girl" parents would speak about on their drives home because they'd forgotten my name, while their own kids went to an after-party?

I'd expected my declaration of allegiance to Laurinda to be easy, especially since Mum and Dad wouldn't be there to witness their daughter telling everyone about the awfulness of her ordinary life in order to demonstrate the ways in which this extraordinary school had lifted her out of it. I had to do this because I hadn't yet accomplished anything illustrious for Laurinda. All year I'd just been trying to survive. All year I'd been searching for a sense of belonging. All year I'd been looking for my voice. And now here it was, going out clear as a bell to hundreds of people, and I didn't even recognize it. At Christ Our Savior, I'd never had to spin some tale of triumph against the odds because we had all been in the same boat.

I kept reading. "Leadership assumes that you have certain exceptional skills, and the confidence to make decisions that will affect other people. It assumes you possess wisdom, discernment and good judgment. Laurinda is a school that cultivates leadership in all its students. . . ."

All year we'd heard dozens of clichéd leadership speeches, and here I was making another one. It was all bull, and I saw red. I'd been a leader before, and I knew that it was not this rubbish about how everyone could be one if only they participated in enough public-speaking, merit-scoring activities. It was not about increasing my profile or clawing my way past rivals or crawling out on top of the competition heap. I glanced down at my speech and knew in a heartbeat that I could not deliver the rest of it. I wasn't even anxious anymore. Peering out into the audience, into all the satiated faces and encouraging smiles, I began again.

"I used to be a leader," I said. "At Christ Our Savior I was a leader because my peers respected me enough to vote me onto the student representative council. At home I was a leader because my parents treated me like an adult with responsibilities. But when I arrived at Laurinda, my mentors here told me that leadership was all about standing out. You had to stand out here because this is supposed to be an *outstanding* school. But I don't have any special talents like my friend Trisha. I'm not a history buff like Katie, or a debater like Brodie. *Nothing about me stands out.*

"However, I have a letter from Laurinda which my dad keeps in a special photo album with all my childhood pictures. It's a letter saying that I am the inaugural recipient of the Laurinda Equal Access scholarship. That means something to him, my dad who has no idea what 'inaugural' means because he didn't even finish high school. So I thought long and hard, and realized that what makes me special at this school is that I come from Stanley, and no one else at Laurinda comes from there.

"Stanley is a place where many people work in banking and advertising—that is, their mums clean banks and their brothers put Safeway ads into mailboxes. It's a place where people have four cars in their driveways—but only one that is working. It's a place where the bogan and the bog*asian* sometimes coexist peacefully, but more often don't."

Whereas before everyone had been half dozing, a few students and teachers now chuckled awkwardly. But not Mrs. Grey. I could see her at the front table, her hand clamped tightly around her upright fork, a disapproving metal exclamation point. The speech I'd shown her was still in front of me, but it didn't matter anymore—not the passage about tradition and unity, not the accompanying out-of-context Confucius quote, nor the final cliché about how what lies ahead of us is nothing compared to what lies within us.

Sure, I had just told a self-deprecating joke, but it was no more of a joke than the entirety of my prepared speech. Sure,

I was not as polished as Markita White or Brodie, but at last I had my true voice back.

"So you can understand that when I first came to Laurinda, I wasn't sure whether I'd ever be up to scratch. All year I've been scared of not being good enough, smart enough, of not being 'leadership material.'"

I looked around the room and could see many students nodding.

"I had so much to learn about my new school, my teachers and the new friends I would make. I wanted to understand the people who seemed so different from my friends back in Stanley. For nearly all of the students here tonight, graduation simply means moving on to the last two years of high school and then, hopefully, on to university.

"But for some of my old friends, graduating from Year Ten will be the last of their formal education. Many of them will never come to a dinner where they use three different forks. In the future, the only politics they will know will be from the television. The last literature they will read in their lives will be their Year Ten English texts. The only professionals they will regularly see will not be their friends, but their family doctors.

"We are all born into a particular set of circumstances— a home, a family, a neighborhood. And to adapt to new circumstances takes time. At Laurinda I had to start from the beginning, and to take baby steps again. So I knew I wasn't going to shine straightaway and make this school proud."

I didn't dare look at Mrs. Grey at all now.

"But teachers like Ms. Vanderwerp and Mr. Sinclair showed me that good leadership does not necessarily mean loudly stamping your boots," I continued. "It can also mean treading lightly like Aung San Suu Kyi. She said that if you have enough inner resources, you can be by yourself for a long time and not feel smaller because of it.

"I have a baby brother. I'm responsible for looking after him a fair bit when I'm not at school. When I walk him through a busy street, he'll suddenly stop in the middle of the footpath and squat down, not caring that people's legs are swirling past him. His attention will be completely focused on a dropped bubble gum wrapper, or a snail, or a dandelion growing out between the cracks of cement.

"I used to tug his arm to get him going again because he was wasting time, but one day I just stopped and squatted there with him. I realized he was learning by being still, by noticing all the small, discarded things that we usually pay no attention to.

"So, while we are all aiming high and marching forward in harmony, I think we should remember that looking down does not mean you'll get vertigo and feel sick and lose your footing." Oh my God, I thought, that was a really terrible, stumbling metaphor, but I had to continue. "It might also mean you notice what is good and what keeps you grounded. You don't make wrong judgments based on the opinions of others."

I had to finish the speech before I ruined it, before I let loose with a profanity and told people where to go.

"So for me, leadership is about building your own character before you start influencing anyone else. To be a true leader, I think you must first learn what it is like to follow, even if it means squatting on the ground with a toddler to look at old things in a new way. And to follow without losing your own moral compass, you have to know yourself and appreciate where you come from.

"My name is Lucy Linh Lam. Thank you for listening."

Phew.

"That was such a great speech," said Brodie when she came up to me afterward, and for the first time ever I knew she meant it, because it came through gritted teeth and she threw in a backhanded compliment: "I didn't know you had it in you."

They were just words, I thought. I would go home this evening to a mother who couldn't even write me a note, and I'd know exactly where I stood. But I also knew now what I had always doubted: that I could make it at Laurinda.

Chelsea and Amber suddenly appeared too.

"Oh my God!" squealed Chelsea. "Lucy Lamby, who could have guessed that you were such a sly little fox? *Following* us all year to suss out how we *led* the school! Ooh, ooh, Brodie, we'd better watch out." She gave me an affectionate punch on the shoulder, but Brodie looked as if she wanted to punch me in the face.

"Do you want a picture with us?" Amber asked.

They still thought they were the school's illuminati, granting me access to their world. I'd proven myself to be a worthy competitor and now they wanted me on their side. I looked at them—Brodie decked out in so many school medals that her torso looked bulletproof, Chelsea still referring to me by pet names, and Amber with her camera ready to immortalize me in their ranks. They looked kind of ridiculous.

"No, thanks," I replied, and walked away.

★ ★ ★

Mrs. Leslie and her cluster were standing near the bar with glasses in their hands, their daughters nowhere in sight. "Very surprising for him to have won the Pulitzer," she was saying to her group of Laurinda ladies, "because the last book, as I recall . . ." She then noticed me. "Lucy, you star!"

Even Mrs. White gave me a gigantic hug. "Chelsea could take a leaf out of your book," she told me. "Where are your mum and dad? We want to congratulate them!"

"Oh, they couldn't make it tonight," I said, ignoring their pitying expressions.

"You're the girl who taught us how to make rice-paper rolls!" declared Mrs. Newberry. "My, you're a dark horse." I had no idea whether that was a compliment or an insult. "Thank you," she added, "for being such a good influence on Brodie."

"Oh, I wouldn't say that," I laughed, wondering whether Brodie had told her how I'd sworn at her at the school gate.

I looked around. Everyone was being so pleasant to each other, filled with good cheer and good manners. The final words of a play I had once read came back to me: *They were not good. They were not bad. They were just nice.*

"Congratulations, Lucy," came a familiar voice from behind me. "Spoken like a true Laurindan."

Mrs. Grey.

And with those words, it hit me that she was the only adult here who knew what I was really capable of. Unlike Mrs.

Leslie, who just saw me as a sweet girl who wanted to do well in life, Mrs. Grey appreciated that my ambitions were larger than even I had recognized. She had taken a chance on me instead of choosing the more malleable Tully, and against all expectations, she had let me deliver the closing address at the dinner. Only she understood the insinuations in my ad hoc speech; only she recognized how deeply I understood the machinery of her school.

And only she appreciated how far I had truly come—from the startled girl who had blurted out all her feelings when nudged, to this *true Laurindan* who now layered her words with care and cunning. She was the only person in this room who had peered into my heart and recognized my dark and secret need to be acknowledged.

It was then that I finally accorded her the respect she was due.

And so here we are, Linh, at the end. You like to think that within you there is quiet courage and conviction, a sense of righteousness that is not judgmental. That's what you like to think about yourself. But you're wrong. You are not truly good until you are tested, and even then you might become a worse person.

I'd seen how the top-performing girls at Laurinda were cultivated like hothouse strawberries—bright and lush. Out in the real world, they would bruise. I wanted to see how the Cabinet would cope in two years' time, when they would be in the same classes as my most driven and hardworking Christ Our Savior friends, and the most tenacious and gifted public school students, the hardy evergreens and olive trees and root vegetables that would last all through winter.

In Stanley, we all knew that going to university guaranteed that we would never have to work like our parents did in the factories or garages. Yet I still think about that day on the 406 bus and how we backstabbed that poor girl with teeth like brittle toffee who gave her bag its own seat. When Tully had turned and muttered, "Look at her, Linh. So selfish," an older woman behind you had yelled, "Stop speaking your own bloody language on a public bus—youse don't belong here!"

"Of course I don't," Tully had calmly said in our secret language. We knew you couldn't put someone like that in their place by yelling back. "One day I'm going to be out of here, out of Stanley, and I'll pull my parents out too, and we'll never look back."

But it was I who got out, and Tully who stayed.

So, this is my last letter to you, Linh. See, I promised it would be a long one. It's the last one because you've been with me a year longer than I thought you'd be, and for that I am grateful. I learned that to have integrity means piecing together all the separate parts of yourself and your life.

So goodbye, my constant friend. I am grateful that I carry a little piece of Stanley with me wherever I go, wherever I end up.

Love always,
Lucy

Please provide a written response in argumentative, expository or imaginative style to the image below:

There are colors everywhere. Although it seems dark in this room, the woman and the baby who spend most of their day here know where to look for the colors. Down on the floor there are sweeping traces of a hundred gowns in multitudinous hues. Up against the metal sides of the shed there are rolls and rolls stacked like wallpaper.

The woman must make sure that the baby does not crawl on the concrete and swallow seed pearls or inhale an emerald sequin from the floor. But these days they are seeing less and less of the sequins. These days they get boxes and boxes of polar fleece or rolls of stretch material because now people want pants to salute the sun. The window is high and bolted shut so thieves can't come in and steal the colors.

337

Beneath a fluorescent bulb glowing like an upside-down mushroom, dust motes rain down like furry spores. The woman is turning a collar-shaped piece of iron-on interfacing over in her hands. This woman has never picked up a book in her life, but that piece of man-made fiber is her special script.

She is an olden-day smith of trade and skill, and she can tell the difference between silk and nylon-blend satin without needing to conduct the burn test that we are taught in science. She knows how to cut across the grain with her eyes closed. She knows what kind of stitch is needed for denim if the overlocker breaks down. She knows how a piece of jersey will drape across a chest, and she can cut a winter coat from a piece of wool weave without a pattern. What she does is classified by those who have authority to classify jobs as "unskilled labor," but only the second half of that is true.

People think that if you sit in a dark and silent shed all day working, your internal universe must be equally dark. It is quiet in this room, but it is a good life, because the woman and her baby get to spend the whole day together every day, surrounded by all these colors.

ACKNOWLEDGMENTS

Thank you to Chris Feik, my editor of thirteen years: as always, the silent alchemist behind all my books.

Thanks to Julian Welch for his extraordinary attention to detail in making sure *Lucy and Linh* is the best version of itself.

Thanks to the wonderful team at Black Inc. for all their enthusiasm, their hard work and the perfect cover, and thanks to Clare Forster at Curtis Brown for her support and encouragement.

To all the resilient teenagers in the western suburbs I've known over the years, who were the inspiration for Linh: thank you for letting me into your lives. Thanks also to the countless teachers who good-humoredly shared their horror stories with me, yet continue to dedicate themselves to their profession. They are true unsung heroes.

Thanks to the staff and students of Janet Clarke Hall for creating a culture opposite to that of Laurinda, for proving it can be done and for showing this writer so many examples of kindness and integrity every day.

Thank you to John Marsden and Melina Marchetta, whose books guided me safely through my own teenage years, and whose hard-won wisdom I still carry with me as I write. I know I stand on the shoulders of giants.

Thank you, KBH, my friend, for being my first reader and the one person who I knew would "get" it. Finally, there will never be enough thanks for my love, Nick, who is an oasis of patience and calm, who listened to the plot unfold for over two years and who watched *Mean Girls* with me in celebration—you are a champ.